before the sunset

Cottonwood Cove ~ Book 4

laura pavlov

On the Shore
Cottonwood Cove, Book 4

Laura Pavlov
https://www.laurapavlov.com

Cover Design: Hang Le
Cover Photography: Madison Maltby

Message from the Author:
Click the link below for content warnings.
https://dl.bookfunnel.com/eato56owlo

Created with Vellum

To the Romance Readers Retreat Girlies,

Thank you for the love and support for my books! I hope that Finn lives up to all your book boyfriend dreams! I am forever grateful for you!

Cheers to good friends, good books and many more girls weekends!!

XO, Laura

one

. . .

Finn

IT FELT DAMN good to be back in Cottonwood Cove. Fall was in full swing, and I had a break before we started filming season two of *Big Sky Ranch*. Our first season had far exceeded everyone's expectations, mine included. I'd bought a house in my hometown with the money I'd made when I signed on for season two.

But now I had a whole new set of issues I was dealing with. Along with the success of the show had come a lot of attention, both positive and negative. My costar, Jessica Carson, had gone on a crusade to take me down. She'd been a guest on every talk show that would have her, bashing me for breaking her heart.

Never happened.

Well, unless you count the fictional world of *Big Sky Ranch*, where my character had ended things with her character. But she'd decided to have life imitate art, I guess.

My agent, Angelique, and I were putting out fires right and left, and the producer of the show was not happy with the shitstorm that she'd started.

She could have had her five minutes of fame if she'd just let her work, and our work as a cast, do the talking. But now she'd created so much drama around it that no one on set was happy with her.

Most of all, me.

And I was a happy dude 99 percent of the time, so it took a lot for me to get pissed off.

I opened my computer as it was time for my Zoom call with Angelique.

"Hey, Finn. How's the house coming along?"

"It's great. They just finished the kitchen renovation, so we should be good for a while," I said, glancing over at the sleek, modern kitchen that I'd renovated with the help of my best friend and interior designer, Reese, who was currently living abroad but due home this week.

It couldn't happen soon enough.

This last year had been one of the most challenging of my life, and I was fairly certain it was because she hadn't been here. We'd grown up together. We'd gone to college together. We'd always lived in the same city, often even as roommates.

This had been the first time we'd been apart, and it had been way too long.

"I saw the photos. Reese has a good eye. The black cupboards give it a modern look, but it's still very homey."

"Who are you and what have you done with my agent?" I teased. Angelique was normally all business, but she'd become a close friend over the last year since my career had taken off.

"Yeah, yeah, yeah. It's all about balance," she said with a chuckle. "Reese is coming home in a few days, right? I'm sure you're happy about that."

So maybe Angelique was a part-time agent, part-time therapist.

Yes, my mother was also a therapist. I was surrounded by women who wanted to analyze my every thought. I had two younger sisters, Brinkley and Georgia, and they were both nosy as fuck.

And I wouldn't have it any other way.

My brothers, Cage and Hugh, stayed out of my business unless I asked them for advice, which didn't happen often. But with this Jessica Carson bullshit, everyone was getting involved.

Go public.

Fight back.

Stay silent.

Let it blow over.

Watch your back.

Ask the producers to fire her.

Press legal charges against her for defamation.

I'd heard it all. But I'd always sort of been a believer that if you don't add fuel to the fire, the flames will eventually burn out.

It just hadn't happened yet, because Jessica fucking Carson continued to pour gasoline on said flames every chance she got.

"Yep. I could use some normalcy in my life. But I'm guessing you didn't ask me to talk today to discuss how happy I am about my best friend coming home. I'm assuming this has something to do with Jessica's recent accusation."

"Ah… yes. The one where she told Len Steckman that you weren't capable of having a real relationship. That you didn't have any depth. That you'd lied to her and promised her forever before leaving her high and dry, just like your character had done to her character on *Big Sky Ranch*. Is that the one you're referring to?" Angelique groaned and shook her head. Len Steckman was the host of the *Midnight After Show*, and her comments had gone viral since she'd made the ridiculous statement.

"Yeah, that's the one." I scrubbed a hand down my face.

"Here's the good news. Len countered back. Asked her why they'd yet to hear from anyone from your past that suggested her accusations were true. And that's important,

Finn. Trust me. She's digging for it. Not one woman from your past has come forward to say anything negative about you. People are noticing that she is the only one making these claims. And Jessica has a pretty bad track record. Did you see her last costar, Dominick Nichols, came out and defended you? Said she had a similar crusade against him and nearly ruined his career."

"Yeah, I saw that. He reached out to me. Told me to just keep my head down and stay out of trouble for now."

"Well, let me tell you. Charles and Sadie are not happy with her. I can't even imagine how it's going to be for her when you go back to filming soon. Everyone is furious with her." Charles and Sadie were the directors of *Big Sky Ranch*, and they'd had a couple of successful series before this, but nothing as big as what our show had become after just one season.

"Yeah, but my name is tied to this bullshit drama. No one wants to work with a train wreck, and she's pulled me into her mess." I let out a long breath. I didn't let shit get to me most of the time, but Jessica was threatening to take me down with her. "And she keeps calling me. She wants to get together."

"Do not reply. Stay away and keep your distance. Nothing good could come out of seeing her right now. She'll post a picture and make up some twisted story."

"Agreed. And we have some time before we start filming season two. But I'm hoping we won't have many scenes together, seeing as the two characters broke up."

"If she keeps pulling these stunts, I think they'll write her off the show. She's blowing up her own career. Hell, she would have gotten plenty of attention if she'd just promoted the show. I don't think she expected it to be the most-watched show on Netflix, not only here but in several other countries. She started this campaign against you back when the show first premiered, so she's probably kicking herself for it now."

"It's hard to stop a freight train once it's already moving down the tracks, right?"

"Correct. But sometimes, that freight train is moving so fast, it's going to crash and burn. She's not making any friends or presenting herself as someone to hire in the future. You've remained silent. Taken the high road. You're going to be fine."

"I've got a few interviews coming up, and I know they're going to ask about it. Do you want me to just continue to say *no comment* every time someone asks if there is any truth to her accusations?"

"Well, you know what I think, but I'll keep saying it. If you could share that you're in a committed relationship, it would go a long way right about now."

"It's a little tough to date at the moment." I laughed. "Some of these fans are pretty aggressive. That's why I'm happy to be back in Cottonwood Cove. But I'm keeping to myself for the time being. I don't know who else might pull a stunt like Jessica and try to get their own five minutes of fame. Or sell a bullshit story."

I'd never had any trouble with women in the past. Hell, I was a big fan of women in general. I hadn't had a serious relationship, but not for any particular reason. I'd never met anyone who made me want to dive into anything that lasted longer than a few casual dates. But I loved women. I was a serial dater and a fabulous fucking lover.

If I do say so myself.

But it had been a while for me now. Even before the whole Jessica scandal broke. I mean, I couldn't just take a woman out for dinner and then rock her fucking world because I didn't trust anyone outside of my family and Reese at the moment. But it had been almost a year since I'd actually had sex with anyone, aside from my almost oops with Jessica Carson. I doubted anyone knew or would even believe that I'd been abstaining for quite a while now. I don't know.

Maybe it was the fact that my career had changed, and I was taking things more seriously. Or that I was tired of the same old shit. Or that Reese had been gone, and I'd just been in a funk.

Hell, she was probably the reason that I haven't had a real relationship.

She was the only girl I liked spending endless amounts of time with. She'd been my best friend for as long as I could remember. Our birthdays were just a few days apart, our moms were best friends, and we'd always just been close.

Literally, since birth.

She was my person.

We'd never crossed the line physically, and not because she wasn't gorgeous.

Reese was the most beautiful woman in the world, as far as I was concerned.

But I would never do anything to fuck up what we had.

We'd made a pact when we were barely teenagers to always protect what we had, and we'd both stuck to it.

And our friendship was the best relationship I'd ever had.

So, yeah, I dated women, showed them a good time, and then talked to my best friend about everything under the sun.

I didn't need a relationship with a woman because I had Reese.

And this year with her being gone… it had shown me just how much I needed her.

"Maybe you'll meet someone in Cottonwood Cove. They already know you there. They aren't going to be looking for a story." She chuckled. "You need to show the world that you aren't this calloused playboy she's made you out to be. You're the best guy I know, Finn. I wouldn't work for you if you weren't."

"Well, I don't have any long-term relationships that I can talk about because that isn't my thing. And I'm not looking for it. My dad always says that you'll know when it happens.

It hasn't happened. So, I don't know how I'm going to suddenly jump into something. It's just not realistic."

"Just keep an open mind. Can you do that?"

"Sure."

"And if it's not anything that's going to go anywhere beyond the bedroom, keep your dick in your pants. *The tip and all."* She smirked.

It was an ongoing joke in my family. I hadn't slept with Jessica. We'd drank too much tequila because I'd been having a shit day, and we made out a little. Things had gotten heated, and before I knew it, we were getting ready to do the deed. I'd barely had the tip of my dick wrapped in a condom and teased her entrance when she'd bitten my shoulder so hard I'd nearly lost my shit. Pain wasn't my thing.

I'd always been a lover, not a fighter.

She'd said all sorts of crazy shit, like she wanted to fuck me into oblivion and marry me and have my babies.

All from the tip of my dick.

I'd quickly lifted her off me and got the fuck out of there, red flags going off in every direction. And that was when the war started. She hadn't taken the rejection well, and I'd avoided her ever since.

And my family… well, they'd had a field day with the whole thing.

It was the tip of the iceberg.

Don't dip your pen in company ink… tip included.

Here's a tip for you: Don't mess around with your coworker.

Does anyone have a tip of the day for Finn?

The jokes were endless. And I'd been forced to share all the gory details with my agent because she couldn't put out a fire if she didn't know what she was dealing with.

"Got it. I'll keep you posted."

"All right. Looks like things are going full steam ahead with that movie deal, so once we get the negotiations figured out, I'll send everything over to you. Keep it on the down-low until then. But it looks like you're going to Tokyo the first week in January, and they think you'll only need to be there for four weeks, so you'll be back in time to start filming season two of *Big Sky Ranch* in mid-February."

"I'm relieved that they didn't try to back out with all this Jessica Carson bullshit. That's a good sign, huh?" I scrubbed a hand over my face. This would be my first lead role in a major motion picture.

"I told you. You're going to be fine. I'll talk to you soon. In the meantime, no funny business. Find yourself a future wife, or stay home."

"Great advice." I rolled my eyes before ending the call.

My phone vibrated, and I glanced down to see the family group text that was ongoing with all my siblings, at all times.

GEORGIA

Oh my gosh. Did you guys hear the latest gossip about who Carl Barley is dating? I mean, Dr. Barley.

Carl Barley was Reese's ex-boyfriend. Actually, ex-fiancé. The guy was such a tool. I never understood why she stayed with him for so long. But I knew she was still upset about the breakup, so any news regarding Carl was going to be a big deal to her.

BRINKLEY

Who? Don't leave us hanging.

CAGE

Why the fuck do we care who that asshole is dating? I never liked the guy. I tolerated him for Reese.

HUGH

Is that because he said you weren't a real doctor? <laughing face emoji>

CAGE

Amongst other things.

Who the fuck is he dating?

GEORGIA

Christy Rae Lovell.

BRINKLEY

I can't stand her. And why does everyone call her Christy Rae Lovell? Like, why does she need three names? When people ask about me, they just say Brinkley. Why is she so special?

CAGE

Ask Dr. Douche. Apparently, he's a big fan. Still not sure why we care. Random gossip is not something that we have time for in our group chat. I've asked you guys to refrain from meaningless texts.

BRINKLEY

Bite me, Dr. Grump. I love random gossip. It's my favorite. We care because Reese will care.

HUGH

Do you think she'll be upset, Finn?

Fuck yeah. She hates Christy Rae Lovell. Dr. Douche dated her when they had that brief breakup a few years ago. I always thought there was some overlap there, but Reese never believed it.

CAGE

Why the fuck does she care what he does now? They aren't together, correct?

GEORGIA

They called off their engagement because he didn't support her decision to go to London for a year. It was a once-in-a-lifetime opportunity. I don't think she thought he'd stick to it.

BRINKLEY

I agree. I think she thought they'd get past it and get back together. He sucks for not supporting her, though. I'm glad she went. And she's coming back in a couple of days, right? You better give her a heads-up, Finn.

HUGH

You're awfully quiet, brother. You still there?

I just got a text from Reese. She already knows. Olivia told her. I've got to go.

Olivia was Reese's sister, and I wasn't surprised she'd told her. She was protective, and she wasn't a fan of Carl, since he didn't support her sister's decision to go to London.

I tried dialing Reese three times, but she wasn't picking up.

My chest squeezed because the thought of her hurting, and me not being there, didn't sit well with me.

She'd always been my ride or die.

There wasn't anything I wouldn't do for her.

two

. . .

Reese

I LAY CURLED up in a ball on my bed in my tiny flat in central London. Boxes were stacked in the room, as I was leaving in a few days to head back home.

Taking this job had been the experience of a lifetime.

I had applied for a design fellowship with Elaine Bronstein, a woman whose design had been an inspiration to me since discovering her in *Design Beautiful* magazine when I was in college.

I now felt prepared to pursue my dreams back home. I had the tools I needed to start my own business. I wasn't sure how it was all going to happen, but I'd start one client at a time. I knew I didn't want to be working for my ex-fiancé Carl's family's party supply business any longer.

I'd been completely unfulfilled for the last few years, and Elaine had taken a chance on me.

Unfortunately, Carl had been furious when I'd told him that I was going to take the opportunity that I'd been offered.

I'd tried to explain that I needed this. Needed something for myself. I'd supported his dream of becoming a doctor, giving up my amazing job in San Francisco to move back to

Cottonwood Cove, where he'd accepted his residency. He didn't want us to be living apart any longer, so I'd made the choice to go back home.

For him.

He was the man I was going to marry, after all. So, I did it.

I hadn't been able to find a job in design back home, so, per Carl's urging, I'd gone to work at Barley's Party Supplies —heaven forbid anyone in his family come up with an original name.

At the end of the day, I'd spent the last few years making balloon arrangements and witnessing meltdowns every single weekend at children's birthday parties.

When Kressa Warren, one of the famously awful twins of Cottonwood Cove, had chucked a cupcake at me, causing it to smear all over my favorite skirt, I knew I was done.

Ever try getting red dye out of a pink silk midi skirt?

Not happening.

There was nothing wrong with making balloon animals or hosting parties. It just wasn't what I wanted to do with my life.

I thought if I drew a line in the sand, if I took a stand about how important it was to me, he'd eventually come around.

I still wanted to get married. Still wanted to do everything that we'd planned together.

I wanted children and a family and all the things that my parents had given my sister and me.

All the things that I'd planned to do with Carl.

We'd spoken weekly since I'd left, and though he'd been angry that I'd made the choice that I had, we'd both talked about getting back together when I returned home.

Even though we were currently not together… officially.

Obviously, I wasn't really clear on what exactly that meant.

I thought I'd return home inspired and ready to start my own business, and he'd ask me to wear my engagement ring again, and we'd go back to wedding planning shortly after.

We had a wedding venue reserved already, and they'd agreed to allow us to use the deposit at a later date.

He'd asked me for forever just eighteen months ago.

Did he seriously change his mind because I didn't do what he'd wanted me to do?

Was I that easy to get over?

Apparently so.

My sister, Olivia, had just called to inform me that he was dating someone, and she'd seen them together.

And he wasn't dating just anyone.

He was dating *Christy Rae Lovell.*

The girl he'd hooked up with when we were "on a break" in high school.

His words, not mine.

Had he not watched *Friends,* like everyone else on the planet, and not known that being "on a break" does not mean you hook up with a girl your ex-girlfriend despises?

A break was not a hall pass.

It was about taking some time while you figured things out.

Kind of like what I thought we were doing right now.

I couldn't imagine going back and seeing Carl with her.

We lived in a small town.

They would be everywhere.

And Christy Rae Lovell was a nurse, so they'd make the perfect couple.

A doctor and a nurse.

How very *Grey's Anatomy* of them.

I would vomit if I had the energy to hold my head over the toilet.

The tears continued to fall, and a sob escaped.

My phone dinged, and it was a text from Finn, also known as Chewy. He'd had a slight obsession with *Star Wars* when we were young. He still considered Chewbacca to be the reason he'd gone into acting. Growing up, we'd take turns every single weekend watching his favorite movie, or mine, the best movies known to man—*Harry Potter* and *Star Wars*. I couldn't even begin to count how many times we'd watched those movies, and how many Halloweens we'd gone as Chewy and Hermione. So, I'd always called him Chewy for as long as I could remember, and he'd called me Miney because he'd dropped the Hermione when we were in middle school.

CHEWY

I've called four times. Why aren't you picking up the phone?

I can't talk right now. I'm not feeling well.

CHEWY

I know Olivia filled you in on Carl. I just found out. I told you he's an asshole. Don't let this set you back. You've got a plan when you come home. And it's a good one.

My plan was to open my own business, hang out with my best friend as much as possible, and resume my relationship with Carl.

I wasn't getting any younger.

I was twenty-nine years old, and I'd invested more than a decade with Carl. I'd only ever had one boyfriend, and it had been him.

So, I'd never imagined he'd seriously start dating someone else. What we had was good—at least I thought it was. We were comfortable.

We'd been talking about moving in together before I'd left, because Carl hadn't wanted us to live together before we were engaged, and then I'd been stuck in a lease that I couldn't break without losing a substantial amount of money. So, I'd assumed he'd want me to move in with him when I got back home. *But seeing as he had a girlfriend now, I'm guessing that would be a little awkward.*

Olivia said they were all over each other at Cottonwood Café, and apparently, Christy Rae Lovell told her friend that they're practically shopping for rings already. How is that possible?

CHEWY

Have you ever considered that he might not be the guy for you?

I covered my mouth with my hand as another sob escaped my throat. I hadn't ever considered that. We hadn't lived by one another during undergrad and medical school, but we'd maintained our relationship long-distance. We'd always had a plan. Once he'd gotten his residency back home, he'd said it was time for us to be together all the time, and I'd agreed. Long distance was exhausting. Though I'd had my best friend with me. But it didn't help that Finn and Carl didn't get along, as neither cared for the other.

No. I've been with him for eleven years. Obviously, I've invested close to half my life with the guy.

CHEWY

You weren't even living near one another for most of that time. He didn't support you when you wanted to pursue your dream. He's a narcissistic asshole.

I wasn't in the mood for a Carl bashing. It was Finn's favorite pastime. My best friend was the most happy-go-lucky guy I'd ever known—unless we were discussing Carl. I cried into my pillow some more, and the lump in my throat was so thick it was painful to swallow.

I can't do this right now. I have to go.

CHEWY

You're coming home in three days, Miney. Do not let him mess that up for you.

I couldn't fathom how uncomfortable it would be to see them together. She'd love to rub it in my face. I couldn't believe Carl was with her.

I can't come there and have their relationship thrown in my face every day. I'm single, jobless, and homeless. Now I'm going to have to move back in with my parents at thirty years old. How am I going to face them?

CHEWY

Fuck them. And you're not thirty; you're barely twenty-nine. You don't have to live with your parents. You can move in with me. I have a big house now. I'll be with you every step of the way. Answer your damn phone, Miney.

My heart ached. Had I made a huge mistake? Had I been selfish by chasing my dream to come here?

I'll call you later, Chewy. I don't want to talk about it right now.

CHEWY

I'll give you a day. But you better pick up your damn phone tomorrow.

I'd spent the next two days in almost the exact same position on my bed. Carl had texted me to let me know that he was in a relationship and thought it best I heard it from him.

Long after I'd heard it from multiple people.

He'd told me that he'd hoped we'd find our way back to one another but that he'd gotten tired of waiting, even though I was coming home this week.

He'd claimed that I hadn't made him a priority and she had.

It was like a knife to the heart.

I'd made so many sacrifices for him, and he couldn't give me this one?

I'd barely eaten, and I'd never felt so low, at least not since I'd been sick in college, but that was a different kind of low.

Finn was having a fit because I'd yet to pick up the phone. He'd left numerous messages and sent multiple texts, but I'd stopped responding. I glanced down to see a new message.

CHEWY

Damn it, Miney. What the hell is going on?
Are you coming home tomorrow?

I reached for the roll of toilet paper that I had in bed with me and blew my nose. I'd canceled my flight for tomorrow because I didn't feel like I could get up and go to the airport.

Nor could I get myself together to face my ex-fiancé and his new girlfriend.

I'm not coming home right now.

CHEWY

What the fuck are you talking about?
Why not?

A cry escaped my lips, and I let it out. I lay on my tear-soaked pillow, wondering what the hell I was going to do with my life, and I responded with the only thing I could.

I told him the truth.

I'm frozen.

And I let myself sleep because it was the only time that my aching heart found a reprieve.

three

. . .

Finn

I'D LANDED at Heathrow Airport and took a car to Reese's place. She really hadn't gotten on that plane yesterday, and everyone was worried about her back home. So, I'd tossed some clothes into a duffle and jumped on the first flight I could.

I'd visited her four times over the last year, and she'd come to my opening when *Big Sky Ranch* premiered.

Her ex-fiancé, *Carl "The Shit-Turd" Barley,* hadn't come one time to see her.

He'd been too busy pouting because she'd left, and then he'd grown impatient and jumped in the sack with the one woman he knew would hurt her the most.

Reese was so hell-bent on marrying the dude, and every time I'd pressed her about it, she had the same answer.

I've invested more than a decade with him.

So the fuck what?

He's an asshole, and he didn't deserve her.

So, I was going to get her and bring her home.

"You look familiar," the dude driving me said with his English accent, making it sound far more formal than it should.

"Do I?" I chuckled.

"You're that bloke from *Big Sky Ranch,* aren't you?"

"I am. Yes. Thanks for watching."

He pulled up in front of Reese's building.

"Ahh… this is amazing. And you snogged that costar of yours, didn't you?" He barked out a laugh, and I winced internally. This was what I was known for now.

Snogging Jessica Carson.

Which never even happened.

"No comment," I said, reaching for my duffle bag before handing him cash for the ride.

"Listen, everyone knows it's a bunch of rubbish. She's a dodgy bird, isn't she?"

I chuckled. "I think calling her a dodgy bird is probably accurate, even if I don't know for sure what that means."

"Yeah. You're a cool bloke. You're all right."

"You, too, buddy. Thanks for the lift." I saluted him after agreeing to take a quick selfie with him.

I was still getting used to being recognized wherever I went.

"Are you staying long?" he called out before I closed the door, and I leaned my head back in.

"Nah. Just here to pick up a friend."

"Ahhh… I'm guessing it's a beautiful bird by the way you're seeming so anxious to get into that building."

"You'd be correct. She's the best girl around. Take care." I knocked my knuckles against the roof of the car and closed the door.

I entered the old Victorian building and jogged up the three flights of stairs before banging on the door. Now that I was here, I couldn't get to her fast enough.

This year apart from Reese had been difficult for me. More so than I ever could have imagined.

"Damn it, Miney. Open the door."

"Chewy?"

"Of course. Does someone else call you Miney?"

The door flew open, and there she stood. Her eyes were puffy, and her skin was paler than usual, but her green eyes met mine, and all the tension left my shoulders.

I dropped my duffle right there in the doorway as she stepped into my arms. Her body quaked, and I just held her there. When the sob escaped her throat, I pulled back, using my thumbs to wipe away the falling tears.

"Hey. You're okay."

"I can't believe you're here. I missed you."

"I missed you, too."

She stepped back, and I pulled my bag into her apartment and pushed the door closed before dropping my ass onto her bed as she sat beside me. She leaned her head against my chest.

Her small studio apartment had a kitchenette, a bathroom, and her bedroom, which was also her living room. But she lived in downtown London, and the location was everything she'd wanted.

"You just flew to London on a whim?" she whispered. She fell back onto the bed, so I lay beside her. My feet were still on the floor, but the rest of me was sprawled on the bed. I rolled to my side just as she did. It was something we'd always done since we were kids.

"You needed me," I said, kissing the top of her head. "We made a deal years ago. I wasn't about to break it now."

She tipped her head back to look at me. *"You call. I come.* And vice versa."

"Yep. Think of how many times you've rescued me."

"That time Cammie Watkins tried to tie you to her bed, and you didn't have a car. That goes down as my all-time favorite. I was the perfect getaway. You came running out in your tighty whiteys." She chuckled as her eyes locked with mine. I saw the sadness there, but I knew getting her to laugh was the best thing for her right now.

"Good times. That girl was… a lot. She lured me to her house, saying she didn't want anything but a one-and-done, and then she tried to tie me up while I was sleeping. I ran and took cover in the bathroom until you got there." I shivered dramatically, which made her laugh harder.

"You sent me that 911 text, and I came running. I hadn't even brushed my teeth." She laughed a real, genuine laugh, which gave me hope that she was going to be okay. "I remember you charging down that driveway with her chasing after you."

I stroked her hair. Damn, it was good to see her. Reese was my girl in every sense of the word—minus the sex.

She was the one I shared everything with and who I trusted with my deepest secrets.

My best friend and my favorite person.

"You sure did. So, I'm just returning the favor. I knew you were hurting, and I came to bring you home. We're flying out in two days." I glanced around to see most of the tiny place was already packed up.

"Thanks for coming, Chewy." She blinked a few times, and I saw tears welling in her pretty sage-green eyes again. "I can't stand the thought of seeing them together."

"Stop worrying about them. It's your home. This isn't you, Miney. You don't curl into a ball on your bed and throw in the towel. You're the strongest person I know."

The shit she'd overcome was more than most could ever wrap their head around. I'd watched her fight cancer. I'd watched her beat cancer. Ever since then, Reese had always known what she wanted for her life. Family. Kids. That whole fairy tale. And she fought hard for it. Almost gave up a part of herself to claim it.

"Don't go flattering me. I don't hold a candle to Brinkley," she said, and the corners of her lips turned up.

Now it was my turn to laugh. My sister was tough as

nails, but she wasn't dealt the shitty hand Reese was. "Brinks is a tough one. But so are you."

"I don't feel so tough at the moment."

"How about we start with food? I'm starving, and the way those jammies are hanging on you tells me you haven't been eating. Let's go get some burgers at that place up the street that we ate at the last time I was here." Reese had always been thin, and not eating for a few days had her looking slightly gaunt. Anytime she lost any weight or looked pale, I couldn't help but let that fear seep in. I'd never admit it to her, but Reese's battle with Non-Hodgkin's Lymphoma had changed me in many ways. I'd been with her every step of the way, from her first treatment, until we'd been told that she was in remission. It was the first time in my life that I'd been overcome with the fear of losing someone that I loved fiercely. So, yeah, I worried about her. All the fucking time.

"I could eat. I haven't had anything outside of dry Cheerios in the last three days."

"Up," I said, pushing to my feet and tugging her to stand. I reached into my duffle bag and unzipped it. "I brought you a surprise."

The corners of her lips turned up when I pulled out her favorite white cowboy boots. She hadn't thought she'd need them when she'd left for London, but Reese was a country girl at heart. She loved her boots almost as much as she loved her horse.

"Ahhhh… Do you remember the day my parents gave me these?" She held them against her chest. They were slightly dinged up, but they were her favorite.

"Yep. You wore them every day for a month, even down to the cove in your bathing suit."

"Hey, good boots are like a good man. They're even better when you break them in." She chuckled, but I still saw the pain in her eyes.

"I'm here. The boots are here. Let's eat."

"Fine. Give me five minutes to change and brush my hair."

"All right," I said as I scrolled through my phone and answered a few emails.

Five minutes later, Reese came strolling out of the bathroom, wearing a pair of jeans, a navy hoodie, and her white cowboy boots. Her golden-brown hair was pulled back into a braid that hung over her shoulder. Her face was clean of makeup, and she was fucking gorgeous.

She'd never had to try. She'd always been the prettiest girl I'd ever known, and I'd told her as much more times than I could count.

"Better?" she asked.

"Well, you don't smell like despair anymore," I said, wrapping my arms around her and breathing her in. She smelled like violet and amber.

It had always been my favorite scent.

Reese Murphy had always smelled like home.

She laughed and took a step back, reaching for her phone and purse as we made our way out into the crisp fall air.

Once we were settled at our table, we both sipped our iced tea and waited for our burgers.

My phone vibrated multiple times, and I glanced down to see several messages from my agent.

ANGELIQUE

You're in fucking London? I talked to you a few days ago, and you were chilling at home. I'm guessing you went to get Reese?

ANGELIQUE

When I said to find a girlfriend, I didn't mean for you to leave the country to make it happen. But I am so here for this.

There were several texts from my siblings in the group

chat, with screenshots of the selfie I'd taken with the driver who'd given me a ride from the airport.

"Good Christ. The fucking driver posted a photo of me and him, saying I was in London to see my girl," I groaned.

She put her glass down just as the burgers were set in front of us. "What did you tell him?"

"That I was in fucking London to see my girl." I reached for my burger and took a large bite.

"Well, you're a superstar now, Chewy. You can't say things like that. What is Angelique saying? Does she want you to clear it up?"

"Hell, no. With this whole Jessica Carson disaster, she wants me to be in a relationship. But you know I haven't been going out. I've been keeping a low profile."

"Don't let Jessica force you into hiding."

"That's the thing. Like I've told you before, I just haven't felt like it. I don't know. I guess I'm enjoying some downtime, you know? It's been a tough year with you gone, and now that I'm done filming for a little bit, I'm not busy at work, and I guess I just haven't had any desire to go out on a date."

She nodded as she bit off the top of a french fry. "I get that. I've been in a real funk, too. I mean the work… I told you that it was amazing. But I haven't gone on a single date in the past year because I thought I was kind of still engaged. I just didn't think it was really over. So, it looks like we're both in a rut."

"You still want to get back with that dude after this?" I asked, shaking my head and crossing my arms over my chest.

Reese and I didn't disagree often. We'd always had one another's backs. But when it came to Carl, we didn't see eye to eye.

I'd never cared for the guy.

"I'm the one who left. I put my job before my relationship. He's not the bad guy here, Chewy."

He was always the bad guy in my mind.

"You did something that you wanted to do. He's always done what he wanted to do, and you've supported him."

She shrugged. "You've hated him ever since senior year soccer tryouts."

"Damn straight. It was a timed two-mile run. He cut it short one lap. It was the honor system. I never trusted him after that."

I'd set the record that year for the fastest two-mile run on our soccer team, and that bastard cuts a lap and tries to say he beat me? I led the whole goddamn race. It took a lot to piss me off, but the fact that he was a cheat and dating my best friend—I'd never forgotten it.

It's all about integrity, man.

And Carl Barley didn't have any.

He might be a doctor now, but the man would always be the guy who not only cut the run short but also said that he'd set the record for the fastest time. He'd tried to double down. Thankfully, Coach Dugger was paying attention. Carl then pretended it was an oversight.

Oversight my ass, you cheating bastard.

She chuckled before letting her teeth sink into her bottom lip. "It's good to see you."

"Yeah? So, you'll come home with me?"

She closed her eyes, leaning back in her chair. She hadn't had more than two bites of her burger and a few french fries. "I'm a mess. I have no plan now."

"Bullshit. You'll live with me. I was hiring you anyway to decorate the house. The renovations are done, and now I need to finish furnishing the place, get window coverings, and all of that. You'll be living there while you get it put together. It's a perfect plan. And I'll be the first client at your new business, so get ready for everyone in town to be knocking down your door."

"Okay," she whispered. "That doesn't sound so bad."

"It's all coming together."

"It's a start. I'll just do what I can to avoid them. I'm not ready to see him with her, you know?" I heard the hurt in her voice, and rage coursed my veins. I'd always been protective of Reese, and that would never change.

"I've got you. Don't worry about a thing."

"I'd be lost without you, Chewy."

"Well, you'll never be without me. And I'd be the one who'd be lost. It's been the best year of my life professionally, and I felt really—off. I didn't like you being gone. I mean, don't get me wrong. I'm proud as hell of you, but I missed you like crazy, Miney."

She smiled. The first real smile I'd seen since I arrived.

"That's because we're peas and carrots, right?" she teased. It's what our mothers had always said since we were young.

And damn, had they been right.

Because this girl had always completed me in a way I'd never understood.

"Damn straight. Eat up. No more of this pouting shit. Starting today, you hold your head high. No more grieving over a dude who doesn't deserve your time or your tears."

She sighed as she reached for her burger. "Easier said than done. This is one area that you don't understand because you don't want the same things as me. You don't want marriage and kids. And I found the person I thought I'd do all those things with, and it hurts like hell to think of him with someone else."

"I never said I don't want to get married and have kids. Hell, I love kids. I just never met anyone I wanted to keep going out with. But who knows? It could happen. The difference between you and me is that I don't worry about shit like that. If it's supposed to happen, then I'll get knocked on my ass. You're trying to force it."

She shook her head. "I'm hardly trying to force it. I said yes to marrying him. But I changed the plan and left. That wasn't fair to him. So, I'm trying to fix what I broke."

I shrugged. We could agree to disagree. That shit was already broken; she just didn't want to see it.

We spent the next few hours catching up after we headed back to her place. Reese showed me her portfolio of the projects she'd been working on, and I was in awe of her. She had an eye for design, always had.

My phone continued to blow up with texts, as apparently, the driver's post had gone fucking viral.

Angelique was thrilled.

It was the first time in several months that the attention I was receiving wasn't about Jessica Carson.

The problem was that everyone thought I had a girlfriend now.

And it wouldn't take any sort of detective skills to realize that my best friend was the girl who lived in London.

But at the moment, I didn't give a shit.

I was just enjoying my time with her.

That's the way it had always been with us.

four

. . .

Reese

"OH MY GOD, CHEWY!" I squealed.

"Stop shouting. I'm dreaming," he groaned, wrapping his arm around me a little tighter.

"Yeah. I'm aware. You've got yourself a little *morning situation.*" My voice was still groggy after sleeping through the night for the first time in days. "And Chewy Junior is poking me in the butt."

I glanced over my shoulder to see him open one eye as he took me in. His chest was pressed against my backside, which meant his raging boner was pressed against my ass. We'd fallen asleep tucked into my small bed, and we'd spooned one another as we'd done more times than I could count.

But this would go down as the first time he'd ever woken me up with a ginormous erection pressed against me.

Finn had always had a natural charm. Too much sex appeal for his own good.

He was gorgeous.

Tall and lean, with just the right amount of muscle. His brown hair was shorter in the back and longer on top and effortlessly styled. He always donned day-old scruff that really worked for him.

He was sexy as hell, and he knew it.

Country boy style with city boy swagger.

Girls were always swooning over him, and that was how it had always been.

He loosened his grip on me, and I sprung to sit forward. My head fell back in laughter as he rolled onto his back. His eyes widened as he took in his erection, which was standing straight up.

My eyes gaped at the sight. He wore a white tee and a pair of black boxer briefs that were doing nothing to hide his morning wood.

His hair was messy but managed to look like he was ready to pose for an underwear ad, and his gray gaze locked with mine.

"Damn. It's been a while since I've gotten laid. I guess your tight little ass was teasing me all night." He smirked.

"Oh, this is my fault?"

"If you ask the big guy, I'd say that's a hard yes. *Pun intended*." He pointed down at his impressive package.

I whistled as I hustled to my feet. Finn showing up on my doorstep yesterday was the best surprise. I felt slightly human this morning for the first time in days. Like things were going to be okay.

And he and I had never stood on ceremony. I knew every embarrassing thing that had ever happened to him, and vice versa for me.

I moved to the bathroom to brush my teeth as he called out to me from the bed. "Damn, the internet is going wild about me coming to London for a girl. Everyone is commenting on how it was about time I got myself a real girlfriend. Apparently, they've figured out that it's my best friend who lives here and that we've miraculously fallen in love. This ought to shut down Jessica for a little while," he said, and I could hear the humor in his voice. "At least until we set the record straight."

I thought about what Carl would do if he heard. He'd always hated how close Finn and I were. It was the one thing I never allowed his opinion to influence me about. I was open to compromise on most things in my life because relationships were all about that. You had to give a little. Choose your battles. But my friendship with Finn had always been something I treasured, and there was no budging in that department.

Did I tell Carl every time Finn and I slept in the same bed? No.

He would have lost it.

I didn't feel guilty because nothing had ever happened between Finn and me. We were the best of friends, through and through. We'd made a pact to never cross the line, and we'd stuck to it. So there was no reason to say anything and stir up unnecessary drama.

I tied my hair up in a bun and went back to the bedroom to get my phone.

"Oh my gosh," I whispered as I dropped to sit on the bed. Finn moved quickly, hovering behind me as his chin rested on my shoulder.

"What's wrong?"

"Carl texted me seven times during the night." I quickly scrolled to read the texts. I hadn't responded to him since he'd told me about him and Christy Rae Lovell.

"That douchesack. Of course, he's all over you now. I've got to give it to him. He's definitely predictable."

I waved Finn away as I read the texts.

CARL

Are you really dating Finn Reynolds now? I knew something was up with you two.

CARL

I can't fucking believe this. I always suspected it.

I checked the time, and the next text came in two hours later, which would have been two o'clock in the morning his time.

CARL

I'm happy for you if you're happy, Reese.

My chest squeezed.

"I just puked in my mouth. I can hear him using that baby voice when he talks to you," Finn grumped from behind me, and I moved to my feet and stared down at my phone as I continued reading.

CARL

I miss you. I've tried not to. I want to give my new relationship a try. Your leaving really hurt me, Reese. But I'd be lying if I didn't admit that I'm struggling. I thought dating someone else would help me get over you.

CARL

How serious is this with you and Finn? You know he's not really a relationship guy. Jessica Carson is living proof of that. Even you said that he would probably never settle down. Why go there?

CARL

Can we have lunch when you get home? I think we should at least talk. You know, for closure and all that. We were engaged, after all. We'd be married by now if you hadn't left.

A tear ran down my cheek, and I swiped it away.

"What is that dick-nugget saying now?"

"He misses me. We would have been married by now, Chewy. He wants to know how serious this is between us." My fingers hovered over the keyboard to text him back and tell him that it was all a big misunderstanding.

But I stopped myself.

My head snapped up to meet Finn's gray gaze.

He raised a brow. "What? I know that look. Let me guess. You're desperate to get home now and win him back."

"Don't be a hater."

"Fine. Tell me."

I dropped my phone onto the nightstand and moved to sit beside him on my bed. "Just hear me out."

"All right."

"You said Angelique wants you to date someone, right?"

"Correct. What's your point?" He eyed me suspiciously.

"Well, you already planted the seed."

"Are you referencing my sperm? It hasn't been planted anywhere, Miney. I keep that shit wrapped up at all times." He smirked.

I waved my hand and feigned disgust, although I had to fight the urge to look down and see if his erection was still there. "Don't be gross. I'm talking about the seed that the driver planted. Painting the picture of a man who couldn't get to his girl fast enough. That's what they're saying, right?"

"Planting seeds and now we're painting? What are you talking about?"

"I'm talking about us. Let's go with it. Pretend that we're dating. It's a win-win."

"How is it a win-win? Will we be having sex in this scenario?"

My mouth fell open. "Of course not. We stick to the pact at all costs. I'm offering you the chance to fake date me."

"Why would I want to do that?"

"Well, your fans will see you as a relationship guy and not some bed-hopping whore."

He barked out a laugh. "Did you just call me a whore?"

"I mean, you aren't one, but Jessica has painted that picture. *A whore.* A womanizing bastard. A selfish prick who chases his own pleasure," I said as I tried to really bring it home.

"Who said anything about me chasing my own pleasure? I haven't even gotten laid in a year outside of the whole tip disaster, which doesn't even count. I'm practically a celibate monk."

"A celibate monk who needs a girlfriend. And clearly, Carl can't stand the idea of you and me being together, because now he wants to meet up for '*closure*,'" I said, making air quotes around the last word.

Closure, my ass.

The man was jealous, and I was here for it. We'd been together so long that we'd lost all the excitement. That was part of the reason that I'd wanted to take this job in London. Life had grown stale and boring, but that didn't mean I still didn't want to marry him and have a family. Maybe this time apart would actually be good for us in the long run.

Aside from the fact that he really was dating someone else, and my relationship was fake.

"So, you want to use me?"

"Totally," I said over a fit of laughter. Hell, this was the best I'd felt in days. Finn's showing up had lifted my spirits, and now I actually felt hopeful. "You said you haven't felt like going out anyway. You asked me to move in with you, so outside appearances will look like we're a real couple. Everyone's always suspected it back home anyway. Let's go with it."

"You really think that we can pull it off, Miney?" He raised a brow in question.

"You're the best actor I know. People will eat this up. Childhood besties-turned-lovers!" I squealed as I fell back on the bed. "Hell, your cousin Ashlan could sell this story, and it would be a bestseller. Carl is going to shit himself and beg me to take him back." Honestly, I still hadn't gotten over how quickly he'd replaced me, and with *her*, of all people. So, I wouldn't mind making him sweat a little bit if, in the end, we found our way back to one another.

"And what do I get out of it?" he asked as he fell back next to me on the mattress, and we both rolled on our sides to face one another.

"An image makeover. You'll look like the swooning boyfriend. It'll be great for your career. All mentions of Jessica will fade to black."

"Fade to black? That's a bit dramatic, yeah?"

"Hey, my best friend is an acting genius. It must be rubbing off on me." I couldn't hide the smile spreading across my face. "Come on. It's a great plan."

He scrubbed a hand down his face. "What about our mothers, who are going to freak out? Are we really going to lie to them? They've always wanted this, and it will break their hearts when it all comes to an end, and you go back to marrying Dr. Prickdick."

This was a fair point. I thought it over.

"Reynolds-Murphy code of silence. We call a family meeting. Get everyone on board."

He groaned. "You're pulling the code of silence card? You know that's only for emergencies."

When Cage had gotten full custody of Gracie, we'd all taken a code of silence, and not one of us had ever shared who her mother was. She'd signed over her rights to Gracie, and as far as everyone in Cottonwood Cove knew, she was just a woman he'd had a one-night stand with. No one knew that she was one of the biggest fashion models of our generation.

Code of silence was a real thing.

"My future husband is dating another woman. That's an emergency."

"Fuck, Miney. There's so much wrong with that statement, but I think we're playing with fire. What if Carl doesn't care when it's all said and done?" I knew he was saying it to protect me. He didn't want me to get my hopes up if it really was over between us. And for some reason, it didn't hurt as much as it did a few days ago.

I wasn't alone. Finn's presence had healed a lot of my hurt already.

"Then you and I are just doing what we always do. We were going to live together anyway. We'll have an amicable breakup when the time is right, and we'll just continue on like normal. *Besties for the resties.*"

"You don't want to try dating other people for real?" he asked.

"I don't. I'm not ready to date. Even if this doesn't work out with Carl, I don't want to date anyone else yet. I need to figure out who I am. Carl and I have been together for so long that I think I've lost a bit of myself. Besides, I'd just be spending my time with you anyway." I cleared my throat as the thought entered my mind. "Oh. You probably want to date, right? Or at least hook up with someone?"

"Nah. I'm taking a break from all of that anyway. I'll be fine."

"So, we're really doing this. We're going to be fake lovers." I pushed up as excitement coursed my veins. "I want to really pour it on. You know, all sorts of public PDA, and we'll act like we're both all sexed up all the time." A maniacal laugh escaped my throat.

Clearly, I was ready to throw some salt in Carl's wounds as he'd had no problem being with a woman in front of everyone that I knew back home. The awful, obnoxious person I tried my best to avoid at all costs—really, how could he?

Well, if there was one thing that I was certain of about my ex-fiancé…

He was jealous as hell.

He couldn't stand the thought of me with anyone else, any

more than I could stand the thought of him with someone else.

Why hadn't I thought of this sooner?

"Have you ever been all sexed up?" Finn asked. "You guys didn't seem to have a very exciting sex life."

"How the hell do you know?"

"Because that last time I got those tequilas in you, you told me you'd never had an orgasm during sex. That doesn't sound very impressive."

"That's a *me* problem," I said, pushing to my feet in a huff. "Maybe this is exactly what Carl and I needed."

"Personally, I think you need to have a real orgasm before you worry so much about winning that dicklicker back," he said dryly.

"No. This break was what we needed. I came here to find what I wanted to do with my life, and now we'll both realize that we missed one another. Hell, maybe it'll make him hot for me again, and we'll have passionate makeup sex."

"He doesn't strike me as a real passionate guy. I mean the dude couldn't even run eight laps around a track."

I chuckled. "Drop it, Chewy."

"Oh, is this where I need to listen to *my woman*? Are you going to boss me around now?" He stood up and tossed me onto the bed before climbing on top of me and hovering above me. "You sure you can handle me, Miney?"

"I've never had a problem handling you, have I?" I said, but my words came out all breathy. And was that his erection poking me in the lower belly again? My God, my best friend was such a horndog. "I think you might be the one who has a problem handling me."

"Never. You've always been my girl. A little fake dating isn't going to change that. I'm a professional actor, for God's sake. Carl's going to lose his shit when he sees me with my woman. You're mine now," he said. His voice was all tease as he leaned down and rubbed his scruff against my neck.

I broke out in a fit of giggles, but something was stirring between my legs. Something foreign. Maybe it was the excitement over my new fake boyfriend and making Carl jealous. My breaths were coming hard and fast, and I shoved him off me. He barked out a laugh as he pushed to stand.

"You all right?" He quirked a brow with a cocky grin on his face.

"I'm fine. Now, let's finish packing and come up with a plan." My eyes moved down to the elephant in the room.

Finn's enormous penis.

My God, that thing had a mind of its own.

He followed my gaze and looked down.

"Looks like you're going to have your hands full. Literally and figuratively." He waggled his brows.

I pointed to the bathroom. "Cold shower. Now."

"You want to join me, Lover?" he teased as he walked slowly to the bathroom, and I stood up and glanced in his direction.

He turned the water on with his back to me and tugged off his shirt and waved it around in the air before whipping it in my direction. Then he turned around and dropped his briefs. My eyes widened as I stared at his chiseled, toned ass. He looked over his shoulder and smiled before he stepped into the shower.

I walked the short distance and pulled the door closed before fanning my face.

My new fake boyfriend was not going to make this easy on me.

five

. . .

Finn

WE'D JUST ARRIVED in Cottonwood Cove, and we were on our way to my parents' house for Sunday dinner, where we were going to explain the ridiculous plan that I'd been talked into. Reese's parents would be there as well as her sister, Olivia, and my entire family. We hadn't even stopped by my house yet, and we were well past exhausted. But with both of our families texting us nonstop with questions about the media frenzy currently going on about me dating my childhood best friend, we knew we needed to explain in person what was up.

"Are you fine with me bringing Millie over to your place? You said the barn is all set up, and I know you're looking for a horse. I just figured if I'm staying there, I'd love to be able to ride her every day," Reese said with a yawn.

"Yeah, it's all ready, and Millie would love it there. I can't wait to show it to you. I know you've seen it on FaceTime, but in person, with the mountains right behind the barn and the water not too far away, it's really something."

I came to a stop at the light. Reese had her cheek resting on the seat beside me, and she smiled. "It feels good to be home."

"Good. I'm glad you agreed to come back with me." I pulled into the driveway of the ranch house where I'd grown up. Reese was already stepping out of the car when I came around to get her door. Her white cowboy boots clacked against the cobblestone walkway leading to my parents' house.

"Looks like everyone is here." She smiled as she pushed open the door.

Loud chatter came from the kitchen, just like it always did. My family home was a gathering spot for anyone and everyone in Cottonwood Cove who wanted a good meal on Sunday. Olivia, Reese's little sister, came charging around the corner and wrapped her arms around her.

"Well, if it isn't the British prince himself," Cage said with one brow raised as he walked toward me.

"Hey, what can I say? I ooze royal charm."

Cage wrapped one arm around Reese's shoulders, giving her a bit of a man-bro hug before turning his attention back to me. "Well, you made quite the impression with your quick weekend jaunt abroad."

The dude oozed sarcasm.

It was his love language.

"All for the greater good."

"I'm sure it is." He smirked.

The cocky bastard.

Before I knew it, little Gracie was hauling ass as she ran toward me, all wobbly and adorable. Her arms flailed as I scooped her right up and spun her around. My niece owned my heart in every way.

"You smell like pumpkins," I said, kissing her cheek.

"Grammie and Pops and me carved pumpkins today." She placed a hand on my cheek and smiled before reaching for Reese.

My best friend scooped my niece into her arms and

hugged her. Reese had babysat Gracie dozens of times over the years, as she was one of the few people outside of our family that Cage trusted with his daughter.

"I'm happy you're home, Ree Ree." My niece settled her head of curls on Reese's shoulder.

"Me, too, Gracie girl. I've missed you big."

"Are you Uncle Finny's girlfriend now?" she whispered, and I raised a brow at Cage.

"Don't shoot the messenger. The whole town is talking about it." He shrugged.

Reese's sage-green eyes found mine, and for the first time, I saw the doubt. This was all fun and games, but she'd never do anything to hurt Gracie.

I gave her the look that I knew she needed from me.

It's fine. There won't be any broken hearts when it's done.

We'd always been able to communicate without words, and she nodded.

This was temporary.

No one was going to get hurt.

There would never be anything that could come between me and Reese. Not even her dickhead ex-fiancé.

When we entered the kitchen, all hell broke loose. We made our rounds hugging everyone, and in typical Reynolds-Murphy fashion, we all talked at the same time, but somehow it worked for us.

When they were all done fawning all over Reese, we made our way to the table. My mom had made chicken marinara, and after the long flight, I was ready for a home-cooked meal. The dinner conversation was light as Gracie, who was sitting between her dad and Hugh, filled in Reese on how her first few weeks of kindergarten were going.

"I can't believe you're in Mrs. Clifton's class. She's been teaching for so long. She was my favorite," Reese said, shaking her head. We'd all been in her class back in the day.

"She's the best," I agreed.

"Just don't try to tell her how to do her job." Brinkley reached for her glass of red wine and took a sip. "She told Mom that I was too bossy."

My mother's head fell back in laughter. "She had something to say about each of you, but it always came from a good place. She thought Brinks needed to be reminded that she wasn't the teacher."

"Well, my girl does things better than most people, so it only seems right that she would take control of her classroom." Lincoln chuckled as he leaned over and kissed the top of her head. He was the best quarterback in the league, and we were all hoping he was going to lead the New York Thunderbirds to the Super Bowl this year. They tried to fly home to Cottonwood Cove on the free weekends that he didn't have a game and Brinkley could work remotely.

"Can't argue with that." My mother gazed around the table, her eyes landing on her firstborn, my older brother, and a wide grin spread across her face. "And she said that Cage needed to work on his patience. I think we got called in several times about that."

"Didn't Cage pop someone in the nose because they cut him in line? He got sent home for the afternoon if I'm remembering right," Dad said, and the table erupted in laughter.

"You got suspended from kindergarten, brother," Hugh said with a chuckle.

"Tony Landry cut me in line one too many times. A kid can only take so much." Cage rolled his eyes before looking at his daughter with a brow raised. "But you're better than Daddy ever was as a kid, so don't do what I did."

"Sounds like the kid had it coming," Maddox said. He and my sister, Georgia, had been married for a few weeks now, and they were ridiculously in love. "What did she have to say about Mrs. Lancaster?"

"I think I recall her telling us that Georgie was a bit of a daydreamer," my father said as he smiled at my youngest sibling.

"Yes. She said that Georgie had her head in the clouds sometimes," my mother added.

More laughter.

"I've always liked the clouds and the stars," Georgia said, smiling at her husband.

"Didn't she call me a stubborn child?" Olivia huffed, looking from her father to her mother.

"Yes. She'd said Reese was a people pleaser and that you were too stubborn for your own good," Jenny said.

"What can I say? I was ahead of my years. I would not be put into a box."

"Power to the woman!" Reese, Georgia, and Brinkley shouted at the same time.

"Damn straight. And since when is being a people pleaser at five years old a bad thing?" Reese said over her laughter.

"Okay. We get it. It's the year of the woman." Cage raised a brow. "And let me guess. Hugh and Finn were perfect angels?"

My father barked out a laugh. "I don't think Mrs. Clifton thought any child was perfect. What did she say about Hugh?"

My mom thought it over. "Hugh was not a big fan of full-day school. He'd fall asleep every afternoon during circle time."

My sister-in-law, Lila, smiled up at her husband. "Awww… he was a tired bear."

"Thanks, baby. If memory serves, I thrived at recess and lunch, and work time had me tapping out for a little siesta."

Gracie was giggling so hard and clapping her hands. "What about Uncle Finny?"

"Uncle Finny was a chatty little guy," my father said. "What did she call him?"

"She said that he was the mayor of the classroom. Always

buzzing around from table to table. And, do you remember, Jenny?" My mother smiled, turning her attention to her best friend. "She'd said that Finn couldn't handle being separated from Reese in line."

"I sure do. They had that fire drill when Reese was in the bathroom, and Finn was frantic that Mrs. Clifton was going to leave her."

"Awww… you always had my back," Reese said.

"Always. That will never change."

"You two were ridiculous back then," Olivia said over her laughter. "Do you remember when Reese found out that she and Finn weren't going to be in the same class in second or third grade, and she cried so hard that you had to go to the school and get them switched into the same class?"

"That was third grade, and it would have been the first time that we weren't together." Reese shrugged.

"Which leads us to the elephant in the room," Cage said. "Time for you to go watch a movie for a little bit, munchkin. And then we're heading home. You've got school tomorrow."

"I'll go get her set up," Lila said, pushing to stand and leading Gracie to the family room where she'd get her settled on the couch while the grownups harassed us.

Of course, my siblings were ready to pounce. They all had the patience of a toddler on a sugar high.

"Okay, let's get into it." Brinkley rubbed her hands together. "Is this the real deal?"

"I've got money on this, so you best tell the truth." My oldest brother turned his attention to me.

"You're betting on us now?" I said over my laughter.

"That was Cage's idea," Hugh said.

"Well, I tossed in ten bucks. I think this is some sort of stunt to get that annoying ex of yours back," Olivia said, crossing her arms over her chest as she looked at Reese.

"Let's not talk poorly about Carl," Jenny said. "And let them speak, for goodness' sake."

Lila came back and took her seat beside Hugh. "What did I miss?"

"Well, this is a 'code of silence' moment. So everyone here has to agree to keep this a secret." Reese glanced around the table.

"What happens at the Reynolds' house stays at the Reynolds' house," Georgia said.

"I don't know that we can say that. You and Brinks have had too many slips to put that slogan on a T-shirt," Cage grumped.

"Don't be a hater," Brinkley said, shooting him a warning look. "A Reynolds-Murphy code of silence is different. Obviously, we will all keep our mouths closed."

"Finn and I are just going to have some fun. I wasn't ready to face Carl and his new girlfriend," Reese said before clearing her throat. It was obvious that even the mention of them dating caused her pain.

"Whom we shall leave unnamed because the fact that she uses a three-name title is annoying as hell." Olivia held her wine glass up, and everyone raised their glasses and chuckled as they clinked them together.

"It's not that big of a deal. She wants to make Carl jealous because he can't stand the idea of her being with me. And it will clean up my image and hopefully put Jessica's claims to rest. She's going to live with me anyway, and we're always together, so it's a win-win. We'll keep up appearances for the next two months, and then I'll head back to filming after the holidays, and Reese will get her happily ever after." I shrugged.

I saw the disappointment on our mothers' faces, but they both nodded.

"Well, I'm not paying until the gig is up and they end this thing," Cage said, throwing his hands in the air.

"Listen, if you want to pull this off, you can't be sloppy," Brinkley said after she set her wine glass down. "You've got

Marilyn there cleaning your house, and you know she's a gossip. She's best friends with Mrs. Runither. So Reese better keep her things in your room and make it look like she's staying in there with you."

"I often wonder where that devious mind of yours comes from. How do you think of these things?" Cage asked as the table erupted in laughter once again.

"I'm a reporter. It's my job to think of these things," Brinkley said, unable to hide her smile.

"Wouldn't change one hair on your head, sweetheart." Lincoln wrapped an arm around her shoulder and tugged her closer.

"So, what's the plan? Finn cleans up his image that Jessica has tainted, and Reese gets back together with Carl?" Georgia asked.

"That's the plan. Now that I know what I want to do with my life professionally, I want to move forward in my personal life, as well. It was never that I didn't want to marry Carl. I just wanted him to support my dreams the way I've supported his."

"And you think he's done that?" Olivia asked, and she didn't hide her irritation. I knew she wasn't a fan of Carl because she'd opened up to me at Maddox and Georgia's wedding in Paris when Reese had stepped out of the reception to take a call from her ex. Olivia and Carl used to be close, but since he'd ended the engagement, she was most definitely protective of her sister.

"He supports me. He just didn't like us being apart for a year. There's a difference."

Everyone at the table shared a glance, and I saw the uncertainty. But they all loved Reese, and they'd agree because they didn't want to say what was really on their minds.

That her ex had behaved like a selfish prick, and he didn't deserve her.

I knew it.
They knew it.
My best friend wasn't there yet.
But I was going to help her get there.

six

• • •

Reese

I LEANED FORWARD and wrapped my arms around Millie's neck as we approached the stable. Finn had done a great job of getting this place ready, and I felt very lucky that my mare was the first one to move in. He'd hired Silas a while back to manage the property while he was on set, and Silas would take over caring for the horses once they filled the stalls. Silas was thrilled to have Millie here now. He was a local who had worked on many ranches in the area, and I could tell he was happy to be working for Finn.

Finn was striding toward the barn, and I waved. His baseball cap was turned backward on his head, and his smile was like sunshine on a cloudy day. He'd always had a way of grounding me and making me feel like everything was going to be okay. He wore a pair of faded jeans and a black hooded sweatshirt. You wouldn't know that Finn Reynolds was going to be on the cover of the most popular entertainment magazine in the country in just a few weeks. He was just… Finn. The same as he'd always been. Fame hadn't changed a thing about him. I knew it wouldn't because this man had always had a strong sense of who he was. It was something that I'd always admired about him. While the rest of us were trying to figure out who we were and what we wanted to do with our lives, Finn just trusted his gut. He didn't think twice when he started pursuing his acting career while we were still in college, cutting his course load back significantly. He no longer wanted to study business and he'd made that change suddenly after I'd gone into remission after months of chemotherapy and treatment. He'd just said he was done pursuing things he didn't want to do and he was ready to go after what he wanted, and he'd completely changed course. He'd agreed to stay in school part time, as he knew his parents would want him to finish what he started, but he pursued acting from that point on. He never questioned his decisions, and there'd been many times in my life that I'd wished some of that could rub off on me.

We'd only been home for forty-eight hours, but I'd yet to venture out beyond going to get my horse and see family. But we were planning on going to Cottonwood Café for lunch, so I'd taken Millie out for a ride to calm my nerves.

I knew it was inevitable that I'd run into Carl. He'd been texting me ever since the news broke about me and Finn, and I'd only responded once. I had to play things right, not act too interested, and not show how hurt I was if I ran into them together.

Millie trotted into the stall, and I hiked my leg over and slid down until my feet hit the ground. The smell of hay and wood flooded my senses, along with the slight mix of pine that was present this time of year in Cottonwood Cove. The crisp air was just starting to get too cold to go without a sweater. I was thankful that I'd slipped on my black cashmere turtleneck before I went out because when Millie broke out in a full run, the wind did nothing to keep me warm.

"Hey, how'd she do?"

"I think she missed me," I said as I gave her one last hug and ran my fingers across her gorgeous brown and amber mane.

"I think we all did," he said, closing the stall as we made our way toward his house.

"Yeah? It feels good to be home. I still think it's a bit much that all my stuff is in your bedroom and bathroom," I said with a chuckle. Brinkley was always one step ahead of everyone else, so we'd decided to trust her suggestion to make it look like we were staying in the same room.

"It doesn't really matter where your stuff is. Hell, you could sleep in my room if you wanted to." He pulled the door open, and I stepped inside.

"No way. With you not having sex, you've got a chronic issue going on in the morning, and I can't subject myself to that."

He barked out a laugh as I grabbed my purse and glanced down at my cowboy boots, which I'd planned to change out of, but I was still chilly, so I decided to leave them on.

As we made our way out to the garage, I paused at the door. Finn caged me in with both arms. "You haven't stopped talking about my morning wood since we left London. Does Carl never get an erection? Why do I feel like the only dick you've seen, aside from mine, was less than impressive?" He smirked.

"I told you that Carl has that issue with the medication he takes." I cleared my throat. "So, I guess seeing how… excited your penis was, well, I suppose that was new for me."

His gaze searched mine. Finn's gray eyes were like none I'd ever seen before. They were this steely pewter with a ring of citrine gold around them.

"That's a shame, Miney. The excited penis is not something anyone should go without. It's my favorite quality about myself." His knuckles rapped against the wall above me, and he stepped back and tugged the door open. I'd been living far away from my best friend for a year now, and something about him was different.

Or maybe it was me.

I'd always known that he was good-looking. There was no question there.

But he was… just more.

Sexier.

More confident.

Sexier.

Did I say that one already?

It could also be the fact that I hadn't had sex in over a year. It would be normal to notice the opposite sex, even if it was Finn.

I felt the need to defend Carl because this tinge of guilt was sinking in that I was looking at my best friend and noticing things I hadn't noticed before.

How about we focus on the man you want to marry, huh?

"Well, I'm not saying that it isn't excited sometimes. It just doesn't show off the way yours does. Some can be more understated," I said as he pulled open the passenger door, and I climbed into his big red truck.

"Mine has always liked to show off," he said when he settled into the driver's seat and winked at me before turning on the engine.

"Of course it has," I teased as we drove toward town.

"Did taking Millie out help settle your nerves?" he asked as we turned down Cottonwood Cove Drive, where all the shops and restaurants sat. The town was decorated for fall. Tall corn husks were tied around every light post, and most of the shop windows were decorated with pumpkins and harvest décor.

The small town was not lacking charm, much like the man beside me.

"Yeah. Your house is on such a beautiful lot. You've got all the pines on one side, and we made our way down near the water. It's gorgeous. It felt good to be outside. I've been spending most of my days going between an office and a tiny studio apartment."

"See, you did the right thing coming home."

He parked in the side lot of Cottonwood Café, and I let out a long breath as I tugged my braid over one shoulder. "So, how are we going to play this?"

"You want to show everyone we're together, so that's what we'll do."

"And if we run into Carl?"

"Then I'll show him what he's missing," he said, waggling his brows before hopping out of the truck. He came around and opened my door, helping me out.

"Relax. I'm a professional actor. We've got this. Just go with it. If we don't see him, we'll just act normal. It's not like I have sex in a booth at a restaurant when I'm with a woman."

I laughed as he pulled open the door to Cottonwood Café. The place was always booming during the day, while Reynolds' Bar and Grill, Finn's brother Hugh's restaurant, was always booming at night.

"Well, if it isn't the couple of the hour." Mrs. Runither, the owner, clapped her hands together. "It's about damn time you two figured it out. Don't get me wrong, Dr. Studmuffin is easy on the eyes, too. But Finn Reynolds, I mean… he's the whole package."

"Damn straight." Finn puffed out his chest and smirked. "You've always had my back. Bring it in." He held his arms out, and the horndog, Mrs. Runither, couldn't get there fast enough. My eyes gaped open when she made no attempt to hide the fact that she was squeezing his ass. My head fell back in laughter. This was what I'd missed about being home. The comfort. The laughs. Cottonwood Cove was my home. My happy place. I just hadn't liked the job I had when I was here. I wanted to go out and experience something new, be my own person, and find myself. But I always wanted to come back. Home was where my heart was. My family. Finn. Carl. All my friends.

Why couldn't he have just understood that?

"Wow. You got the whole cheek in there, didn't you? You don't want to make my girl jealous, do you?" he teased as he pulled back and kissed the older woman's cheek.

Very few people tolerated Mrs. Runither, but Finn had always embraced her.

He didn't mind that she was a dirty old bird and completely unprofessional in the way she violated her customers.

He shrugged it off.

That was the beauty of Finn.

He didn't take life too seriously.

I hoped he'd never change. He was the eternal Peter Pan.

But he didn't always understand my internal clock and the timeline pressure I felt to achieve the things I wanted out of life.

"Oh, that's right. You two are bumpin' dirties now, aren't you?" she purred, and I couldn't help but zone in on her tangerine-colored lipstick that was drawn so far outside the lines of her lips that it looked like clown makeup.

"I mean, look at her. Do you think I could contain myself around her?" His tongue swiped out to wet his lips, and Mrs. Runither groaned as she watched him.

Damn. He really was a good actor.

"Okay, Finn, we should probably get to our table," I said, anxious to sit down and get away from this awkward conversation.

"Yes, baby," he said. His tone was so sexy that my eyes widened. "Her ex isn't here, is he? We don't need any fights breaking out in this fine establishment of yours."

He'd always been good at getting information out of people.

"Not that I've seen today, but he and his new lady friend do come here often. Christy Rae Lovell is a big fan of my mac 'n' cheese."

"Well, if they do come in, we'd appreciate you sitting

them far away from us." Finn kissed her cheek, and I swear I could see hearts appear in the woman's eyes.

This was why women needed to be careful with Finn.

He'd broken more hearts than either of us could count, but he'd always managed to walk away still loved. He didn't lie about who he was, and women found that endearing.

She led us to the table in the back, and I stopped to say hi to several locals. Matilda, the owner of The Tipsy Tea, jumped to her feet to hug me. She'd always been one of my favorites in town.

"I'm so happy you're back home, Reese," she said as she hugged me tight. My favorite birthday party of all time was the tea party at her shop when I was eight years old. Of course, Finn had been the only boy in attendance, and he'd been just fine with it. She'd owned that store for as long as I could remember.

"It feels good to be home." I pulled back and smiled at her.

"And this," she said with a wide grin as her gaze moved from me to Finn. "I always suspected you two would end up together."

A sharp pang hit my chest at the realization that we were lying to a lot of good people. Before I could react, Finn's arms wrapped around me from behind, and he nipped at my ear, which made me squeal.

What the hell was he doing?

He didn't need to pour it on this thick when Carl wasn't even here.

"I always suspected it, too, Matilda. I just wasn't mature enough to recognize it before now. But the heart wants what the heart wants. And I'm all in."

I dug my nails into his hand in warning.

And for the love of God, I felt his massive boner press against my lower back again.

I knew my best friend was a big fan of sex, but this was out of control.

"Well, there's nothing better than finding your soulmate and holding on tight. You two enjoy yourselves, and please stop by the store next week so you can tell me all about London."

"I will. I'm looking for some office space downtown this week, so I'll definitely come by and see you." I shoved Finn back as casually as I could and hugged her one more time.

He chuckled as we walked to our table. I dropped my butt into the booth, and he slid in beside me, which was not the norm.

"Why are you sitting on the same side of the booth as me?" I said under my breath.

"Because we're lovers, Miney." He chuckled as his lips grazed my ear again.

"Carl and I never sat on the same side of a booth."

"Exactly. I'm a much better boyfriend than he is. I don't like any distance between me and my woman."

"He's not even here. Tone it down," I said over my laughter.

"This is a small town. Everyone talks. I can't have people thinking I'm a selfish lover," he whispered before leaning back in the booth and grabbing the menu on the table.

I leaned close to him. "Speaking of selfish lovers… I think you might need to see a doctor about that situation you've got going on. That cannot be comfortable. Chewy Junior was poking me in the back again."

He barked out a laugh before leaning close again and talking just above a whisper. "It's been a while for me. The longest I've ever gone in my adult life without sex. So, you're going to have to deal with it. You're in a relationship with a horny dude now."

I glanced around to make sure no one was listening. The place was going off as usual. There was an Elvis Presley song playing from the jukebox, and conversations were going on all around us.

"I've gone a year, and you don't see me acting like a teenage horndog."

"What can I say? My girl does it for me." He smiled so wide that I couldn't help but smile back.

Because Finn Reynolds really was my favorite person on the planet.

seven

. . .

Finn

REESE and I stepped outside of Cottonwood Café, and I reached for her hand when the cool breeze hit us right in the face. She stopped, her back pressed against the brick building, and rolled her eyes.

"I swear you just let Mrs. Runither round second base with that hug she gave you when she said goodbye," she said.

I chuckled and reached for the zipper of her coat, tugging it all the way up.

"Do you even know what rounding second base means? An ass grab does not count as a base." I saw something out of my peripheral vision, and my head turned the slightest bit before I realized who it was. On instinct, I leaned forward and covered her mouth with mine.

She gasped against me, her hands gripping my coat as my tongue slipped inside and tangled with hers.

Only Reese could taste minty after eating a Cottonwood Café burger. The girl was always prepared with mints and lip gloss and sunscreen.

I shouldn't be surprised.

But I didn't know she would taste so good.

I liked the way her lips felt, the way they melded with mine.

My dick was out of control, and this kiss was the equivalent of a missile launch countdown. He was ready.

I definitely needed to get laid. Between no sex for the last year, and then not even so much as a make-out session with a woman since Jessica launched this psychotic campaign against me, and now fake dating my best friend—there was no light at the end of this tunnel.

Or should I say, light at the end of this missile launch.

"Reese," a voice growled, and I smiled against her mouth before pulling back.

She blinked up at me several times before her gaze slowly moved to find her ex-boyfriend, Carl, standing there.

He stood with his arms folded across his chest.

Christy Rae Lovell was beside him, her eyes moving between us.

"Carl," Reese said, clearing her throat and squaring her shoulders like she was preparing for battle.

Atta girl.

"Hey," he said awkwardly, raising a brow at me as he moved closer as if he wanted me to step back so he could hug her.

That wasn't going to happen.

She was mine now, at least as far as everyone knew, and I wouldn't do anything to help him out.

Reese would have to make the move if she wanted to hug him.

Of course, she shot me a look and slid away from me, giving him the world's most awkward hug.

Well, second to my hug with old lady Runither, who goosed me on my way out the door.

She stepped back quickly and then nodded at the woman beside him, and they both said an awkward hello.

"I texted you," he said before glancing at his girlfriend

and then back to Reese. "Christy knows that we're going to get together for some coffee and some closure. Oh, have you not told Finn that we're meeting up? I hope I haven't caused any trouble."

"Are you kidding? My girl told me all about it. We don't have secrets." I clapped him on the shoulder. "Yep, when we were soaking in the tub last night with glasses of wine in our hands, she mentioned it. *Briefly.* You know, we had more important things going on at that moment."

Reese's foot pressed down hard on top of mine, and then she tried to play it off as if she'd slipped. "Oops. Sorry about that, Finn."

"Can't get close enough to your man, can you, baby?" I said, wrapping one arm around her and pulling her to me.

Carl just stood there with his mouth hanging open.

Clearly, the dude had never soaked in a tub with her because apparently, he had the libido of a corpse and a dick that required batteries.

Christy Rae Lovell's eyes widened as she took us in. "Well, I trust my man, so it's fine with me. I can't keep him on a leash, can I?"

I felt Reese stiffen against me.

"If you want to pull out a leash, I wouldn't mind if you tied me up, baby." I leaned down and kissed her cheek, and she chuckled.

I was ridiculous when it came to Reese. I couldn't stand the idea of this dickless wonder hurting her any more than he already had.

"All right, well, just let me know when you want to meet. It was good to see you both," Reese said, stepping out of my arms and reaching for my hand.

Carl looked surprised that she was ready to walk away, and I loved seeing the bastard squirm.

"Yeah. I'll text you, and we'll get that scheduled. I'm glad you're home, Reese."

She nodded casually, as if it didn't matter when he texted her, and I fucking loved it. We walked hand in hand toward my truck, and I waited until we were around the corner of the building to speak. "You okay? You handled that well."

She nodded, and I helped her into the truck. Her eyes watered the slightest bit, and she shrugged. "It's just weird, you know? We were supposed to be married by now. Did I mess everything up by leaving? Was I not worth the wait, Chewy?"

And that fucking did it. The first tear streaked down her face, and a sharp ache moved across my chest. I slipped my hands beneath her knees and her neck, and I lifted her just enough so that I could slide into the truck and drop her onto my lap. I tugged the door closed and wrapped my arms around her.

"You're okay, Miney. You didn't do anything wrong. It's his loss."

"It doesn't seem like it is, does it?" she croaked. "He seems to be doing just fine. He's already got a new relationship, and they look happy."

"No, they don't. He looked fucking miserable and jealous. Did you see the way he was staring at me when I had my arms around you? He was struggling to control himself."

She sniffed, and her phone vibrated in her purse, which was sitting beside us on the seat. "Really? You think so?"

"Hell yeah, I do. There is no one like you," I said. "He can try all he wants, but I know it, and he knows it. Christy Rae Lovell doesn't hold a candle to you."

"She's pretty; you can't deny it."

"I honestly didn't notice, Miney. Because my eyes were on you."

She sniffed once more and then tipped her head back to look at me. "You're the best fake boyfriend in the world, Chewy."

Her phone vibrated again, and she reached into her purse

and pulled it out. I glanced down at the screen to see a lengthy text from Dr. Limpdick.

"I think you might be right about him being jealous," she said, her tone lighter now. "He wants to meet during the week. *For dinner.* It was supposed to be coffee, but he said we have a lot to discuss."

"There you go. See, everything is going to be fine." I kissed her forehead, and I shifted to get out of the truck, but she surprised me by wrapping her arms around my neck and hugging me even tighter.

"I'd be lost without you. Thank you for always having my back."

"Always will, you know that. Now, how about we go home and watch our two favorite movies and chill out?"

"Let's do it. I think we should watch *Star Wars* first because you just saved the day," she said as I moved her off my lap and climbed out of the truck.

Once I was in the driver's seat, I glanced over. She was still staring down at her phone as he continued to text her.

It bothered me that he kept fucking with her head. He'd cut her off, had gotten fully into another relationship, and didn't have a care in the world about Reese.

Until he found out that she was coming home and that she was with me.

And the minute he thought she was happy without him, he wanted to swoop back in.

That didn't sit well with me, but I wasn't about to take this moment from her. She was happy, and I'd just have to deal with it.

"How exactly did I save the day?"

"Well, that kiss clearly sent him sideways." She chuckled, tucking her phone back into her purse.

"Yeah. It was a spur-of-the-moment decision."

"It was a good one."

"Good decision or good kiss?" I chuckled as I pulled into my garage.

She turned to face me. "I mean, I haven't kissed anyone in over a year, and you are a trained actor."

I barked out a laugh. "Damn straight. And I've always loved kissing, so obviously I'm good at it."

"If you say so, Romeo." She jumped out of the truck, and I slipped out and shut the garage door.

"Well, I didn't say it first; you did. Just admit it. Best kiss you've ever had."

"I'm not going to say that."

"Because it isn't true, or because you feel guilty admitting your ex-boyfriend is a terrible lover?"

She set her purse down on the kitchen island and gaped at me. "I never said that. I said he has some medical limitations with certain things, but he's a great lover. I mean, not that I have anything to compare him to. You know that he's the only guy I've ever been with."

"That still breaks my heart," I said, pressing my hand to my chest dramatically. "You should have had a fling in London. Had some fun. Only being with Carl would be like never eating anything but a peanut butter and jelly sandwich."

She rolled her eyes and crossed her arms over her chest. "Just because I'm not like you does not mean my way is the wrong way. I found a guy I loved my senior year of high school, and I like monogamy."

I grabbed two bottles of water from the fridge and motioned for her to follow me to the couch. My home had one big open great room with a large brown sectional couch that Reese had picked out a while back. I set the water bottles down and kicked off my favorite cowboy boots and sat down. Reese did the same and reached for the throw blanket on the back of the couch.

"I'm not saying you have to sleep around. I'm just

saying… being with one person, especially Carl, for your entire life—never having an orgasm…" I shrugged. "Where's the fun in that?"

Her cheeks pinked, but I didn't regret saying it. Reese and I had always been honest with one another. I wasn't going to stop now.

"I never said that I've never had an orgasm. I said I've never had one with Carl." She raised a brow.

My motherfucking dick responded like a caged bull breaking free after the gates opened. He sprung to life and was ready for action. I adjusted myself as inconspicuously as possible, but her eyes moved down, and she shook her head.

"You're unbelievable. All it takes is the slightest breeze, and there he is again, showing off."

But it wasn't a breeze my dick was responding to.

It was Reese.

But I'd write it off to my lack of sex lately.

"Let's finish this intriguing conversation," I said.

"Only you would find a conversation about orgasms intriguing." Her tongue dipped out to wet her lips, and I couldn't look away.

Had she always had such pouty pink lips?

"I will not apologize for knowing the importance of the orgasm. I always make sure my lady climaxes first. I'm a generous lover. So, tell me, when was the last time you orgasmed?"

"Oh my God, Chewy. Why are we talking about this?"

"Hey." I held my hands up and laughed. "You want to fix things with the asshole, and part of that will be improving your sex life. Trust me, Miney. If the sex had been fabulous, you wouldn't have considered leaving him for a year."

"Why?" She pursed her lips, not hiding her irritation. "You apparently have fabulous sex, yet you leave everybody."

Damn. Shots fired.

"You wound me," I said, both hands on my heart. "I don't leave anyone that doesn't know what the score is, and you know that. I'm a straight shooter. I love women. I just haven't found one I loved for longer than a weekend... aside from you, of course."

She rolled her eyes. "Fine. You want to talk about it. Let's talk about it."

"Have you and Carl never talked about sex?"

"No. He doesn't like to talk about it, and neither do I."

Bullshit.

That prim and proper prick has made her feel ashamed to talk about what she wants.

"Well, there's no shame in talking about it. I always ask my partner what they like. What they want. What makes them feel good. And I take my time getting them off. I don't just fuck and run."

She groaned and fell back against the couch. "Carl and I do not fuck and run, either."

"All right, so tell me. He never made you come? I know it didn't happen during sex, but what about other things?" I asked, and I was suddenly dying for her to answer.

"I'm going to tell you something, but if you bring it up or throw it in my face, I will never discuss sex with you again."

"Well, I like that we're talking about it now, so I won't risk that." I smirked, moving closer to her like she was about to tell me her darkest secret.

"I've only orgasmed by myself." Her cheeks flamed pink, and she looked away.

That fucking selfish prick.

I reached for her, settling my thumb and pointer finger beneath her chin, and turned her face toward me. Her sage-green gaze locked with mine.

"There's no shame in that, Miney. I get myself off all the time. Hell, my right hand is getting a real workout lately." I laughed. "But I want you to know that having an orgasm with a partner is better. More powerful."

"If you say so," she whispered. "It doesn't bother me that it hasn't happened during sex. Lots of women don't orgasm during sex."

"I don't know if that's true, but I know there are other ways. He couldn't even get you off with his fingers or his tongue?"

Her mouth fell open, and I suddenly wondered what it would be like if those lips were wrapped around my cock.

What the hell was wrong with me?

"Jesus, Finn. I'm done with this conversation."

"Just answer the damn question."

"We don't do… you know—that."

"What does that mean? He doesn't go down on you?"

"He went to medical school; he knows too much." She shrugged.

"Oh, for fuck's sake, Miney. Lots of doctors eat pussy."

Her head fell back in laughter, and I couldn't help but join in. This was a ridiculous piece of information.

What kind of man didn't like pussy?

I guess the same kind of man who doesn't like pleasing his lady.

"Okay, can we please start the movie? That's enough show and share for the day."

I reached for the remote and turned on the TV. I searched for the movie and then leaned back against the sofa.

"Hey, you don't have to put on *Harry Potter* first. I said we could start with *Star Wars*."

"That was before I knew your pussy has been deprived all these years. So, we're watching *Harry Potter*, Miney. But when you get back together with that selfish prick, you're going to make some demands, and I'm going to help you."

"Deal," she said, extending her hand to me just as the movie started. But instead of shaking it, I tugged her close, and her head settled against my chest. My arms came around her on instinct.

For a moment, I wondered what it would be like if she didn't go back to Carl.

And she stayed here with me.

Forever.

eight

. . .

Reese

THE LAST WEEK had flown by. Finn had found a gorgeous three-year-old colt whom he'd named Han Solo.

Go figure.

We'd taken him and Millie out on a long ride today after Finn had gone with me to check out two office spaces downtown. Starting my own business was both thrilling and terrifying, but I was ready to take some risks.

To feel something.

The prices were a bit high for me, and I could potentially start the business off remotely. Meet people at their homes.

Finn felt strongly that I needed to show that I was serious. Find a space and get things rolling.

It had been so long since I'd been excited about what I did for a living, and going to London had changed all that for me. I wasn't going to waste that lesson. I was going to make it happen.

"Hey, I just thought of something. Have you ever thought about the fact that someone might name their horse Wyatt after your character on *Big Sky Ranch*? I mean, you just named your horse Han Solo," I said as I made my way into the kitchen, where he was cooking chili.

I'd just gotten ready in Finn's bathroom. Sometimes it was just easier since all of my belongings were in his room. Turns out, Brinkley was right because Georgia had been at Cottonwood Café and overheard Mrs. Runither and Marilyn talking about me and Finn living together. Marilyn had cleaned his house three days ago, and clearly, she'd paid attention to where my things were.

"Wow, look at you," Finn said with a whistle.

It smelled like fall in here, with the fresh log burning in his fireplace and the seasonings from the chili flooding the kitchen.

"Thank you. You approve, *Lover*?" I teased as I twirled around. I was wearing my new cream sweater, which fell off one shoulder, my dark skinny jeans, and my lucky cowboy boots. My hair was pulled back in a messy knot at the nape of my neck, and I felt put together for the first time since I'd found out Carl was dating someone else.

It felt good to put on makeup and dress cute again.

After our long conversation about orgasms, my mind wandered to Carl and his current girlfriend. It was nauseating to think about, for sure, but I couldn't help but wonder if our lack of connection had something to do with me. Maybe I don't appeal to guys in a sexy way. Maybe I'm safe or something like that. Finn and I have been friends forever, and never once has he tried anything sexual—not in a serious way, anyway. Maybe Carl didn't get excited over me either… That was a depressing thought.

"I sure do, Lover," he said as he held a hand beneath the ladle and motioned for me to come taste.

Living here had been so easy, and I knew I'd be sad when our little arrangement came to an end, but it was for the greater good. I'd still get to see Finn every day, at least when he wasn't filming. And it was time to figure out things with Carl.

I sealed my lips over the spoon and groaned as the garlic

and peppers hit my tongue. Finn had become a really good cook since all the drama with Jessica had him keeping a low profile at home.

She'd gone silent since our relationship had gone public. But she kept calling Finn, who continued to ignore her calls. He was not looking forward to filming with her again in the new year. And I was dreading him not being here, where I could see him every day.

This last year had not only shown me that I was ready to spread my wings professionally, that I was ready to get my relationship with Carl back on track, but it also showed me how much I'd missed my best friend.

My ride or die.

And I'd missed being here, in Cottonwood Cove, more than I'd ever imagined.

"Damn. That is so good. I kind of wish I was going to stay and eat here."

"So, stay and eat here," he said, setting the spoon down and crossing his arms over his Henley-covered chest. His muscles pressed against the fabric, and I took him in. He really was a beautiful man. He had fans and women that fawned all over him, but he was still just Finn.

The boy who'd convinced me at the young age of five years old that if we left food out at night for our gummy worms, they would come to life while we were sleeping.

The boy who'd gone with me to get my ears pierced when I was ten years old because I was too afraid to go alone.

The boy who'd always saved a spot for me at lunch right beside him, from kindergarten through high school.

Even when I was dating Carl our senior year, he'd still hold that spot for me, just in case I didn't want to sit with my boyfriend that day.

He was also the boy who went to every single chemo treatment with me for months. He never missed one. A lump formed in my throat at the memory—how Finn had somehow made my treatments tolerable.

"I need to go talk to him and find out how serious things are with him and his new girlfriend." I cleared my throat. "See if we can salvage this."

He studied me for the longest time as I reached into my purse and popped a mint into my mouth. I didn't know what to expect tonight, but I wanted to be prepared. "Yeah, yeah, sure. A lifetime of boring sex and being a doctor's wife sounds really appealing."

"Says the guy who doesn't do relationships. You don't know what it's like out there, Chewy. I don't want to waste years looking for Mr. Right when I'm fairly certain I've already found him."

He nodded and looked away. "I just want you to be happy, Miney."

"I am. I've been so happy being back home and here with you. With the holidays coming up, it just feels really good."

"It does. I'm glad you're here. But I've got to say, I don't think it's cool that he changed the plans to dinner tonight."

I pursed my lips and studied him. "Why does that matter?"

"Because you're my woman, right? I mean, as far as he knows. He can't just take you to dinner without running it by me. That's all I'm saying."

"I think that chili pepper has made you a little crazy. You don't need to play the role of the caveman boyfriend. This is what we wanted to happen, remember?"

He turned away and huffed, and I couldn't help but laugh. He was being ridiculous.

The doorbell rang, and we both startled. "He's here. He insisted on picking me up."

"I'll bet he did. What a fucking gentleman." He made no attempt to hide his irritation as he tried to shove past me.

"You do not need to walk me to the door," I whisper-hissed, moving in front of him.

"What kind of boyfriend would I be if I didn't make sure that he knew I was paying attention?"

I shook my head and grumped. "The fake kind?"

"Hey. I take my role very seriously. Don't underestimate me."

Finn opened the door and immediately glared at Carl as I slipped into my jacket.

"Hey. You look—" Carl paused and looked at Finn before turning his attention back to me. "Nice."

"Nice observation. But she always looks nice. Come here, baby." Finn reached for my hand and spun me until I slammed into his chest. He tipped my chin up, and his lips covered mine. We hadn't discussed any pregame kiss, but he was the professional actor, so I'd follow his lead.

His lips were soft, just like the last time he'd kissed me. I'd thought about it a lot since it had happened. The man could definitely kiss.

His tongue slipped in, and my hands moved on instinct to his hair as I urged him closer.

God. I'd never been kissed like this, not before Finn.

A loud noise pulled me from my daze, and I realized Carl was clearing his throat, reminding us that he was there.

Finn pulled back. "Don't stay out too late, Miney. I'll be waiting for you."

"Yeah, of course," I said, my words breathy as I patted my bun into place, and Carl pulled the door open and walked briskly away from us toward his car.

I turned around and gave two thumbs-up to Finn as I couldn't hide the smile spreading across my face, and whispered, "So freaking good. I think we're getting under his skin. Have fun with your brothers."

I tugged the door closed and jogged down the walkway to where Carl was holding the passenger door open for me.

"Sorry about that. He just can't keep his hands to himself sometimes," I said as I slipped into the car and reached for the buckle.

"I can see that." He closed my door and was in the seat beside me quickly. I noticed the way his jaw clenched as he stared out the window at the road.

The drive to the restaurant was quiet, and I suddenly felt a little awkward. It had been a year since we'd spent any real time together. So much had changed, and I didn't know how to feel about that. There was this nagging fear that we might not be able to get back to what we had before, and then what? I'd be single for the rest of my life and living in my best friend's guest room?

Don't overthink it.

You were engaged to this man.

You want to spend your life with him.

He surprised me when he pulled into the driveway of his house and came around to open my door.

"Oh. I thought you said that we were going to Reynolds'?"

"I just figured we'd have so many people in our business if we went there, and I ordered us takeout from your favorite Italian restaurant. It'll be delivered in fifteen minutes."

My heart squeezed at his words.

He remembered.

He'd made an effort for us to be alone because he missed me.

"The ravioli and the Caesar salad?" I asked.

"Of course. It's what you always chose when it was your turn to pick." He put the key in the door and pushed it open for me to walk in.

I sucked in a breath. I was supposed to be living here by now.

It looked exactly the same. Mid-century modern décor. I'd helped him decorate it when he'd bought the place, even though I found his style to be a bit cold for my liking. I'd planned to warm it up once I'd moved in.

"I could have just driven here. You just mentioned that Finn's house was on the way to the restaurant," I said, slipping my coat off and hanging it on the coat rack by the door.

"I wanted to come get you." He shoved his hands in his pockets and studied me. "You look good, Reese. I think London agreed with you. Or it's just that your new boyfriend makes you really happy."

Here we go.

Should I tell him the truth?

My heart raced, and the words were on the tip of my tongue.

But for whatever reason, I couldn't say them.

He was dating someone. Carl's relationship was real. I wasn't ready to admit that mine wasn't.

"He does make me happy. And it appears Christy Rae Lovell makes you very happy."

He nodded, but something in his blue gaze told me things weren't that simple. This was exactly what I was hoping for. A chink in his armor.

"Come on. Let me get you a glass of wine."

"I'm assuming your girlfriend is okay with me coming to your house for dinner?" I answered, following him toward the kitchen.

"I told her we were getting together tonight. I didn't mention where we were going because it's not important. She's working the night shift at the hospital." He poured me a glass of Cabernet and handed it to me.

"She hasn't moved in with you?"

"No. You know how I feel about that. I didn't want us to live together before we were engaged. I see Finn doesn't mind making up the rules as he goes."

"I think everyone's allowed to make up their own rules, Carl. If you recall, I wanted to move in with you sooner. That was your rule, and I respected it. But I have my own rules that I live by now."

And when we got back together, I would not hold back from sharing what I wanted moving forward.

"Just be careful, Reese. He's not the kind of guy who wants to take things the whole way. I mean, have you not watched any of the interviews with Jessica Carson? He really did a number on her."

I rolled my eyes. "I think I know Finn pretty well, don't you think? He'd never do anything to hurt me. And Jessica Carson is just looking for her five minutes of fame. They never slept together. She's making all of this up for attention."

Those words came easy for me because I knew that they were true.

Defending Finn had never been difficult for me.

He put his hands up in apology. "I'm sorry. I overstepped."

The doorbell rang, and he excused himself and went to the door to get the food.

I pulled out my phone and sent a quick text to Finn.

OMG! He took me to his house. It's all working. He definitely misses me. Love you, Chewy.

CHEWY

Fuck him. He's got some fucking nerve taking you to his house without telling me.

I chuckled and tucked my phone back into my purse when I heard him close the door.

Once he returned, he set everything up at the modern table in the dining room and lit a few candles, which shocked me. Seemed a little over the top for two people who were no longer dating, but I wasn't complaining.

Carl was trying. That much was obvious.

I carried my wine glass into the dining room, along with his sparkling water.

"I'm on call tonight, but I've got someone covering for me so I could spend some time with you. I just don't want to risk it if there's any kind of emergency."

I respected the hell out of how seriously he took his job.

We spent the next two hours talking about London and all that had happened while I was gone. I filled him in on my plans to start my own business and told him about the spaces I'd been looking at. He seemed genuinely happy for me, and that felt good.

"Your mom says business is going well for them," I said as he poured me a second glass of wine.

"Yeah, they've been busy, but they're managing okay. I didn't know you'd spoken to my mom since you'd been back."

"Yes. I gave her a call yesterday. I didn't want things to be awkward between us now that you and I aren't together. I'm sure I'll be running into them. I don't want hard feelings."

I'd been close with Carl's family, but they hadn't taken me leaving any better than their son had.

"Of course, there are no hard feelings. They've always loved you. You know that." His gaze locked with mine, and I saw the sadness there.

"Are they close with Christy Rae—" I said, but he cut me off.

"Let's just call her Christy. The three names are exhausting." He chuckled. "And I know it's her own fault, as she's always insisted everyone call her that. But I can't hear it one more time."

Now it was my turn to laugh. This was the Carl that I'd missed. He could be really funny when he wanted to be.

"I get it. So, are they close with her?"

"Not the way that they were with you, if that's what you're asking." He let out a long breath. "What I have with her isn't like what you and I shared. I miss you. I'm not going to lie. We have a history, Reese. This isn't easy on me either. But maybe this is good for us. Maybe you were right about going to London. I shouldn't have tried to hold you back. I own that. I wasn't looking at things from your side. I was wrong. But maybe me dating Christy and you dating Finn is something we both needed. We've always only been with one another, aside from a few short breaks over the years."

I nodded, and a lump formed in my throat. "Are you happy, Carl?"

"As happy as I can be when I'm not with the person I always thought I'd be with. But that doesn't mean that this is forever for either of us. But I'm different with her, you know?" he said, and his voice cracked.

"Different how?"

He scrubbed a hand down his face. "I don't know. Maybe you're experiencing it, too. We've technically been broken up for a year, and I don't know what you did when you were in London by yourself."

"I didn't do anything because I didn't stop loving you, Carl. I just wanted to take a professional opportunity that had come my way. I wanted something for me to feel good about. I still wanted us to be together. But I'm guessing you've done plenty since I've been gone." I braced myself for what he was going to tell me.

He refilled my wine glass, and his gaze locked with mine. "You and I were so young when we first met, Reese. I was your first... *everything*, and I think I just didn't ever want to do anything to scare you off. Or hell, maybe I was the scared one. But my relationship with Christy is different than ours was," he said, clearing his throat before letting out a long breath. "There's more passion, physically, I guess. I don't hold back with her because she's more experienced than you were. But I don't feel like it's going to be a long-lasting thing, if I'm being honest, so I don't think about every little thing when

I'm with her. There are no rules. We don't have the same emotional connection. Maybe this is what you and I needed. To experience something different."

Oh my God.

Did he really just admit that he has good sex with his new girlfriend while our sex life was vanilla at best?

A dull ache settled in my chest.

"Wow. I did not see tonight going like this," I said, reaching for my glass and taking a long sip, downing most of the liquid in one gulp.

"Come on, Reese. You can't tell me you don't agree."

"Oh, I agree, Carl. But I was the one that always wanted to try things, and you were the one who kept throwing your medical background in my face when it came to our sex life." I crossed my hands over my chest and leaned back in my chair.

"I just always looked at you as the woman I was going to marry. The future mother of my children. I didn't want to tarnish that," he said, his gaze searching mine.

"You didn't want to tarnish our future with orgasms?" I hissed.

His eyes widened. "I'm guessing your relationship with Finn is also different. I'm assuming you're sleeping with him?"

This was the moment of truth.

Come clean or keep the lie going.

But after hearing what he'd just shared, I wasn't going to admit that I hadn't had sex in over a year. Hadn't had sex with anyone but him. That I'd waited for him while he was out having fabulous sex with Christy Rae Lovell.

If we were going to end up together, it wouldn't be me begging him to come back. He would need to do the begging. He's the one who ended things. He's the one having all the good sex with someone else.

"Of course I am. He's my boyfriend, after all. And obviously, he's very experienced, so…" I chuckled as I reached for the bottle and filled my glass with what little was left in the bottle.

I was well on my way to drunk town, and I was going to let him know all the ways that Finn Reynolds was rocking my world.

He nodded. "I figured you were. I can't lie, Reese. The thought of another man touching you makes me sick."

"Well, the feeling is mutual. You jumped first, though, Carl. You can't expect me to sit around and wait forever. And Finn and I—" I paused and looked toward the kitchen for dramatic effect. "We're explosive together. I guess we're both exploring new things, huh?"

His tongue swiped out to wet his lips, and I smiled because I knew the jealousy was eating him up.

"I miss you." He shrugged. "But I guess we'll just have to see where things go for both of us."

My phone vibrated, and I glanced down to see a text from Finn.

CHEWY

I can't believe the dude went behind my back and took you to his house. I'm still pissed off. Miss you, Miney. It's country night at Garrity's. Hugh and Cage don't want to go. You want me to wait for you? We'll go dance our asses off?

Normally, I'd say no and stay here with Carl. But at the moment, I had a good buzz going, and the thought of dancing to some good country music with my best friend sounded a hell of a lot better than hearing about the great sex Carl was having with someone else.

Let's do it. Heading home in five minutes.

"Well, I'm not sure where things are going for either of us in the future, aside from having lots of rocking good sex with other people," I said. Were my words slurring? Was rocking good sex a real thing? "But my boyfriend wants to take me dancing, so I need to get home."

He nodded. "I miss the nights we used to go dancing."

"Yeah. Well, now we have new partners, Carl. And that was your doing."

His eyes widened. He wasn't used to me being so confrontational. But the new me was done being a doormat. If we were going to have a future together, things did need to change. He was right about that.

He'd have to make the effort if he wanted to get me back.

Right now, there was only one place that I wanted to be.

Dancing with my best friend—my fake boyfriend and the guy who would take my mind off the fact that the man I planned to marry had just shredded my heart.

Again.

nine

. . .

Finn

"FOR FUCK'S SAKE, dude. You need to chill," Cage said as he carried our empty beer bottles to the kitchen. "She said she's on her way home. Isn't she your fake girlfriend? Wasn't the plan for her to win Dr. Douchesack back?"

"It's Dr. Limpdick now. It's more fitting. And yes, that was the plan, but I don't like the guy."

"Agreed. He's an asshole." Cage dropped the bottles into the recycling bin.

"You two fuckers are being a little dramatic. Carl is not that bad of a guy. Reese wouldn't want to marry him if he was as awful as you're making him out to be. Yeah, he's a little arrogant, but you just hate him because he's dating your best friend," Hugh said, pointing at me before turning his attention to Cage. "And you never got over the fact that he said you weren't a real doctor."

"I'm offended both for my best friend and my brother," I said, throwing my hands in the air.

"That's a bit of a stretch," Cage said. "You laughed when I told you he said that. I think you're actually jealous of him being with Reese."

I gasped and made all sorts of sounds to let him know

how appalled I was at the suggestion that I could be jealous of a dude like Carl.

"Not a fucking chance. He doesn't deserve her. He never has. But after the way he treated her for chasing her own fucking dreams, I don't know why she's even trying to get him back."

"Yet you agreed to go along with the plan. Interesting." Cage had a smug look on his face.

"It's not that interesting. I'm protective. Plus, I'm supposed to be dating her. So what kind of fucking loser boyfriend would be okay with her being out with her ex this late?"

"A guy who's *pretending* to be her boyfriend," Hugh said over his laughter. "You seem to be getting really worked up. Didn't she say she was on her way home and she wanted to go to Garrity's with you?"

"Yeah. Thirty minutes ago. The asshole lives five minutes away," I said, looking down at my smartwatch. "I'm not going to let Carl treat me like I'm his little bitch. This is too much." I stormed to the window and gasped when I realized his car was parked in my driveway.

That bastard thought he could try something with my girl in my driveway?

Not a fucking chance.

"Damn straight. You tell him, brother!" Hugh shouted. My brothers both laughed hysterically as I reached for my coat and whipped the door open.

Carl had fucked with the wrong guy.

I stormed toward his *I'm-an-insecure-prick* red sports car and saw them facing one another as I approached. I banged my fist against the passenger window, and Reese jumped in her seat.

Her eyes widened as she turned to look at me before putting the window down.

"Hello, Lover. Did you miss me?"

Was she drunk?

Reese was a goofy drunk, and I'd always loved when she got a little tipsy because she was a lightweight, and all she did was laugh when she was intoxicated. But Carl was looking at her like she was his next meal, and I was fucking livid.

Did I have a right to be this mad?

Hell yeah, I did. What kind of actor would I be if I allowed shit to go on under my nose?

"I don't know what the fuck is going on here, but I suggest you take your ass home and meet up with your own woman," I growled.

Reese unbuckled herself, and I tugged the door open. When she stepped out, I wrapped an arm around her neck and covered her mouth with mine. Her lips parted immediately, inviting me in. My tongue tangled with hers, and she molded her tight little body against mine.

I pulled back and stroked her bottom lip with my thumb. "Better?"

"Yeah," she said, her voice breathy.

I slammed the car door, leaned down to look at him through the window, and flipped Carl the bird before leading her inside. He sped out of the driveway as I pushed the front door open.

"Chewy! You really are the best actor. That was brilliant!" Reese squealed once we were inside. She hurried over to hug my brothers before sitting on the couch beside Hugh. "You guys should have seen him. He acted all pissed off and possessive. I thought Carl was going to wet himself when you pounded on that window."

"I won't be disrespected in my own home," I said as I took the seat beside her and tried to tone down my anger.

"How was dinner?" Hugh asked.

"He took me to his place and ordered takeout, poured me

a few glasses of wine, and lit some candles. It was all very romantic." She waggled her brows.

I pushed to my feet and ran a hand through my hair. "That was not the deal, Miney. I don't appreciate some dude that you used to date making you romantic dinners when we're supposed to be together."

She fell back in a fit of laughter. "Right? It was a ballsy move. He said he really misses me. I'll tell you the rest on our walk to Garrity's. Let me go put on my jean skirt. I'll be right back. Are you guys coming with us?" she asked my brothers.

"Nope," they both said at the same time and then followed it up by saying that they had to get home.

She hugged them goodbye and jogged toward my bedroom to change her clothes.

"You do realize this is all getting a little complicated," Cage said once Reese was out of earshot.

"No, it's not. It's fine. I'll have to set some boundaries. I'm not going to stand by and allow him to shit on my turf."

"Your turf?" Cage raised a brow.

"Yeah. He thinks we're dating, and he's trying to move in on my girl."

"Isn't that the goal?" Hugh asked, keeping his voice low.

"I'm not sure about that." Cage barked out a laugh.

"It is the goal. But not like this. He can't just walk in and disrespect me. He's going to have to work a lot harder than that."

"Let me get this straight." Cage pulled the door open, and I followed them out to the front porch. "You're fake dating your best friend so that she can get her ex back. But now that he's interested, you have a problem with it?"

"I have a problem with the way he's doing it. Plus, this is supposed to improve my image. What kind of boyfriend would I be if I allowed him to move in on my woman right in front of me? Not a fucking chance."

"I don't think you have the same goal as Reese. You don't

want her to get back with him at all," my oldest brother said with his brow raised.

"That doesn't make you a fucking rocket scientist. Newsflash. I don't like the guy." I shook my head.

"I know you don't, brother." Hugh clapped me on the shoulder. "You haven't been yourself since she left for London. Maybe things have changed between you two."

"Oh, I haven't been the same? I wonder why. Let me see… My costar tried to poison the world against me. My best friend got her heart broken by a pussy-hating-narcissist. Could that be the reason that I'm a little on edge? I haven't been laid in almost a year, and I just want to protect my best friend from getting hurt again. Is that not enough?"

Hugh nodded. "All right. We've got your back. You know that."

"Well, I'm not as easily swayed as the big teddy bear over here. I'm not buying it. No one is that good of an actor." Cage smirked.

"I hope your dick shrivels up and falls off on the walk home," I said over my laughter because dick threats made me laugh every time.

"Chewy, are you outside?" Reese shouted from inside the house.

"Yep," I called back.

"I think I need to take a lover, and I may need your help with that," she said as she stepped out onto the porch before she proceeded to hiccup no less than six times in a row.

Like I said. Drunk Reese was always a good time.

"My point has been made. Nothing about this is normal," Cage said under his breath so only Hugh and I could hear him. Reese laughed hysterically, either that my brothers had just heard her confession or that she couldn't control the noises coming from her mouth. She had a bottle of water in her hand and unscrewed the top and took a long pull.

"See ya," I said, saluting them as they walked down the driveway.

Reese was shouting her goodbyes as I locked the door and turned to face her.

"You sure you want to go dancing? You seem a little drunk. That bastard better not have been driving you around if he was drinking."

"He didn't drink. He was on call. And I'm fine. I want to go dancing with you, Finn Reynolds. I can't even remember the last time I went dancing."

I turned toward her and zipped up her coat, glancing down at her bare legs that were covered up to just below her knees with her white cowboy boots. I led her down from the porch, and we walked toward Garrity's, the bar my family owned, which was only a three-block walk from my house.

"Tell me what happened," I said as her hand found mine. We'd always been affectionate with one another. It was just the way we were when we were together.

"He's sleeping with her," she spewed, not hiding her disgust.

"Did you really think the guy was going to go a year without sex and then get a girlfriend and not sleep with her?"

"Well, I haven't slept with anyone."

"Because you've never had good sex, so you don't know what you're missing."

She came to a stop and faced me. "You're right. That's why I need to take a lover. Carl thinks we're both having good freaking sex. He basically called me a boring lover. I'm the one who kept trying to do new things. He didn't think his," she paused and held up her pointer and middle fingers and completely over-accentuated the air quotes, "'future wife and mother of his children should be curious about sex.' Well, guess what, Chew?"

"What?" I smirked.

"I'm curious. I wanted to find a profession that challenged

and excited me. And I want to get drunk on a Tuesday night just because I can and then go dancing at Garrity's with my best friend. And the biggest shocker of all…" she said, raising a brow and waiting for me to beg for it.

"Yes?"

"I'm curious about sex. About all the orgasms. About trying anything other than boring old missionary with a few heavy grunts that is nothing to write home about. So, maybe Carl's right. Maybe we will become better people while we're apart, and when we find our way back to one another, we'll be better for it."

"Let me get this straight." I moved closer, my mouth just a breath from hers. My gaze locked with those familiar sage-green eyes. "You want to go bang a random dude, experience real sex, and then go back to your boring boyfriend who doesn't please you?"

She rolled her eyes. "He pleases me in many ways. We want the same things. A family. A home. A happy life."

"And the sex?"

"Well, Carl claims he's having all the good sex now. And he likes it. So maybe when we both know what that actually is, we'll be able to have it together. But I'm not going to be the only one who doesn't have it while he's out there doing it with Christy freaking Rae Lovell," she said, her voice louder now.

"Don't you dare add a fourth name to that monstrosity." I chuckled before putting an arm around her shoulder and leading her toward Garrity's. "I think you should experience some goddamn fun and a whole lot of good lovin'. It's going to be life-changing."

"Yeah? Well, he asked me if we were sleeping together."

"You better have talked me up, Miney. I'm a fabulous fucking lover."

"I told him you were amazing. That we were explosive together." She paused to hiccup several times again before continuing. "I wasn't about to look like a pathetic, sexless woman, sitting home pining over my ex, who was talking about all the good sex he's having. That's what sold me on this new idea. While we're apart, Carl won't be the only one living it up. If he doesn't like it, I guess he'll have to get his shit together and beg me to come back."

"Well, I've got bad news for you."

"What's that?" she asked as we approached the bar, and I reached for the door.

"As far as everyone in Cottonwood Cove knows—and the rest of the world, if I'm being honest," I said, pausing as she rested against the door and looked up at me, waiting for me to finish what I was saying. Country music boomed from the bar.

"Yeah?"

"You're my woman. And I can't have you out there looking for a random man."

Her lips turned up in the corners. "You want me, don't you, Chewy?"

I did, didn't I?

Cage was right.

The thought of claiming Reese in a way I never imagined possible didn't have me running scared.

I wanted her as more than my fake girlfriend.

As more than just a best friend.

I wanted to make Reese Murphy feel good in a way her boyfriend never would.

Even if I knew I couldn't keep her forever. Eventually, she'd go back to Carl because that was who she wanted to spend her life with.

And my life would return to normal.

Dating and having a good time.

But for this short time… I wanted this.

"Bah! I got you." She patted my cheek and chuckled. "You should have seen your face. The fear. Don't worry. I'm more than aware that this isn't real, Chewy. So, we'll just have to figure out how we're going to find me a lover that I can sneak around with. Come on. Tonight, I just want to dance with you."

She led me to the dance floor, and I wanted to stop her and tell her she was wrong.

Because for the first time in my life, I realized I wanted a woman who didn't want me back.

ten

. . .

Reese

I WOKE up with my mouth dry and my head pounding. I'd had several tequila shots at Garrity's, and if memory served, Finn had tossed me over his shoulder and walked all the way home when he'd insisted that I'd had enough.

And then I remembered that he'd tucked me into my bed and put a glass of water on the nightstand for me. I felt around for the glass, and just as my dehydrated mouth started to water, I knocked the glass onto the carpet and spilled the water.

Damn it.

This was why I'd never been a big drinker.

But I'd had a lot of fun.

Too much fun.

Finn and I danced for hours.

I stumbled to my feet and found my phone. It was three o'clock in the morning, and I'd been asleep for less than an hour. I made my way to the kitchen and poured a large glass of water, chugging it beside the sink.

I heard a noise.

It sounded like someone was groaning.

Finn was known for sleepwalking, and I couldn't even

count how many times he'd wandered around when we were kids and when we lived together as adults.

"Chewy?" I whispered as I tiptoed down the hall toward his bedroom.

The house was dark, but a light was coming from beneath his door, which was cracked open. I stood beside it and heard a deep moan.

I pushed the door open the slightest bit and saw the lamp sitting on his bedside table was turned on, providing just the slightest bit of light. I heard the gruff noise again, and I tiptoed toward the bathroom. I was still drunk enough that my walk felt a little wobbly, but I was sober enough to be curious about what was going on.

Was he sleepwalking?

Did he have a woman here?

We'd come home alone together.

I held my breath as I moved through his dimly lit bedroom. The bathroom door was ajar. The light from his closet must have been on, because there was just enough light to make out his silhouette. He stood over the sink, head down, boxers shoved down as he gripped his dick and stroked himself.

I'd never seen anything more magnificent in my life.

He wasn't wearing a shirt, and the muscles in his back strained with each pump of his hand.

I pushed into the bathroom further, and he froze for a moment before glancing over his shoulder.

"You watching me, Reese?"

"I am," I whispered.

"Come here." He turned toward me, stroking himself slower now. "Does this turn you on?"

I nodded because it did. Carl and I had never discussed touching ourselves. He'd certainly never let me watch him get himself off.

But Finn had always been more confident in his own skin.

It was one of the things that I loved most about him.

He continued sliding that big hand of his up and down his engorged shaft. It was long and thick, and I moved on instinct, stopping directly in front of him.

"It's normal to want to feel good. There's nothing to be ashamed of," he whispered.

"I'm not ashamed. I want to feel good." My voice was quiet, but it sounded huskier than normal. My head was still fuzzy, and the tequila was clearly still present or I'd never have had the nerve to be standing here.

"Slip your hand into your shorts and touch yourself." He continued to slide his hand up and down his erection.

I squeezed my thighs together because I was so turned on, I couldn't think straight. I slipped my hand beneath my pink pajama shorts and closed my eyes as my fingers grazed along my most sensitive area, and I let out a deep breath.

A deep groan left his mouth. "Are you wet?"

"Yes."

"You like watching me, don't you?"

I opened my eyes for a moment and nodded, but the sensation between my legs was like nothing I'd ever experienced. I'd never been turned on like this before.

"Keep rubbing those fingers over that pretty little pussy." His voice was so sexy and gruff. My hand moved faster in response. I stepped closer to him and forced myself to open my eyes, even if I couldn't believe what was happening.

"What are you thinking about, Finn?" I asked as my fingers pressed in circles against my clit.

Faster.

"I'm thinking about what it would be like to touch you. To taste you," he said, as he started sliding his hand faster and faster up and down his shaft. "To fuck you until you cried out my name over and over."

"Oh my God," I said as my hips started bucking against my hand, and my head fell back as I groaned. I was so close.

"Do you like that I'm thinking about that tight little pussy that hasn't even been tasted yet?"

"Yes," I said as his hand grazed along my shoulder and down over the fabric of my tank top. His thumb stroked over my hard nipple, back and forth.

I couldn't think straight; the sensation was so overwhelming.

White lights exploded behind my eyes and a moan that I barely recognized as my own left my lips as I went over the edge.

I cried out as I rocked against my hand over and over.

"Fuck, Reese," he hissed. My gaze snapped open, and I watched as he worked himself faster now. I stared in wonder as a feral sound escaped his lips, and he went right over the edge with me. White liquid pooled over his hand, and he just kept stroking himself. His head fell back, and I watched his Adam's apple bob in his throat as the muscles in his chest bulged and his chiseled abs flexed with each thrust into his hand.

I was still tingling. I'd never felt anything close to this before. My legs wobbled, and I pulled my hand from my shorts and gripped the counter to keep myself upright.

A layer of sweat covered my forehead, and Finn just watched me like I was the most beautiful woman he'd ever seen. When he was done riding out his pleasure, he took two steps back and grabbed some tissue, cleaning himself up before tucking his dick into his boxers.

I couldn't help but stare because it was still hard.

I turned to the sink because suddenly, the realization of what we'd just done was settling in.

I'd just gotten off in front of my best friend while he'd done the same thing.

I hadn't been surprised that he had a filthy mouth because I knew Finn better than I knew anyone.

What surprised me was that I liked it.

Hell, I liked it a lot.

Hearing him talk about the things that he wanted to do to me.

Did he mean it? Or had he just said it because I'd walked in on him?

Finn was a player. He'd never been in a relationship longer than a few days.

And it wasn't because he didn't have endless women chasing after him.

The problem was that no one could hold his attention for long.

He was a heartbreak waiting to happen for anyone who fell for him.

"Shit," I whispered as I shifted toward the sink and turned on the water, reaching for the soap and cleaning my hands.

What the hell had I just done?

This was a line that Finn and I had vowed we'd never cross.

Along with my family, my best friend was the most solid relationship in my life, even before things blew up with Carl. What he and I had had always been different.

This man was my confidant, the one person who never judged me.

"You all right, Miney?"

I shook my head. "I'm drunk. We're both drunk. That was not a good idea. I'm sorry. I shouldn't have walked in on you."

"There's nothing to be embarrassed about."

"You're right, because nothing happened. This never happened. Goodnight, Chewy."

I couldn't even look at him.

I padded through the house, back to my bedroom.

What the hell was I thinking?

I squeezed my eyes shut and tried to think of anything

other than what we'd just done. My body was still tingling from the sensation.

I could still vividly see the muscles in Finn's arms straining as he stroked himself.

The way his eyes had watched me with a hunger I'd never felt before tonight.

No. No. No. No.

This was a stupid, drunken mistake.

We hadn't touched each other—well, aside from a little nipple graze.

Tomorrow we would just act like it never happened. I could do that.

There was no other option.

I'd snuck out of the house early this morning to take Millie for a ride. I'd been unable to get Finn out of my mind now that I'd seen him the way that I had last night. I'd always known he was sexy and that women fell to their knees for him—I'd just never allowed myself to imagine why.

But I liked it, didn't I?

The things he'd said to me.

The way he'd made me feel.

Watching him fall apart right in front of me.

What kind of woman was I? Here I was, trying to win back my fiancé, and I fell asleep last night, thinking about my sexy best friend.

Millie trotted into the barn just as Finn stepped out of Han Solo's stall. He had on a pair of faded jeans, his worn cowboy boots, and a navy-blue Henley. His tan baseball hat was turned backward, and the man just oozed sex appeal. It shouldn't be legal to look that good without even trying. He smiled, flashing his white teeth at me, while his eyes hid behind his gold aviators.

"Did you take her down to the water?" he asked, his tone light, like nothing had happened between us.

It was what I'd asked of him, but I didn't know how to pretend I hadn't made a massive mistake myself.

"Yeah, it's gorgeous down there. It's a little cloudy today, and she loved it. What are you doing out here?" I asked as I slid down Millie's body, and he wrapped both hands around my waist and set me on my feet.

"I came to find you," he said, waiting for me to turn around and face him. He chuckled, like whatever he saw on my face was funny. He leaned forward and rubbed his thumb above the bridge of my nose between my eyes. "Stop worrying, Miney."

"Is that what you came to tell me? To stop worrying?"

"No. I came to tell you that I spoke to Maddox about an investment property he'd asked if I wanted to partner up with him on, and I thought it might be something that could work for your office space."

I tucked my hands in the back pockets of my jeans and shifted on my boots. "Really? That was nice of you."

He leaned forward, his forehead resting against mine. "Stop acting like you committed a crime. It's not a big deal."

"What would Carl think of me?" I asked, and he reared his head back like I'd slapped him.

"What would Carl think of you? The dude is probably banging his girlfriend right now. He told you as much. And weren't you the one talking a big game about finding yourself a lover? You touched yourself. You didn't rob a bank. Stop overreacting."

I looked out toward the doors of the stable with views of the gorgeous mountains. I loved being home. Breathing in the mountain and ocean air. That perfect mix of pine and salt water. Seeing the snowcapped peaks in the distance.

"I was drunk. It was a really stupid thing for me to do."

"It's never a bad thing to let yourself feel good. You were

having fun. You aren't dating Carl right now. So what if you have a good time? He's not worrying about what you think, Miney. You don't know what's going to happen, so stop letting what he thinks depict what you do. Do what makes you happy. London was the first time I've seen you do that in a long time."

I cleared my throat. "I guess I've just had this vision of who I was going to be in my head for so long. And then I took a risk and accepted that position in London, and it cost me everything that I wanted."

"I disagree. I think you've been so hell-bent on believing that Carl is the only way to have the future you want, that you've tried to be who you think *he* wants you to be. And the minute you didn't do what he wanted, he jumped ship on you. That's the guy you want to spend your life with?" His words were harsher than usual, and it caught me off guard.

"Says the guy who hasn't had a relationship that lasted more than a hot second," I hissed and stormed toward the doors.

I was not going to take relationship advice from Finn Reynolds.

Nor was I going to admit that there was a lot of truth to what he'd said.

He chuckled behind me and wrapped his fingers around my wrist before turning me to face him. My chest bumped into his.

"Don't compare me to Carl. I'm never going to lie to you, Miney. I'm just calling it as I see it. But I'm not the one who left you when you chased your dreams. Hell, I've never left you. Not when you spent months going through chemo treatments. Not when you cried yourself to sleep, thinking it could affect you having kids in the future. Not when I held you when we found out that you'd most likely be fine. Not when you dated that douchesack. Not when you chose to leave your amazing job in the city because he asked you to come back home with him. Not when you went to London. And not when you slipped your hand down your pajama shorts and touched yourself. *I don't fucking leave,* Miney. I'm not the one trying to make you into someone you're not. I've always known who you are." His breaths were coming hard and fast, which was not the norm for Finn. He was a chill guy. He rarely got this worked up. And he was right about every single thing he'd said. He'd been there through it all.

A lump formed in my throat. "I don't know who I am right now, Finn."

"Yeah, you do. Stop overthinking it. If he loves you, then he'll love you even more for being who you are. You don't want to spend the rest of your life pretending."

"Says the actor," I said with a chuckle as I swiped at the tear rolling down my cheek.

"That's my day job. I don't hide who I am from the people I love, and you know that. What you see is what you get. I don't waste my time trying to fit into someone else's box. And I've watched you do it for a long time." He ran a hand through his hair. "If you want to be with Carl, and you want me to pretend to be your boyfriend to win him back… I'll do it because I love you. But I won't watch you beat yourself up for doing things that you want to do. I won't let you feel guilty about what happened last night. You're the best fucking person I know. You and Carl are the only ones who don't see it."

A few more tears streamed down my face. "I love you, too, Chewy. Thank you for being the best friend I could ever ask for."

He wrapped his arms around me and hugged me. "That will never change. And if you want to look at my dick again, you just say the word."

I pulled back as my mouth fell open, and I swatted him on the arm. "That was a one-and-done."

"All right. But you know I'm not dating anyone right now,

so I can't promise I won't be in the bathroom doing that every single night from now until we stop fake dating in a few months and I have sex again. So, if you don't want to see it, I suggest you don't wander around at night."

"Every night, huh? Thanks for the heads-up." I looped my hand through his arm as we walked out of the barn toward the house.

"Damn straight, woman. Now, let's go check out this office space so you can get things going."

I wasn't sure how I'd gotten so lucky to call Finn Reynolds my best friend.

But there'd never been a day that I hadn't known how lucky I was.

Because even when I felt lost... he always felt like home.

eleven

. . .

Finn

WE'D RUN by Maddox and Georgia's house to grab the key. My brother-in-law had told Reese that the place was hers if she wanted it, and I'd agreed to go in on it without even seeing it. The location was exactly what I'd been looking for, and if Maddox thought it was a good investment, I wouldn't argue with that. We'd both made it clear to her that the first year would be rent-free, and we weren't negotiating that. Of course, she'd argued, because that was Reese. I'd told her that we'd discuss changing the terms in a year once she was on her feet, and that was the deal. It was a good investment, and Maddox knew how much she meant to me, and he had no problem with the arrangement.

She was quiet on the drive over to the storefront. When we'd stepped inside, she'd gasped and turned slowly as she took in the space.

Reese's sister, Olivia, had met us over at the location, barreling through the door just as I turned the heat up. She'd come to check it out, as well.

"Wow, Finny, you went in on the place?" Olivia asked.

"Yeah. I've got to do something with the money I'm making, and I was looking for an investment. I figured this would be the perfect fit for Reese." I turned to face my best friend.

Reese's eyes watered, and she lunged at me, her arms wrapping around my neck. "I can't believe you did this."

"This is great. You've got a little office space, and you can use this open area for your design center." Olivia continued moving around and taking it all in.

"Yeah, it's really perfect. But I don't know why you're insisting on me taking it rent-free for the first year. I've got savings, and I want to pay what I can to start off. And then we can stick with the plan of increasing the price next year when I'm turning a profit." Reese shook her head in disbelief.

"I told you that those were the terms. Take it or leave it." I crossed my arms over my chest, giving her a hard look. I was rarely serious with Reese, but I was about this. My current financial situation allowed me to help her out. It was a no-brainer for me.

"I guess it's good to know Finny boy here, huh?" Olivia leaned her head on my shoulder. "My sister is lucky to have you. You always show up for her, don't you?"

I don't know if her walking in on me with my dick in my hand counts as showing up for her… But I wasn't about to say that out loud.

"She always shows up for me, too. I feel like the lucky one." Reese had been there through everything with me. Through my decision to pursue acting, more drunken nights than I could count after I didn't get the parts that I'd auditioned for over the years, and one of the lowest points, when my father was diagnosed with cancer. After going through it with Reese, it had been an awful blow to me and to our family. And she'd been there, holding my hand and talking me through it. Just like she always did.

"So, I haven't seen Jessica Carson doing any interviews lately. I think you two have shut her down," Olivia said with a chuckle as her gaze bounced between both of us. "You make it all seem very believable."

"He's an actor, Liv. Of course, it's believable," Reese said, glancing around as if she were afraid someone could hear us. She stepped away from me. "I had dinner with Carl last night. I don't think he and Christy Rae Lovell are going to be together for long."

The things I wanted to say in response would hurt her, so I bit my tongue, which I didn't do often.

But for Reese, I would.

"How convenient for him. He punishes you for leaving, and he finds himself a backup, and then he lets you know it's not permanent? Way to play head games, Dr. Dickhead," Liv hissed.

"Hey, I'm the one fake dating my best friend to make him jealous. That's got the makings of an epic head game. I'm no better," Reese whispered, her green eyes wide as she looked between us.

"Well, we're not only doing it to make him jealous. It's helping me, too. So don't beat yourself up. And I don't mind having you at the house. It's been good for me. Plus, my agent messaged me this morning. Apparently, Jessica is trying to get an interview with the *Morning Show*. She can't handle that her crusade against me has pretty much died down."

"Fuck her," Reese snipped, which made me laugh because she didn't get worked up often. "Nobody messes with my man."

Olivia looked from her sister to me, her brows furrowed as if she were trying to figure out if there was more going on here.

Aside from a porn-worthy masturbation session, there wasn't much else to report.

She wanted Carl.

I needed a girlfriend.

This worked for both of us.

Watching one another get off was just a bonus, in my opinion, even if Reese was horrified by it.

I had no regrets. It was the hottest thing I'd ever experienced, and I'd been around the block before, so that was saying a lot.

"Carl is almost as bad as Jessica Carson in my mind." Olivia reached for her purse.

"That's a real stretch, Liv. I understand you guys want to be protective of me, but I'm the one who left. That was my choice. Carl isn't the bad guy here," Reese said, her voice harder now. "And you both need to stop calling him names because when we get back together, it's going to be awkward when you remember all the things you said about him."

"I'm fine with it," Olivia and I said at the same time, and I barked out a laugh.

"Stoooop." Reese rolled her eyes.

"Are you guys nervous about the interview this week? *The Hollywood Moment* is big time. You think you can pull it off?" Olivia asked.

Angelique had asked if Reese would take part in the interview because she thought it was time for us to come out publicly. Season two filming would be starting soon, and everyone wanted this Jessica Carson story put to rest.

"No. Finn's a professional, and I'm just going to act like I always do with him. It's not like they can ask a question that we don't know about one another. We'll be just fine." Reese shrugged. She'd agreed without hesitation to do the interview when I'd asked her about it a few days ago, and I was glad that there was no sign of her getting cold feet. Because they were coming, and if we canceled now, it would look suspicious.

"That's true. So, I'm guessing you can't be out meeting women with everyone believing you two are together. How are you handling that?" Olivia asked, directing her question at me.

"I'm *handling* it just fine. Pun intended." I glanced over to see my best friend's cheeks pink, and Olivia laughed so loud that it echoed through the space.

"Come on, Reese. Don't tell us you've never taken matters into your own *hands*?" Olivia was laughing hysterically now as she watched her sister shift back and forth on both feet as she looked away.

"I'm not talking about this. Anyway, the interview will be great, and hopefully, Carl reads it and seethes with jealousy." She was making an effort to change the subject, and my gaze locked with hers.

"Don't worry about it. We'll make him so jealous he won't be able to see straight."

"Yep. And then everything can go back to normal," Reese said, but her eyes were still on mine. "And all the women will be waiting for Finn with open arms."

"Well, I hope you have some fun before you go back to Carl. He's having his fun. You aren't together. Go do something crazy," Olivia said, and I turned my attention to her.

"I agree. She should live a little right now."

"Well, I have a very serious fake boyfriend at the moment. How do you two suggest I go out and do something crazy?" Reese teased, her gaze finding mine once again.

"You've got the hottest actor playing the role of your lover. I'm guessing Finny knows how to please a lady. Take advantage of the situation, guys. Stop being so morally exceptional." Olivia barked out a laugh. "You're best friends. That's never going to change."

Reese's mouth gaped open, and I reached over and tipped her chin up to close it. "That's a terrible idea. We made a pact years ago to never cross that line, and we would never risk hurting our friendship," she said.

"What's there to hurt? You want to marry Doctor Narcissist, and Finny wants to continue blessing the women of this fine part of the country with his swagger. You want two different things. You want the white picket fence, and Finn wants to have a good time with no strings attached. So, if you go into it knowing that, there's no risk." Olivia clapped me on the shoulder. "Show this poor girl what it's like to have her world rocked."

"Thanks for the commentary, Liv. Didn't you sleep with your lab partner in college who you called your best friend at the time? The whole thing blew up in your face."

"Ahhh… Newman Cock."

"That was not his name," Reese said over her laughter. We were all laughing now because Olivia Murphy had no filter.

"Fine. It was Newman Glock. He wore those thick-rimmed glasses and barely spoke, but the man was a freak in the sheets."

"I want those words written on my tombstone," I said as I winked at my best friend, who was gaping at me.

"Yeah, that's not happening. And where is your bestie now?" Reese crossed her arms over her chest.

"Well, he turned into a stage-five clinger. Started talking about marriage after our little fling got started."

"He broke your door down and sprayed Mace in your date's face. The poor guy got arrested, didn't he?" Reese asked as she studied her sister.

"It was the campus police. It's not like he had a record. But yeah, a restraining order is a real buzzkill for a friendship."

"Are you hearing this?" Reese asked me. "This is who is offering us advice?"

"Listen, she makes a fair point. And nothing would ever come between us, you know that, right?"

"Do not encourage her. It's not happening."

"Think about it. You could go back to Carl and teach him a thing or two. Show him what you like. The man is a doctor, after all. The least he can do is figure out how to find a woman's G-spot," Olivia said.

I barked out a laugh, and Reese pointed at the door. "Goodbye. I told you that in confidence when you got me liquored up in London. No more sex talk. Go find yourself a man and stay out of this."

"So touchy. Or is she just in need of being touched?" Olivia squealed when Reese pinched her arm and guided her toward the door.

"Thanks for coming," Reese grumped.

"That's what she said, Finny!" Olivia bellowed.

"Damn. You beat me to the punch on that one. That's my line, girl."

Reese closed the door behind her sister and shook her head at me.

"You're both insane."

"Are we, though?" I teased.

Because I didn't think it was a bad idea at all.

Hell, I'd had a little preview last night.

And I couldn't get the vision of her out of my head.

twelve

. . .

Reese

FINN HELPED me bring a bunch of things over to the new office this morning, as I'd spent the last week moving stuff over here and getting set up. My parents had surprised me with a desk that had just been delivered. Tonight, we were going to the Bumpkin Pumpkin Fall Festival downtown. It was one of my favorite events in Cottonwood Cove, and Finn and I had been going to it since before we could even walk. This year it was falling on the day before Halloween, which would make it even more fun because the kids would all come in costume and take advantage of the opportunity to dress up two days in a row.

Everyone in town would be there, and the weather was getting chilly, so we'd need to bundle up. Tomorrow was the interview with *The Hollywood Moment*, and I'd be lying if I didn't admit to being a little nervous now that it was so close. I didn't want to do anything to mess things up for Finn.

"I've got macaroni and cheese and cornbread," my dad said as he and Finn walked back inside.

I'd chosen a name, and it was Sunset Cove Design.

I like what it represented.

Three of my favorite things. The water and the sunset and design.

To me, this represented beauty.

I'd minored in graphic design in college, so I'd been working on my logo for a long time—long before I even knew this pipe dream of mine could actually become a reality.

My friend, Maggie, was coming by to paint the logo on the large front window this weekend. She'd done a few of the shop windows in town, and I was thrilled that things were really coming together.

"Oh, good, I'm starving," my mom said. "I just got those pictures hung in your bathroom for you."

"Thanks, Mama. You guys are the best. I don't really have any clients, so it's not like there's any urgency."

"Hey. I take offense to that. I'm your client." Finn set down a large bag of food on the card table my parents had brought over for an extra place to sit for now.

"I know that. But I live with you. So, it's not like you meet me at the office."

"I'm here, aren't I?" He smirked before helping my dad carry the folding chairs and placing them around the table.

I had bins of fabric samples I'd been collecting, along with endless design notebooks and magazines that were stacked on the built-in shelving that had come in handy.

It was a start.

"You just got the keys a week ago, so I think you're doing really well," my father said.

"Thanks. I appreciate you all helping me get set up."

"Always," they all said at the same time before my mom started grilling us about the interview.

"Are you nervous? It's a big magazine. Will they be taking photos of you guys?" she asked.

I glanced at Finn. We hadn't discussed me being in the photos, but he knew I'd do whatever he needed. He'd literally pushed me to get my business going, believed in me probably more than anyone in my life ever had, and was putting his life on hold to help me get mine back.

To help me get Carl back.

"Well, I'm guessing once they meet Reese, they're going to want to take a bunch of photos. I'll leave it up to her."

"You know that I'll do whatever you need me to do," I said, moaning when I took a sip of the best hot chocolate from Cottonwood Café. Finn's eyes snapped to mine, and I cleared my throat. I'd caught him looking at me differently ever since that night in his bathroom. He'd play it off and look away or wink and make a joke of it. But I saw the desire there. Maybe I recognized it because I felt it, too.

But feeling it and acting on it were two completely different things.

I was fairly certain that we were both just lonely right now. It didn't help that we were constantly together, so of course we were feeling things that we didn't normally feel.

But we hadn't acted on anything since that night, and we wouldn't.

My phone buzzed as my dad asked Finn endless questions about filming the new season. *Big Sky Ranch* would be filming season two in Scott's Ranch again, which was located between here and the city. So, he'd be leaving once he got back from Tokyo, and we'd stage our breakup right before he left the country. He wasn't telling anyone about the movie just yet, as he wanted to wait until they announced it and everything was finalized.

I glanced down to see a new text.

CARL

Hey. I heard you found an office space. Mrs. Runither filled me in. So, you're really doing it. Proud of you, Reese. Sorry, it took me so long to say it.

I sucked in a breath, my heart racing a bit at his words.

Thank you. I'm excited to get started.

CARL

I'd like to hire you. I can be your first official client. I'd like to get my office done.

Well, Finn has beat you to the punch, but of course, I've got room on my calendar. I'd be happy to design your office. You just let me know when you'd like to get started.

CARL

Sooner rather than later. I'm off on Monday next week. How about you come over and we take a look?

Sure. Does 9:00 a.m. work?

CARL

That sounds perfect. Will you and Finn be at the festival tonight?

Of course. You know I love it. Are you going this year?

He'd never gone with me in the past. It wasn't his thing, and I'd never pushed it because it had always been something that I did with Finn and our families.

CARL

Yeah, a group of us are going from the hospital. I'm off tonight. I'll see you there.

Sounds good.

"Everything all right?" my mom asked.

I dropped my phone into my purse and reached for my

fork. "Yeah. That was Carl. He just hired me to design his office."

Finn smiled, but it didn't reach his eyes. "That's great, Miney. Sounds like he's starting to grovel. This interview will probably push him over the edge."

I nodded. "Yeah. I hope so."

I should feel happy. But so much was happening right now that I wasn't solely focused on Carl at the moment. I was excited about launching my new company.

And I was enjoying being back home and riding Millie every morning with Finn and Han Solo, spending time with family, and seeing some of my friends who still lived here.

"Well, you know I want you to be happy," my father said as he set his cornbread down on his napkin and brushed his fingers back and forth to get rid of the crumbs. "I've always liked Carl, but I'm enjoying this side of you, sweetie."

"And what side is that?"

"Seeing that passion and excitement for something that you're building. And if you want to get back together with him and he appreciates it, then I'll support it. But don't dim your light for anyone, okay?"

"I won't, but Carl has been more supportive of this new venture of mine. Thanks for coming out today and helping me get set up."

"Wouldn't want to be anywhere else, darlin'." My mother beamed at me before she started asking Finn for some inside on-set gossip.

We laughed and chatted until my parents left to go home, and Finn and I did the same.

"Wow. We stayed later than I planned. Do you think we still have time to take the horses out for a quick ride" I asked as we pulled down his long driveway.

The leaves were changing colors, and Finn's lot was really something. The tall trees were covered in reds and yellows and oranges, and the branches created a canopy over his driveway.

"Of course. It's always been our favorite time to ride. We can make it to the water before sunset."

I chuckled. He hadn't said that in a while. When we were kids, we were allowed to stay out until the sun went down. We lived three houses away from one another our entire lives, and we'd spend every last second outside.

"Remember that treehouse my dad built, and we'd both have to go home for dinner and then we'd meet back out there?" I chuckled at the memory. "We'd sit in there, goofing around before the sun went down and it was time to go home."

"Uh, yeah, I remember," he said, getting out of the truck as we both headed straight for the stables. "You decorated the treehouse like you were moving into it permanently."

I laughed as we made our way to the stalls and saddled up. "I think I would have lived out there with you back then. I hated when it was time to go home."

"Yeah, me, too. We had a damn good childhood, didn't we?" He smirked as he effortlessly slipped onto Han Solo. I dropped my purse in the stall and did the same as I followed him outside.

I waved at Silas as we trotted out of the barn.

The sky looked more like a watercolor painting. The yellows and oranges swirled together with a hint of gold.

"Yep. It was the best. That's why I've always wanted to raise my kids here someday. Give them what I had. It doesn't get any better than Cottonwood Cove."

He glanced over his shoulder and smiled at me, and my stomach did some sort of weird flip. Maybe it was the fact that he'd become a big movie star in the time since I'd been gone, but Finn's sex appeal was on par. Even more so than it normally was.

I was seeing Finn differently these days. Maybe because I

was trying to figure out my future with Carl. Either way, Finn's good nature, kindness, caring for me, and making me feel special were all things I wanted in a relationship, and sadly, I didn't remember having those things with Carl. Things with Carl were never this easy.

"You want to race?"

"You sure you're up for the challenge, Mr. Hollywood? I always was able to beat you, and Han Solo doesn't know you the way Millie knows me." I shifted and grabbed the reins.

"Don't you worry about me, Miney!" he shouted as he took off. "Race you to the sunset."

We were both flying now. I had to give him credit. His horse was new, but Han Solo had some serious wheels. The wind whistled around us, and I looked over a few times to see him smiling as he leaned forward to keep the momentum.

This was my happy place.

Surrounded by nature, the crisp chill in the air, and the smell of the ocean mixed with the pine surrounding us.

And my best friend riding beside me.

Trying to race the sun before it tucked behind the clouds, just like we'd done our whole lives.

My hair whipped around me, and we stayed right beside one another.

Stride for stride.

And we made it to the water… just before the sunset.

Gracie had her little hand in mine, and Finn was holding her hot chocolate as we walked through the maze of pumpkins. Cage had stepped away to take a work call, and we were going to meet up with Olivia, Georgia, Maddox, Hugh, and Lila to go for a hayride in a little bit. Brinkley and Lincoln were traveling for a game and in Chicago right now.

"Can you come to my tea party in two weeks, Ree Ree?"

"I would love to come. I'm guessing it's at The Tipsy Tea?"

"Yep. Bossman got it for me, but I wanted to wait until you got back from the faraway place you went to so I could have my tea party with you, too."

My heart squeezed. I adored little Gracie Reynolds. She was dressed as a bumble bee, and there was no cuter human on the planet. All the kids were wearing costumes, and they'd go trick-or-treating tomorrow night, as well.

"I wouldn't miss it for the world. Who all is coming?"

"My Bossman and Aunt Georgie are coming, and my Bossman called Miss Matilda and made it so I can have all of my peoples at the tea party. So, Daddy and Grammie and Pops. You and Uncle Finny." She paused as she counted on her fingers. "Aunt Lila and Uncle Hughey, and Auntie Brinks and Links are going to fly home just for my tea party. We're going to have tea and pumpkin spice cupcakes." Her long brown curls bounced on her shoulders, surrounding her little cherub cheeks. She really was the most adorable thing I'd ever seen.

"I can't wait. I'll have to find a special dress to wear that day."

She covered her mouth with her hands and squealed. "Yes. I've got a special wedding dress that Links got me, and Daddy said I can wear it to the party."

"I can't wait to see it."

"Yeah, she's been talking about this tea party for months, but she didn't want to have it until Ree Ree got home," Finn said with a laugh, bending down to give her a sip of her cocoa.

"Hey, Reese," a deep voice said from behind me, and I turned around to see Carl waving at me. I glanced at Finn, and he gave me the slightest nod, letting me know they'd be fine if I stepped away.

"I'll be right back, okay?" I said, and Gracie smiled with a chocolate mustache above her top lip, which made me laugh.

"Carl, hey," I said, walking toward him.

His girlfriend stood a few feet away, but her eyes were on me.

"Hi, I thought that was you. Is that Gracie Reynolds? She's getting so big," he said, waving at her. I looked over to see Finn and Gracie both frowning at Carl and a loud laugh escaped.

"Yeah, she's in kindergarten now."

"And she's definitely not a fan of mine. I guess she likes you with her uncle, huh?"

"I think she does, yeah," I said, and my gaze kept moving over to Finn and Gracie. They were laughing now, and Finn dropped her hot chocolate cup into the trash can and scooped her up, settling her on his hip. I'd always loved how much he loved his family.

"She knows a good thing when she sees it," Carl said, pulling my attention back to him. It was a sweet thing to say. But my gaze kept wandering back to Finn and Gracie, watching her head fall back in laughter as he tickled her cheek with his scruff.

"Thank you," I said. "So, we're good for Monday?"

"Yeah, I'm looking forward to getting started. I can't wait to see your new office space, too. That's exciting."

"It is," I said. "I just ran into my old neighbors, the Johnsons, and they said they are looking to do a remodel on their home, so I may have just landed another client."

"Wow. Look at you go. I'm proud of you."

It was all I'd wanted to hear for the longest time, but I was too distracted to get lost in the moment because Gracie was shouting something to me, and Finn was trying to get her to stop yelling for me.

"Listen, we're going on a hayride, and I don't want to make her wait any longer. I need to get going," I said.

"Yeah, of course. I'll see you on Monday." He reached for my hand and squeezed it. He was trying.

This was what I'd wanted.

But I couldn't get back to Finn and Gracie quickly enough.

I gently pulled my hand away and smiled. "I'll see you then."

I was tempted to look back to see if he was watching me, but for whatever reason, my gaze was locked on Finn and Gracie, who were waving at me and laughing.

I had no desire to look back.

And that was unexpected.

thirteen

• • •

Finn

I GLANCED down at my phone after I slipped on my boots. The family group chat was blowing up this morning.

GEORGIA

Big day today, Finny. Are you and Reese excited about the interview?

HUGH

You're going to kill it. Glad you'll have Reese with you. It's about time you tell your side of the story.

BRINKLEY

Agreed. Just act natural. Forget that the whole world will be reading this.

Wow. That's helpful, Brinks. Thanks.

CAGE

Sorry, I'm trying to text, but fucking Maxine followed me into my office, and she's trying to climb me like a tree right now.

HUGH

Maxine Brooks? The librarian? Isn't she, like, eighty years old?

BRINKLEY

Maxine Brooks banned me from the library in high school because I put caution tape over a section of books that I felt were sexist to women.

GEORGIA

I think Maxine Brooks left town with her lover. I heard the guy was, like, forty years younger than her. She's a cougar.

CAGE

For fuck's sake. Maxine Brooks did not move away. I just saw her at Cottonwood Café with her boyfriend, who happens to be older than dirt. The dude is pushing ninety. Check your facts, people. I'm talking about Maxine Langley. Martha and Joe's pig who has a weird obsession with me.

Ahhh... Didn't that pig try to mount you a few months ago when you made a house call?

HUGH

Beggars can't be choosers, brother.

BRINKLEY

Agreed. Don't look a gift horse in the mouth.

CAGE

<middle finger emoji>

GEORGIA

I love Maxine Langley. They brought her to The Tipsy Tea last time I was there with Gracie, and they were buying her a tutu.

CAGE

Yeah. She's wearing some sort of fucking skirt. They dropped her off here for a few hours because Martha claims I'm the only person Maxine will tolerate. Apparently, I'm a fucking babysitter?

Don't you offer to board animals at the clinic?

CAGE

Maxine doesn't like being put in closed quarters. She thinks she's fucking human. So now this is my headache. When we put her in a crate, she squealed like someone was cutting off a fucking limb. So now she's just walking free in my office while her parents are off doing God knows what, and I'm trying to run a business here.

GEORGIA

Maddox and I will come visit. I love Maxine. Did you know that she can play video games? Martha told me she plays with people all over the world, and she wears a headset.

HUGH

You can't make this shit up. How the fuck is a pig playing video games?

BRINKLEY

Maybe she thinks she'll win over Cage with her mad Madden skills?

CAGE

Let's put our attention back on the interview. You're going to do fine, Finny. Acting like you're in love with your best friend won't take any real skill, because I think your fake relationship is not fake at all. There. I said it.

Well, you've said it many times. Doesn't make it true just because Cage Reynolds says it. Although, I'm sure Maxine, the pig who is currently imprinting on you, would listen to anything you had to say.

GEORGIA

Be honest, Finny. Have you never thought about being with Reese?

Reese is in love with Carl.

HUGH

I like the way you avoided that question.

BRINKLEY

I noticed that, too. Maybe Reese doesn't know you'd be willing to date for real. I mean, your track record is a big red flag for someone who likes to be in committed relationships.

I wouldn't even know how to date for real. And I'd never risk fucking up our friendship. We made a pact years ago not to cross the line.

CAGE

Well, you're now living together. The world thinks you're dating. You both can't seem to stay away from one another. I'd say the pact you made in middle school could be amended.

Like a friends with benefits amendment?

HUGH

She doesn't strike me as a girl that would go for that deal. Although, she is technically single right now.

BRINKLEY

That's a risky offer. I wouldn't go there.

GEORGIA

Sex can make things very complicated.

Sex doesn't have to be complicated. I think sex is fucking fantastic. And I haven't had any for a long time.

BRINKLEY

TMI <puking face emoji>

GEORGIA

Maybe you should try to date her instead.

You can't date someone who is actively trying to get back together with their ex-boyfriend. She isn't looking for a replacement. I'm just the dude making the one that she actually wants jealous.

CAGE

Show her what she's missing.

HUGH

You're Finn fucking Reynolds!

GEORGIA

Hell, yes.

CAGE

I can't do this. Maxine just bit my kneecap and squealed so loud I'm certain I have permanent hearing loss. Stop being a <cat emoji> and take a fucking risk for once in your life.

I hope Maxine broke skin and your kneecap falls off. I have to go. They'll be here in five minutes.

A slew of texts came through, but I turned off my phone and slipped it into my back pocket.

"You almost done in there?" I called out to Reese, who was in my bathroom getting ready. I'd be lying if I didn't admit that I loved having her here. Even if I had a chronic case of blue balls.

Reese had been working her magic on my house already. She'd found a bunch of pillows and a few throw blankets for the couch, along with sprucing up my bedroom. She'd hung curtains in the front room and dining room. There were fresh flowers in the kitchen and the family room, and her warmth was all around. She'd been online, ordering new light fixtures, which would arrive sometime next week.

"How do you feel? Are you nervous?" she asked me as she stepped out of the bathroom.

I looked up, and for a brief second, I was unable to speak, which had never happened to me. She looked fucking stunning.

Her hair was in a loose bun at the nape of her neck, with a few stray waves that had broken free, framing her pretty face. She wore a long floral dress that hugged her perfect tits and cinched at her tiny waist, and the full skirt ran down to her ankles. Her white cowboy boots peeked out at the bottom. I looked up just as her tongue swiped out and moved across her plump, pink, gloss-covered lips.

"Wow. You look gorgeous. But you can't be licking your lips like that when they're here." I pushed to my feet, my eyes finding the tops of her breasts that were being pushed up by the dress.

Fuck me.

I was going to be hard as a rock the entire interview.

"What? My mouth is dry. I can't lick my lips because you haven't had sex in months and have a chronic erection?" Her eyes searched mine.

She really didn't have a fucking clue just how sexy she was.

Because her pea-brained boyfriend had never let her know.

I moved toward her. My hand moved under her chin, turning her face so she was looking up at me.

"I don't get a boner when I'm not with you. I never once got an erection on set, where half-naked women were rubbing all over my junk. So don't go blaming my lack of control on anything other than what it is."

"And what is it?" She narrowed her gaze, holding her chin up high, as she watched me.

"Well, for starters, your tits are teasing me the way they're showing off in this dress." I shrugged. "And your fucking lips are too much, Miney. It's too much."

"Too much? My lips? I don't know what you're talking about."

Okay. I guess she needed me to spell it out for her. We'd always been honest with one another; this shouldn't be any different.

"When you lick your lips, I think about them being wrapped around my cock." I raised a brow, and she sucked in a breath, eyes wide. "And these tits of yours? Well, I think about teasing them with my tongue and my lips. Hell, I think about kissing them in the shower and all the things I'd like to do to them."

Her chest was rising and falling quickly, and she whispered, "Oh. I'm, er, I'm sorry about that. Anything else?"

"Yeah. Since you're asking… When you walk around the house in those tiny pink pajama shorts—the ones you wore the night you slipped your hand between your legs," I said, trying not to laugh at the pink hue that was covering her cheeks now.

"I know the shorts you're referencing, Chewy."

"Well, every time you wear them, I have to go take a cold shower because all I want to do is press you up against the wall, drop to my knees, spread your legs, and taste you."

"You need to have sex," she whispered as she fanned her face.

I barked out a laugh. "Yeah. I do. But my girlfriend won't cross the line with me, so I'm fucked."

"Your fake girlfriend."

"Potayto, potahto. I'm a horny dude. You asked for the truth, and I gave it to you. Stop licking your lips. You got it?"

She smiled and nodded, her eyes watering as she looked at me. "You've always had a way of making me feel beautiful, Chewy."

"I've told you many times. You're the most beautiful girl in the world. Now, come on. They're going to be here any minute. Get ready to gush over me."

She opened her mouth to say something, and the doorbell rang.

"Game time, Miney."

I took her hand and led her out to the front room before pulling the door open. There were more people there than I'd expected. Lane Fortworth was the woman I'd spoken to on the phone, and she quickly introduced herself to Reese and me. But there were at least a dozen people behind her.

"This is the lighting and camera crew. I probably should have told you that the whole team was coming, but you'll barely notice them. They'll stay out of our hair." Lane stepped inside when I held my hand out, inviting her in. She wore a navy pantsuit. Her hair was short and cropped around her ears, and she was probably in her mid-forties.

"That's not a problem. The more the merrier," Reese said as we led everyone to the kitchen.

Reese had put out juice and muffins and fruit, and she told them all to help themselves. Lane checked out the space and told them to set up in the kitchen area, and she pulled the chairs to one side of the table.

"There's a lot of natural light in here. This will work well." She motioned for us to sit across from her. "It's nice to meet you both in person. I'm thrilled that you're joining us, Reese. The world wants to meet the woman who stole Finn Reynolds's heart. A heart we'd heard would never be up for grabs."

"Well, I'm happy to be here, and Finn's my favorite topic." Reese leaned her head against my shoulder, and I wrapped an arm around her on instinct.

Lane beamed and waved her hand in the air to adjust the lighting, and she let us know that she was beginning the interview. She held a notepad on her lap, but she also had a device on the table beside her and said that she would be recording our chat, as well. We'd be taking photos afterward.

"Let's do this," I said.

She dove right in, asking questions about Jessica Carson and pressing for a response from me.

"Listen, I don't want to dredge up something that I'd rather put to rest. I will say this… There was never a relationship. We worked on the same set. It never went very deep, and she's painted a very different picture from what really happened."

"There wasn't an ongoing romantic relationship?"

"There was not."

"Do you believe him?" Lane asked, turning her attention to Reese.

"One hundred percent. I've known Finn my entire life. He's the most honest person I know. He's taken the high road, even though his character has been dragged through the mud. That's who he is. He doesn't want to hurt anyone or embarrass anyone. But that relationship has been fabricated, and that's the truth."

"Okay. Good to hear the other side of things. So, how did your lengthy friendship become a romantic relationship?"

Reese glanced over at me, biting down on her juicy bottom lip, blushing at just the right time. My God. She could be a professional actress because the way she was looking at me had even me believing she was madly in love with me.

"We spent the last year apart. We'd never spent time apart before, and I think we both realized how much we missed one another," I said, reaching for her hand and holding it in my lap.

"And you were engaged before. Is that right, Reese?"

I startled the slightest bit, but Reese didn't appear even remotely fazed by the question. "Yes. I had a long-term boyfriend, and we'd gotten engaged before I'd accepted the job in London. I realized that I wasn't happy with my life, and I wanted to take the opportunity that had presented itself."

"Like something was missing?" Lane pressed.

"Definitely. I wasn't on the right path, so I made a change." Reese let out a breath, and I squeezed her hand. I didn't want her to say anything that would mess up her future with Carl, even though I hated the dick weasel. "If my relationship had fulfilled me, I don't believe I would have left. But the person I missed the most when I was away is the man sitting beside me right now."

A tear moved down her cheek, and my fucking chest squeezed.

Damn, she was good.

I leaned forward and swiped at the tear before placing my hand beneath her chin and turning her toward me. I kissed her. It was quick, but it felt right.

Nothing about it felt fake at the moment.

"Oh, my." Lane fanned her face. "You two are just so cute

together. Get ready to swoon, America. The love between these two is palpable."

"Tell me something fun about one another that nobody knows. I mean, you've known one another your entire lives. I'm guessing you know each other better than anyone."

I glanced at Reese and turned my attention back to Lane. "Reese's favorite color is citrine." I chuckled. "Everyone gives her shit about it, saying she should just say that her favorite color is yellow, but I never did because I know the reason."

"And what's the reason?" Lane leaned forward, completely invested.

"We'd race daylight every day when we were growing up. We'd stay outside until just before sunset, and during that last hour, she'd always look up at the sky and point to all the colors. Man, this went on for so many summers over the years. And she'd point out this particular shade of yellow and tell me that it was citrine. She'd call it a gift from the sun."

Reese laughed. "Good memory, Finn. He's also being modest because that wasn't the only place that I would see my favorite color."

"Where else did you see it?" Lane asked.

"Look at his eyes. There's a gold ring around the outside, and if you look closely, you'll see the layers of amber and citrine."

"I do see it." Lane motioned for the photographers to snap a few pictures of us while we were sitting close and having a good time.

We spent the next hour talking about our favorite movies, our nicknames, and telling her about some trouble we got into as kids.

"You got taken to the police station at ten years old? How in the world did that happen?"

We were both laughing so hard now, and I motioned for Reese to tell the story.

"Finn and a few of our friends dared me to run through

the Leonards' farm. I wasn't about to turn down a challenge. But I didn't expect to get chased by a pack of pigs," Reese said over her laughter.

"Yeah. I freaked when I saw them going after her, so I jumped in, and we both slipped in the wet mud and flopped around. I got her up, and we made it to the gate, but a bunch of the chickens and pigs and goats got out, and let's just say, old Mr. Leonard wasn't too pleased. We were taken to the station, and I swear it was worth it because I've never laughed so hard in my life. She was covered in mud and trying to explain that she got goosed by a goat."

We were all laughing, as were the members of the crew around us.

"You two have quite a history. I imagine this one's going to stick." Lane smirked.

"I think it's already sticking, Lane."

And that wasn't a lie.

fourteen

• • •

Reese

"WHAT DO YOU THINK?" Maggie asked as we stood in front of my new office space, looking at the logo she'd just painted on the window.

"I love it. It's perfect. Thank you so much." I took a couple of pictures with my phone to send to Finn, and we both hurried inside as the wind began to pick up.

"It looks so good. This has to make it feel very official." Maggie and I had grown up together, and she owned Buttons & Boots, one of my favorite boutiques just a few doors down. She was an artist at heart, and painting was her true passion.

"It does," I said, reaching into my purse and handing her the envelope with the money inside. "I can't thank you enough."

"Pfft. I'm thrilled that you're making your dream a reality. I knew that working at Barley's Party Supplies was not your end game. I'm proud of you for taking the leap."

I motioned for her to sit in the cute chair that I'd been storing in my parents' garage. It was a white-and-pink floral armchair I'd had recovered shortly before I'd moved, when I thought I'd be moving in with Carl. I took the seat behind my desk.

"Yeah. I was ready for a change."

"You're not kidding. I mean, the job is a big change, but dating Finn…" She clapped her hands together, and the widest grin spread across her face. "I'd say you upgraded with both."

The comment caught me off guard. Not that Finn wasn't the greatest guy I knew, but I didn't know that Maggie wasn't a fan of Carl.

"Thank you. Yeah, I'm really happy. But Carl and I are still friends. I still care very deeply for him."

She winced. "Oh, man. I didn't mean to imply anything bad about him. I just, well, I always felt like he wanted you to be on board with his plan. It always seemed like it was his way or the highway. I don't doubt that he loved you like crazy, as much as a man like Carl can."

A man like Carl?

"What do you mean, 'as much as a man like Carl can'?" I pressed, because I understood my family and Finn having an issue with Carl, but not someone who didn't know all the details of what had gone down between us.

"I just mean that I think Carl thinks very highly of himself. His first love will always be—well, Carl." She chuckled. "But all those years of you and Finn hanging out all the time, it was never like that. You both always celebrated one another in every way. And I saw you do that with Carl, but I never saw him reciprocate that with you."

My heart raced a bit at her words because I knew deep down there was some truth to them. Maybe that was why I'd decided to go to London.

Maybe I hadn't been selfish at all.

Maybe I'd been trying to show him that I was just as important as he was. It was true. It was Carl's way or no way, and after a while, that had gotten old. I'd lost myself and my identity while doing everything for him, his way. There was more to this than I'd realized, and now, talking with Maggie, I was seeing things more clearly.

"Yeah, Finn is a natural at making everyone feel like they're the most important person in the room." I chuckled.

"He's charming, that's for sure. But he's never looked at anyone the way he looks at you. I'd always thought he was in love with you. I'm just glad he finally realized it."

I sucked in a breath.

What was she talking about?

I mean, he was a damn good actor. But we hadn't been pretending before now.

"I don't know about that. This is new for us. We realized our feelings during our time apart."

She raised a brow. "Maybe you did. But I think his were there long before yours were."

I'm guessing she was confusing friendship with romantic feelings. Because I never doubted that he loved me for a minute—but not in a romantic way. Finn had the attention span of a toddler when it came to women.

Everyone knew that.

He wasn't a womanizer like Jessica made him out to be. The man would never lie or risk hurting someone. He was honest about who he was. We'd talked about it dozens of times.

In fact, the only time he'd ever lied in all the years that I'd known him was right now. Because I'd asked him to.

And he'd lied for me.

I remember a time when we were in college when Sarah Hamlin wanted to date him, and he felt horrible that he didn't feel the same. He'd tried to force it, but it just didn't work. She wanted to be angry with him, but he'd told her the truth. He'd tried, and it just wasn't there.

Finn had always believed what his father had told him about meeting Alana, Finn's mom.

That when it happened, he'd know it.

But it just hadn't happened.

And he was fine with it because he'd been so focused on his career, and when he wasn't working, he liked to have a good time.

There was no shame in knowing what you want.

"Well, I don't know about that. Tell me what's going on at the shop," I said, trying to change the subject.

I was lying to so many people I cared about, and it didn't sit well with me. What was everyone going to think when all of this came to an end?

"Business is great, and things always get crazy busy heading into the holidays. Guess who came in yesterday?"

"Who?"

"Christy Rae Lovell." She rolled her eyes dramatically. "It seems she's not too happy about Carl hiring you to design his new office."

Ahhh… trouble in paradise.

"Really? It's not like they live together. He and I are still friends. He's just trying to help me out with the new business."

"I don't know. She was talking to Sally Cauldon, and I was just doing what small-town locals do best," she said with a wink. "Eavesdropping like my life depended on it."

My head fell back in laughter. "Well, I would expect nothing less here in Cottonwood Cove."

"Yeah. It sounds like they get down and dirty at the hospital, though. She was telling Sally that she pulled him into a storage closet, and they went at it in there between seeing patients. Doesn't that feel a little, I don't know… dirty? For a doctor and a nurse to be banging between seeing sick people?"

My chest squeezed, and I made a conscious effort to keep my face even. "I don't know. I mean, that stuff happens on *Grey's Anatomy*, right?"

"True. But that's with McDreamy and McSteamy. This is…

Carl. If Finn were a doctor, I'd think it was perfectly fine. He's got that swagger. You two must be having a lot of fun." She shook her head. "The cowboy boots and the backward hat, and don't even get me started on those abs he showed off in the finale of *Big Sky Ranch*. Ugh. I'm totally fangirling over your man. You know I'm very happy with Brex. I just got a little off track."

We both laughed.

"Hey, I get it. You won't get an argument here. And he's all mine." I fanned my face because my best friend was hot, and I totally understood why everyone gawked at the man. And he'd shared that his lack of sex was making him very horny around me. I'd ignored it, and obviously, we hadn't acted on anything, but I couldn't get what he'd said out of my mind.

"You lucky biotch." She chuckled. "So, what will happen when he goes back to filming? He'll be gone for months at a time, right?"

Yes. We'd stage an amicable breakup. Long distance wasn't easy for anyone, but with him being a famous actor, it would be impossible to maintain at that point.

So, I had until after the holidays to get things back on track with Carl.

"We'll just do whatever it takes to stay together," I said with the confidence of someone in love.

"Good. I like seeing you happy. It's been a while since I've seen you smile like this. It looks good on you." She pushed to her feet.

Hadn't I always been happy?

My light had probably been dulled by doing a job I didn't feel inspired by. I was sure a lot of what she was seeing now was that I had opened my own business. I was doing what I loved.

I started my days riding Millie and ended my days racing Finn down to the beach before the sunset.

That was hard to beat.

"Thank you. I'll be coming by later this week to look for a dress for Finn's work party this weekend."

"Perfect timing. We just got all new inventory. The cutest dresses you've ever seen. And we got a bunch of lingerie in, too. You'll have to get a little something-something for after the party, too." She waggled her brows, and I chuckled. "And we're still on for happy hour with the girls tomorrow night?"

"I think I'll have to take you up on that lingerie, and we are absolutely on for tomorrow night." We were going with a few high school friends to Reynolds' for happy hour. I hugged her goodbye and gathered up my iPad and my sketch pad to head to Carl's for our design meeting.

I wasn't in the best frame of mind after hearing about him going at it with his girlfriend in a closet at the hospital. I couldn't get the man to make out on the beach when we'd been alone, and now he was having sex in public places?

I drove the short distance to his house, and when I walked up the walkway, I glanced over at the plants that he and I had put in together when he'd bought the house.

The home I'd planned to live in, as well.

I reached for the doorbell, but the door flew open before I pressed it.

"Hey, thanks for coming." He stepped aside so I could walk in. He wore a navy sweater and a pair of dark jeans. Even casual, the man looked polished and put together.

"Of course. Thanks for hiring me," I said, sounding overly peppy, which was not how I felt.

"You okay?" He paused and gave me a hug, holding me there a little longer than he should.

"Yeah, of course," I said, pulling back. I searched his gaze, wondering if I even knew this man. The things Maggie had said, outside of his wild sex life with his girlfriend, were running through my mind.

Did he ever celebrate me?

"I'm so proud of you, Reese. You found a space, and you're making it happen. I think it's amazing."

"Yeah? Thank you. It means a lot to me." I followed him to the office. Maybe he was going to prove everyone wrong. Maybe things would be different between us after spending so much time apart.

When he pushed the doors open, I smiled, because it was a clean slate. The walls were white. The floors were covered in a gorgeous natural wood that ran through the whole house. There wasn't a stitch of furniture or anything hanging on the walls.

"I'm giving you free rein. Work your magic," he said, shoving his hands into his pockets as his eyes locked with mine.

"Really? You're not going to give me any direction?" My voice was all tease because Carl was a control freak. He had strong opinions, and he'd never been able to hide them.

"Nope. You just spent a year in London working under a famous designer. I'm sure you know what you're doing."

Maybe he really was changing.

"What about Christy? She doesn't want to have any input?" I asked, raising a brow as I waited for an answer.

"Christy doesn't live here. I'm sure she'd like to have input, but the only one I'm trusting is you."

My heart squeezed at his words. Maybe he was finally seeing me. Really seeing me. Hell, I was capable of doing a lot more than I'd realized.

"Well, thank you for that. I'm going to have a lot of fun designing this room. So, let's just talk about budget, and I'll show you a few inspiration photos I have and get an idea of things you like and don't like, and then I'll work my magic."

"Sounds like a plan." We moved to the dining room and sat in the chairs beside one another as I pulled up the photos on my iPad.

Carl moved his chair closer so we could both see the

screen. His pinky finger brushed against mine before his hand covered mine. I sucked in a breath, but I didn't move.

"Carl," I whispered. I mean, I wasn't in a real relationship, but he was.

"I miss you, Reese."

I nodded, and then I thought of Finn. Real or fake, I'd never disrespect him. I still wanted the life I'd always imagined with Carl, but I wasn't going to act on anything while we were both actively dating other people. I pulled my hand away and turned to look at him.

"Not sure how Christy would feel about that, but I know Finn wouldn't like it." I licked my lips because my mouth had gone dry as my adrenaline started pumping.

It wasn't attraction or a physical pull that I felt toward this man. It was adrenaline. I was pissed. Why was I keeping that to myself?

Here he was, telling me that he missed me, and I knew what he'd been up to.

"I can't stop thinking about you."

"Really? Were you thinking about me when you were fucking Christy in a closet at the hospital?"

His eyes widened, and his face paled. "How do you know about that?"

"It's a small town, Carl." I turned back toward the photos and moved my chair away from him just a few inches. "If you aren't able to work with me, please say so now."

"Of course, I can work with you. I'm sorry." He turned so he was facing me. "I don't know what's going on with me right now, Reese. I'm just kind of lost."

My heart ached at his words. I'd loved this man since we were teenagers. I didn't want to see him hurting, even when he'd hurt me badly.

Even when I'd felt lost, and he hadn't been there for me in any way.

Why was that okay with me?

"Well, I suggest you take some time to figure it out. I'm always going to be your friend, and I'm here for you. But as long as you're with Christy and I'm with Finn, that's all I can be to you."

He nodded. "I get it. I'm sorry. And the truth is, I could use a friend right now. You're the best friend I've ever had."

I nodded. I couldn't say the same back to him because that would be a lie.

"I'm here for you."

"Thank you. Now, show me what you have in mind for my office."

We got back to work, and we spent the next few hours talking about his office, life, and just hanging out.

For the first time since I'd left for London, I didn't feel that horrible distance between Carl and me.

But the closeness didn't feel the way that it should feel either.

I was ready to leave, so I packed up my stuff.

Finn had texted me and said that he'd prepared a picnic for us so we could take the horses down to the water and have dinner out there.

And I couldn't wait to get home.

To see Finn.

And that thought alone terrified me.

fifteen

. . .

Finn

REESE and I had driven to the city this afternoon, as we'd both been swamped with work this week. I'd had several meetings, the most exciting being with my agent, where we'd finalized everything for the big-screen movie production I'd been offered the lead in. My career had really launched since *Big Sky Ranch* was the hottest streaming series out there at the moment. The movie had a tight timeline, and they'd agreed to work around my schedule, which meant I'd be leaving for Tokyo right after New Year's, and I'd be there for four weeks, and then I'd come home and start shooting season two.

I knew that I needed to strike while the iron was hot.

Reese's business was also taking off. She had two clients, one being that dick weasel of an ex, who I doubted was really hiring her because he wanted his office professionally decorated. I had a hunch that jealousy was eating him up, and he would do just about anything to keep her close.

She hadn't said much since her meeting with him at his house earlier in the week, so either he hit on her or said something she wasn't ready to tell me because she'd been tight-lipped ever since.

I was at a fork in the road. I wanted the best for her—first and foremost, that was what I always wanted for Reese.

I was struggling with what to do at the moment. A part of me wanted her to have everything she wanted, and if that was Carl, I wouldn't interfere with it.

But something had shifted in me. Maybe it was the lack of sex. Maybe it was the realization that I'd missed the shit out of her during our time apart. Maybe it was that hot-as-fuck night in my bathroom, or the fact that I wanted her in a way I'd never wanted anyone.

And that was fucking scary.

At first, I thought it was because she was off-limits because we'd made a pact. That maybe I just wanted what I couldn't have, wanting the unknown. But being with her in London and seeing her so vulnerable after not being with her for so long—I think I knew I wanted her with me then. And not just in a friendly way. In a future sort of way… the way she wanted to be with Carl. And that sucked for me unless Carl was to fall by the wayside.

Fuck.

I wasn't a relationship guy, so I didn't have much to offer her. I didn't know what I was capable of, and fucking anything up with Reese would be… unacceptable.

The worst move I could ever make.

Because there was no world that I existed in that she wasn't a part of.

And she knew me better than I knew myself.

The potential for me to fuck things up was high—not that she'd shown any signs of being willing to go there either. Hell, she was still shaming herself for that drunken night in the bathroom weeks ago.

So, it wasn't like I could tell her I wanted to give things a try for real. She'd laugh in my face. And she'd have a damn good reason to.

So, I'd fake date her. Continue being her best friend. And

if the opportunity to cross the line and rock her fucking world presented itself, I would take it. See if we were as good together in the physical way as I hoped we were.

Give her a chance to see me in a different light.

I was older now. I'd played around enough to know what I wanted. I was tired of the game. Sure, I wanted to get laid; I was a sexual dude. But the problem was, I didn't want anyone else.

I wanted Reese.

But it would have to happen on her terms. I sure as fuck wouldn't push her, only to have her end up hating me.

Tonight, we were at a cocktail party at a swanky hotel in the city, and I'd gotten us a suite so we wouldn't have to drive back home. Reese looked hot as fuck in her strapless black cocktail dress that hugged her curves in all the right places. Her hair was pulled back in a knot at the nape of her neck, a few pieces falling out around her pretty face. She'd been off with Angelique, chatting with the crew, while the directors, Charles and Sadie, pulled me aside to talk about the new season.

"Congratulations on finalizing the movie deal. That's big news, Finn." Charles held his glass up and clinked it against mine.

"Yeah. I'm looking forward to it. Thanks for being flexible and pushing the start date back by a few days for me."

"Of course. Are you going to be okay being on set with Jessica?" Sadie asked as she sipped her martini.

The private room they'd rented at the hotel restaurant was buzzing, as everyone was excited to be reunited.

"I'll be fine. Don't worry about me. I'm grateful for the opportunity, and we'll make it work."

"You are a big part of the reason that this show has taken off, Finn. And it's important to us that you're happy. I know you're going to be getting a lot of offers, and I want you to do what's best for you. But you're part of the *Big Sky Ranch* family, and we want you to be with us for the long haul. We'll keep you and Jessica apart on set, and you won't have any scenes together if we can help it." Charles's gaze locked with mine. These two had been great to work with, and I was grateful that they'd taken a shot on me.

"Listen, I know this isn't your fault," I said, looking around, relieved that Jessica hadn't shown up to the party yet. "I appreciate you trying to navigate this to make it easier on everyone."

"Hopefully, it's been put to rest. I heard that interview by *The Hollywood Moment* is getting a lot of buzz. Everyone's excited to read it and meet your new lady, and I've got to say, she's spectacular." Sadie waggled her brows.

"Yeah. They don't get any better than Reese Murphy." My gaze moved across the room to find her with her head back in a full-bodied laugh. The group around her had grown, as people were just drawn to all that goodness.

I could attest to that.

"It's good to see you happy. And I know Jessica is going to make things challenging, but with her contract right now, we don't have a ton of options." Charles cleared his throat. "She's got us all by the balls at the moment. Just know that things are in the works. We've got your back. Now that's enough shop talk. Go enjoy yourself."

I nodded, and they both stepped away just as Lacey hurried over. "Finn, I've missed you."

Lacey did our hair on the set, and she was one of my favorites to work with. She gave me a big hug and glanced over her shoulder to make sure no one was listening. "So, I've got some news. Edward and I have been seeing each other since shooting ended."

Edward was one of several camera guys. Cool dude. I'd planted the seed that Lacey liked him because the girl had been crushing on him for months. He wasn't here today as he'd taken a gig on another set during our downtime. Not everyone could afford to take months off between seasons, so it was common to find other jobs when we weren't filming.

"That's what I like to hear," I said, wrapping an arm around her shoulder.

"We're actually moving in together. Looks like things worked out for both of us in that department," she said, beaming up at me. "And thank God that it shut Jessica the hell up. Everyone is so pissed at the crap she's pulled with this shitstorm she started. I'm so sorry you've had to deal with all that drama. But maybe that's what pushed you into getting into something serious with Reese. I need to meet her. I feel like I've heard so much about her for so long, and now you're a couple. And you're in love, Finny."

She wrapped her arms around me and hugged me again, her head falling back in laughter. She was goofy by nature, and she made work a lot of fun for everyone.

I looked up, and my gaze locked with Reese's. I wasn't sure what I saw there. Was she upset about something? I quickly scanned the room, but there was no sign of Jessica. When I looked back, Reese wasn't looking at me any longer, but her shoulders were squared, and there wasn't the usual lightness there.

A loud ruckus had my attention moving to the door just as Jessica came walking through with an entourage. She had security on each side of her, and her own hair and makeup team behind them, as she refused to use the on-set crew. Why she felt the need to bring hair, makeup, and security to a work event was beyond me. But the girl was definitely not predictable, so I never knew what kind of stunt she'd pull.

The air in the room shifted with her presence, and I excused myself from Lacey and beelined over to Reese.

"Hey, y'all!" Jessica yelled out. "Let's get this party started."

I reached Reese just as Jessica approached her. My hand

came around her protectively as I pulled her back up against my chest.

I'm here.

The lines were blurring for me with Reese, but I needed to keep my head on straight.

Reese's hands came over my forearm that rested against her chest, and she tipped her head back to look at me.

"Well, isn't this just adorable," Jessica said as her gaze locked with mine. "I heard you two did an interview together. I'm sure everyone can't wait for it to release. Way to keep the focus on the show."

"Hey, let's not start any drama. This is a party," Brenna said. She had a supporting role on the show, and she and I had become good friends. Her husband stood beside her, shoulders squared, as if he were ready to defend her at all costs.

I understood that.

"This doesn't seem like much of a party, at least not until I got here." She moved closer, and her security guard stood slightly in front of her, giving her a warning look.

"If you have something to say, you don't need to make a scene. Use your words," Reese hissed, catching me off guard.

"Oh, the little country girl has a voice. How nice." Jessica laughed. "I knew you were trouble when you came to the premiere party, you home-wrecking whore."

That was all I needed. I unlocked my hold on Reese and slipped her behind me, moving into Jessica's space. "You don't get to speak to her. You don't even get to fucking look at her. Do you hear me?"

I barely recognized my own voice. I'd never felt this kind of anger before. But she'd pushed me too far.

"Oh, someone is sensitive about their '*special friend,*'" she said, using two fingers on each hand to make air quotes dramatically. "Were you fucking her the whole time we were together?"

"You seriously need to get help. We were never together, and you fucking know it. What is your obsession with this? You don't get enough attention for your acting skills?" There were camera flashes going off from behind her, and I looked up to see two dudes taking photos that were not part of this party.

How the fuck did they get in?

Jessica glanced over at them and then looked back at me with a wicked smile. She'd brought them. She wanted this caught on camera.

Charles was there with security from the hotel and motioned for them to escort Jessica and her crew out of the party.

"Actually, I'd appreciate it if security could escort us up to our room. We're leaving." I'd had enough. This had all gone too far, and I didn't even know what her end game was.

"Fuck," Charles said under his breath as everyone stood there, watching the whole ugly scene with their mouths gaping open. "I'm sorry about this, Reese."

"I'm fine. I think someone's just a little angry that she didn't get what she wanted," Reese said, looking completely unfazed as her hand remained in mine, and we followed the security guards out the door.

Charles and Sadie were having words with Jessica, who plastered a fake smile on her face and waved at us as we walked by.

Air puffed from my nose as we took the private employee elevator to the top floor, and I tried to tamp down my anger. All three security guards were standing beside us. No one spoke, and when the doors opened and we stepped off the elevator, they escorted us to our hotel room door. I slipped them each a tip and apologized for the inconvenience.

Once we stepped inside the hotel room, Reese moved across the suite and sat down on the couch.

"I'm sorry about that," I said, moving closer to her.

She put her hand up and stopped me from coming any closer. "You don't have to apologize to me for Jessica. I was prepared for her. I've watched her interviews. I know she's putting on a show. She likes the attention that she's getting. She doesn't bother me."

"She's completely unhinged. She called you a fucking whore." I stormed across the room and poured some bourbon into a glass and tipped my head back. "I will fucking ruin her. The gloves are off. How dare she say that to you."

"This is how she wants you to react, Chewy. Don't give her the pleasure. I'm not offended."

How was she so fucking calm?

"Why are you not rattled by what just happened?" I set the glass down on the bar and moved to sit beside her.

"Well, do you think I'm a whore?" She smirked.

"No. That's why I'm pissed."

"She doesn't know me. I don't care what she thinks. We both know it's not true. She's unprofessional, and she's caused everyone a ton of trouble, so no one is even listening to her at this point." Her green gaze locked with mine. "I'm sorry she ruined your night. Seemed like you were having a good time with your friend."

She raised a brow.

"My friend? Who?"

"The beautiful woman that was hugging you and completely into you. I'm guessing you were hoping to sneak off with her tonight?"

I tried to think back to who she could be referring to.

"Lacey Waters?"

"Long, dark hair. Hourglass figure. And dressed to kill. You two were taking selfies or something because she was holding the phone up to get you both on the screen." She pushed to her feet and started pacing in front of me, her hands in fists. "The one you're clearly attracted to, but you're stuck with me, so you didn't act on it."

A loud laugh escaped my lips. "Lacey is dating a friend of mine, Edward. And those selfies were her FaceTiming Edward so we could both say hi. She does my hair on set. She's a good friend, nothing more. As far as she knows, we're both in serious relationships. She was actually really excited to meet you before Jessica came in, raining hell down on the party."

I was fairly certain that Reese Murphy had just shown me her cards.

She was fucking jealous.

"Oh," she whispered, her mouth making a perfect O as she looked at me.

"You weren't jealous, were you, Lover?" I said. My voice was all tease, but I knew she was.

I just didn't know exactly how to proceed.

"Please. Why would I be jealous? This isn't real." She threw her hands in the air and flailed her arms around, making all sorts of noises, letting me know how outrageous I was.

"All right. Just checking. You going to be okay sharing the bed with me tonight?" I asked as my tongue swiped out to wet my lips, and her heated gaze landed there.

Yeah. She wanted me as badly as I wanted her.

She just didn't want to admit it.

"I've slept with you more times than I can count, Chewy. It'll be fine. I'm going to go brush my teeth and put on my pajamas." Her cheeks were flushed, and she turned on her heels and walked unusually fast to the bathroom, and I heard the bathroom door close behind her.

I pulled out my phone. Relationships clearly weren't my strong suit, and I didn't want to fuck this up. Which I most likely would. I sent a text to the brothers-only group chat.

> Do not add Brinks and Georgie to this group text. This is a Reynolds brothers' conversation. I've got a situation.

CAGE

I'm waiting with bated breath. <eye roll emoji>

HUGH

Here for you, brother. Go.

I think I have feelings for Reese. Like real fucking feelings. Not the friendship kind.

CAGE

You don't fucking say? I'm shocked. <blowing smoke emoji>

Don't be a dick. I've never felt like this. Tell me what to do.

HUGH

I get it. It's going to be okay. I think we all saw this coming.

CAGE

Hell, yeah, we did. You aren't that good of an actor. <winky face emoji> I'm kidding. But I've known for a while.

Good for you. You knew before me. It doesn't matter when you knew. What the fuck do I do? This is Reese. She's still in love with that fuckface ex of hers. But I'm fairly certain that she got jealous tonight when she saw a woman talking to me.

HUGH

That's a good sign. She has a history with Carl. I don't think there's anything deeper there, to be honest. Show her what she's missing.

She knows me better than anyone. There isn't much I haven't shown.

CAGE

He's talking about friends with benefits, dipfuck. Stop with the platonic shit. Forget what Brinks and Georgie said. Reese was talking about finding a dude to hook up with when we were there that night after she had dinner with Carl. Or have you forgotten that?

Of course, I didn't forget about that. That was the night things got… complicated. I hadn't shared what happened with anyone.

HUGH

Agreed. Stop holding back. She's single. You're single. Work your magic, dude. This is your wheelhouse. Throw a Hail Mary, and get the fuck out of the friendship zone.

I barked out a laugh. Clearly, I'd never been shy when it came to bragging about my skills in the bedroom when I was talking to my brothers.

This is Reese. I can't risk fucking it up.

CAGE

I thought you said you had real feelings for her. This isn't just someone you want to casually fuck, correct?

She'll never believe it. She doesn't think I'm capable. She'll think I'm just horny because it's been a while since I've gotten laid. A real long while, if you know what I'm saying.

HUGH

Would you go hook up with someone else right now if you could get away with it without anyone finding out? If you could sneak someone up to your hotel room right now. Would you do it?

No.

It was an easy answer. I didn't want anyone else. I hadn't for a while.

CAGE

Then let her know that you're open to a little friends with benefits to go along with this fake relationship. See if she bites. Her ex-boyfriend certainly isn't holding back with his girlfriend. Then once you've taken things to the next level, you can show her that you want it to be something more with your actions and not your dick. But right now, your dick is your best shot at getting out of the friendship lane.

HUGH

Yeah. If you try to say you want an actual relationship right now, it might scare her off, and she won't want to risk messing things up. One step at a time, brother. See if she wants to have a little fun, and then you can show her that you're not leaving.

They made a good point. I'd already made it clear that I was attracted to her, but I hadn't sold it as a real option. Sure, I'd joked about it, but I'd never presented it as something serious to consider.

I was going to take things up a notch.

Okay. I think you're on to something.

CAGE

I feel like a fucking therapist, and I should charge you for billable hours. And then I should smack you upside the head for taking this long to figure this shit out.

HUGH

What he means is... you've got this.

CAGE

Fine. You've got this. And remember, I've still got money on this.

<middle finger emoji>

I turned off my phone when I heard the bathroom door open.

Game time.

sixteen

. . .

Reese

SEEING Finn with Lacey had stirred something inside me that I hadn't felt before. Something foreign.

Sure, I hated the idea of Carl and Christy Rae Lovell. It made me physically ill, but it was different. It hurt because I felt like he'd replaced me.

Like my dream of a family and the future I'd imagined were gone, as well.

But seeing Lacey with Finn had been next level.

It was almost a feral response.

Like I wanted to storm across the room and make sure she knew that he was mine.

But he wasn't mine. None of this was real.

I didn't know what was happening to me. Hearing about Carl in the closet at the hospital with his girlfriend had stung. Angered me even. Because for all those years, I'd tried to get us to have a little more fun, and he'd shut me down, and then he'd experienced them with someone else.

But it wasn't Carl I was thinking about when I closed my eyes at night.

Was I a glutton for punishment?

Fantasizing about my best friend. Knowing that it could never go anywhere.

When I came out of the bathroom, he was unbuttoning his dress shirt, and he turned to look at me, his abs and chest on full display.

Golden and sun-kissed and so freaking sexy.

I stood there gaping before pulling myself out of my daze and walking toward the bed. I did a dramatic stretch with my arms and yawned.

"I'm exhausted. I think I'm going to get some sleep."

"Yeah, me, too." He pushed his shirt off his shoulders and tossed it on the chair in the corner before tugging off his dress pants.

I couldn't keep my gaze from watching as he walked toward the bathroom wearing nothing but his black boxer briefs.

I mean, it would be abnormal for me not to notice.

Inhuman, even.

The man could actually pose for an underwear ad, so how could I not look?

I heard him chuckle as he disappeared into the bathroom and the sink turned on and off. I climbed into bed and pulled the covers over me.

You're just lonely. It's been so long since anyone has touched you. This is perfectly normal to feel these things. It doesn't mean anything.

I could feel him moving through the bedroom, and I heard the click of the lights turning off. The room was dark, and I squeezed my eyes closed because I was fighting the urge to act on my desire.

Something we'd always agreed we'd never do.

The weight of his body had the bed moving as he slid in beside me. His warm breath tickled my cheek from his nearness. He radiated warmth, and I wanted to wrap myself around him.

"You fake sleeping, Miney?" His voice was deep and low, and there was humor there.

"Well, we're fake dating, so it only seems natural." I chuckled.

His thumbs moved to my eyelids, and he forced them open, which made me laugh harder.

"Why are you hiding?"

"I'm not hiding," I whispered. The light from the moon coming through the windows overlooking the city created a halo around his handsome face.

God, he was a beautiful man.

It was only right that he would never settle down. It wouldn't be fair if only one woman got to enjoy this man for the rest of her life.

I was lucky enough to be the woman he called his best friend. So, in a way, Finn did belong to me. But not entirely. He'd never fully give himself to anyone.

He knew he'd tire of them, and he would never want to disappoint anyone. That was the kind of man he was.

"Tell me what's going on. Why were you jealous tonight?"

"I don't know, Chewy. I guess the lines are blurring a bit for me." My tongue swiped out to lick my lips, as my mouth was dry because having him so close to me was torture. "Not in the way you're thinking, so don't panic. I know what we are. I guess I just felt possessive because we're putting on a show and all."

"Yeah? You sure that's what it was?"

"What else could it be?" I asked. His fingers had moved down to my jaw, and he stroked each side in the most soothing rhythm.

"It's okay to admit you're attracted to me. I admitted it to you."

"Fine. I'm attracted to you. I mean, I think every woman with a pulse is attracted to you."

"So, what do you want to do about it?" His leg brushed

against mine as we closed what little distance we had between us so our bodies were flush together.

"Well, admitting it and acting on it are two very different things. We made a pact years ago, and I think we should honor that."

"What is it that you're afraid of?" he asked, but he moved his thumb to press gently against my lips, holding it there for a moment so I wouldn't answer just yet. "I already love you, and you already love me, so that's not going to change. We aren't strangers who might realize they love one another after crossing the line. We already do. So, we'd just be giving in to something that we both want. At least I know I do."

God, I wanted it, too.

"What if it ruins everything? We have a little fun, and then you leave for Tokyo after the holidays, and we stage a fake breakup, and Carl and I get engaged again—it's going to be weird between us. And I would never want to do anything to hurt what we have, because it's everything to me." My voice broke, and a tear slipped down my face.

I was in some sort of horndog hell. I'd never wanted anyone so badly, and I knew in my gut that it would end up destroying us.

I could survive in a world where Carl rejected me. I'd already proven that. And yes, in the end, it would hurt like hell, but I'd move on and find someone else who wanted what I wanted.

But I couldn't survive in a world where Finn and I weren't best friends. It would be dark and cold and lonely. And there would be no way to find another Finn Reynolds.

The loss would be too much for me.

"Reese," he whispered, his forehead resting against mine as he wrapped his arm around me. Our legs were tangled together. His erection was weighing heavy against my lower belly, and desire pooled between my legs. "You will never lose me. There is no world in which I could exist that didn't have you in it. I know that you want to be with Carl. There are no secrets here. But you're single, and I'm single, and all I want to do tonight is make you feel good. You deserve to feel good. And I want you so fucking much I can't see straight. We both know what this is. We're living together, and the whole world thinks we're together. So why not enjoy it?"

My fingers moved up the back of his neck, running through his hair. "You make a good argument. Carl thinks we're having sex anyway, and God knows he's having plenty of it. Maybe you could teach me a thing or two." A nervous chuckle escaped my lips.

My God, was I actually considering this?

"Listen, I don't want to do anything you don't want to do. But if you want me to make you feel good. If you want me to show you all that you're missing. If you want me to make you come so many times you won't be able to see straight, all you have to do is ask. I'm not in the dark about how this ends, so stop worrying. There is nothing that could come between you and me."

Oh my God.

My breaths were coming hard and fast now, and my hips started grinding up against his erection.

We were too close.

This was too much.

"Make me feel good, Finn," I whispered.

His mouth covered mine. His hand was on my neck, tipping my head back so he could get better access. My lips parted, inviting him in. His tongue slipped inside, tangling with mine. We'd kissed for show before, but this was different.

Needy and desperate.

My hands clawed at his shoulders as he groaned into my mouth. He rocked himself against me as he settled between my thighs before he rolled me completely onto my back and propped himself above me. No weight from his body, just the feel of his desire throbbing against my core.

He pulled back to look at me. His hand stroked the hair away from my face, his eyes wild with desire. "Is it too much?"

I shook my head, a husky chuckle escaping my lips. "It's not too much. I want more."

Did I really just say that?

"Good. You need to tell me what you want, Reese. That's the only way this happens."

Jesus. He was so sexy and commanding. This was a side of Finn that I hadn't experienced. How was that possible?

"Okay," I said, my chest rising and falling rapidly.

Desire overpowered all rational thought.

"Tell me what you want." His thumb stroked along my bottom lip.

"What are my choices?"

This sexy, deep chuckle escaped his lips. "I can kiss you some more. Make my way down every inch of your body. Spread your legs wide and taste you. Show you what you've been missing."

"Yes, to all of that," I said, a little too eagerly. "And sex. You didn't mention the sex."

"Not tonight. Tonight, we're going to take our time. There's no rush. You're mine for the next two months, and I plan to make every day count."

I nodded slowly because all ability to speak had left me.

His tongue moved along my bottom lip before he kissed me again. Slowly, this time. Tasting and exploring my mouth like he was memorizing every side. Every angle. I'd never been kissed like this. Like nothing else mattered in the world.

And at this moment, it didn't.

We kissed for what felt like hours, but in reality, it was probably twenty minutes. My body was buzzing, hips moving up and down against him, desperate to relieve the ache there.

Finn pulled back, looking at me with the sexiest smile I'd ever seen. His gray eyes blazed, and his lips turned up in the corners as he watched me. He pushed up, tugging me to sit forward, and raised my arms over my head. He pulled my tank top off and tossed it on the floor. Then he carefully tipped me back and slipped my pajama shorts down my legs, like he was unwrapping a present he'd been waiting for his entire life. His eyes scanned my body as if I were the most beautiful woman he'd ever seen. Goose bumps spread across my skin. No one had ever looked at me like this before.

He pushed to his feet, looking down at me with just my pink thong, the last remaining piece of fabric on my body. My cheeks burned as he stared at me, leaving me feeling more vulnerable than I'd ever felt in my life. I squeezed my eyes closed, desperately trying to gather myself.

This was Finn.

I was baring myself for the boy I'd known my entire life.

"Reese." His deep voice vibrated through my body like a current. "Open your eyes."

I used my hand to cover my eyes before I slowly opened my lids and peeked through my fingers.

He took my hands and moved them beside me.

"No. There's no hiding here. I think you've done enough of that, don't you?"

I didn't think I'd been hiding before now, because no one had ever stripped me down like this and taken their time to savor the moment.

"I haven't been hiding. I'm just not used to doing—this." I shrugged.

"This? Me looking at you like you're the most beautiful thing I've ever seen? Neither have I, Reese. This is just for you."

"Okay," I whispered, and his fingers moved to my breasts,

gently tracing a circle around each one with the tips of his fingers. I was certain my nipples could cut glass right now because they were achingly hard.

"I want you to watch so you can see what I see." He hovered over me, and he sucked in a breath as he stared at my breasts.

"These tits are what dreams are made of, Reese." His voice was husky as he leaned down and flicked his tongue across my nipple, and a shuddering breath escaped. He lapped around the outside of my hard peak, teasing and licking, before he moved to the other breast, giving them equal attention. I could barely contain myself. My back arched off the bed, and my legs squirmed, searching for something to press against, but he kept himself propped above me, remaining just out of reach.

He chuckled against my skin, and his teeth grazed along my nipple.

"Finn," I groaned as my hips jerked up, trying to reach him.

"You're not going to come just yet, so stop trying."

"Why?" I hissed, reaching around to grab his ass as I tried to tug him down toward me.

He pulled back and looked at me. "Because the first time you come tonight will be on my lips."

Oh. Okay, then. I could live with that.

Well, if I didn't die from desperation first.

seventeen

. . .

Finn

I'D BEEN with my fair share of women. I'd had plenty of sex in my lifetime. But this... nothing had ever come close to this.

To her.

To making her squirm and watching her body blush beneath my touch.

To those tits.

Those lips.

This body.

Her sounds and her scent.

Violet and amber flooding my senses.

I'd never been so turned on in my life.

Reese fucking Murphy was more than just my best friend.

She was the woman I wanted to be mine.

I didn't know when it happened, but I knew it now in my gut. I didn't know if she'd ever feel the same about me. But I was going to do everything in my power to show her that we were meant to be together.

I kissed my way down her stomach. Flat and toned and smooth.

Missing her tits the minute I left them.

My tongue traced along the edge of the lacy fabric

covering all her sweetness. Our breaths filled the air around us, and her body writhed beneath me, and I fucking loved it.

"Please," she groaned, and I pushed up on my knees.

"You want me to taste your sweet pussy, Reese?"

"Yes. And I want you to take your clothes off. I don't like being the only one who's naked."

I smiled. I liked her telling me what she wanted.

Her tits were perky and round, and her pink buds were taunting me to wrap my lips around them again. But I didn't. Because right now, her pussy was calling me.

My fingers found the edge of the lace, and I slid them down her legs, pushing to my feet as I grazed my fingers over her thighs and then her ankles before dropping the scrap of lace on the floor.

"Look at you," I said, brushing my fingers over her pussy. "Has there ever been a more beautiful woman?"

Her teeth sank into her bottom lip, and her gaze locked with mine. I gently pushed her legs apart, my mouth watering at the sight of her.

Fuck. Me.

I'd never wanted anyone or anything more in my life.

"I'm going to taste you now," I said, lowering myself to the bed and breathing her in before I buried my face in all that sweetness.

I ran my tongue along her slit, and her body jolted off the bed. My God, how had she gone this long without being touched? I knew she'd had sex, but she clearly had never really been touched. Not the way a woman should be.

Not the way this woman deserved to be.

I took my time, licking and tasting every goddamn inch of her.

If I died right here, right now, my tombstone would read: *Finnegan Charles Reynolds died eating the best pussy of his life.*

"Finn, please. I can't wait anymore," she whined, and I pulled back to look at her. A layer of sweat covered her sweet body, her skin flushed and lips swollen from where I'd kissed her.

Her gaze held mine before I winked at her, pressing my thumb along her clit as my tongue went back to work. Her thighs squeezed against my ears as she bucked like a wild fucking bull.

My wild fucking bull.

I slipped my tongue in and out. Her walls were so tight I didn't know how my dick would ever fit, but at the moment, I was in fucking ecstasy. I pressed my thumb harder, making little circles, somehow knowing exactly what she needed.

I felt her body tense just before she let go. She cried out my name with a gasp. Her pussy constricted around me as she rocked against my face. I sucked and licked and waited for her to ride out every last bit of pleasure.

My hands gripped her hips and kept her right there until she slowed. Her breaths were still wild and out of control, and I let go of the hold I had on her. I raised my head to look at her before moving up beside her, where her head was resting, a layer of sweat covering her cheeks and forehead. Her sage greens locked with mine, and she smiled.

"Wow," she whispered. "I think the friends-with-benefits plan was the best idea we've had in a long time."

"Better than the plan I had in third grade to see who could eat more sloppy joes in one sitting?"

"Well, I vomited for two hours after that brilliant plan, so I'd say this one is much better."

"I'd eat your pussy over a sloppy joe every day of the week."

She covered her face with her hands and laughed. "Oh my God, Finn. Stop."

I wrapped my fingers around her wrists and pulled her hands away. "I'm not kidding. You have a spectacular pussy. Like the gold standard of all pussies. You should be proud. And I got to be the lucky bastard to taste you first."

"Those are words I never thought I'd hear you say." She shook her head.

"Me, too. But after that, I would tattoo those words across my chest."

"Yeah?"

"Yeah. It was that good."

"Thank you for—" She looked away, and I ran my fingers over her tits because I couldn't help myself. Her gaze returned to mine. "Thank you for showing me how it could be."

"There's a lot more where that came from," I teased.

Her hand moved between us as she rolled onto her side and stroked my erection over my boxers. "I want to taste you now, Finn."

"You sure about that? Tonight is supposed to be about you and what you want."

She pushed up on her knees and looked down at me. "I want to make you feel as good as you just made me feel. That's what I want."

"Well, then. I can't turn down the beautiful woman with the magic pussy, can I?"

"At least not until after the holidays," she teased, but it was a reminder that I had my work cut out for me. She thought this was temporary.

I knew that it wasn't.

She rubbed her hands together, and my dick jumped to attention. He was already straining against my briefs, but now the bastard was threatening to tear through the fabric.

She leaned down and carefully tugged my boxers down as I sucked in a breath at the thought of what was to come.

Pun. Fucking. Intended.

"So, I've done this a few times, but I wasn't very good at it. Feel free to give me pointers, okay?"

There was just something about this gorgeous woman with the green eyes and the magic pussy and the perfect tits asking me for pointers on how to suck my dick that literally did it for me.

She crawled onto the bed and waggled her brows before stroking me several times while her teeth sunk into her bottom lip.

"Reese, I'm going to come right here, right now, if you don't stop playing."

"Oh… who's squirming now?" she teased.

My fingers tangled in her hair, and I didn't miss the way she gulped but tried to shake it off. Hell, I knew her too well to be deceived.

"You can't mess it up, Reese. I could come with you just staring at it."

She laughed and shook her head at me.

"I'm not going to stare at it. I'm going to taste you the way you tasted me," she purred, and it was sexy as hell.

"Ahh… someone's bringing out the dirty talk, huh?"

And before I could process what was happening, she leaned down and swirled her tongue around the tip of my dick, and I nearly fucking lost it right there.

There was no more teasing. No more talking.

Because Reese fucking Murphy winked at me before leaning down and taking me in. She sealed her lips around my shaft, and her hand wrapped around the base of my dick, and my head fell back as I reveled in the feel of her.

Her tongue and her lips and fingers all moving in perfect rhythm.

I reminded myself to calm the fuck down. I wasn't a teenage boy getting his first blow job.

But it sure as hell felt like it.

"Good fucking Christ, woman," I hissed. "Just like that. So fucking good."

And just when I thought it couldn't get any better, she took me deeper. My cock hit the back of her throat, but she didn't slow down. She met me thrust for thrust as I bucked against her.

My fingers tangled in her hair, helping her set the pace so I didn't come too quickly.

My body was no longer in my control.

She took me in faster, and I nearly shot off the bed when the sensation moved through my body.

I tugged at her hair, trying to warn her. "I'm going to fucking come right now."

But she didn't pull away. She just continued moving.

My vision blurred. Bursts of light.

The fucking Fourth of July on steroids.

My body was scorching as I unleashed and went right over the edge.

A feral sound escaped my throat as I came harder than I'd ever come in my life.

And she stayed right there.

Taking every last drop without any hesitation.

I was still gasping and shaking when she pulled her mouth away, continuing to stroke me slowly. She used the back of her other hand to wipe her mouth as she stared at me with this questioning look.

"What the fuck was that?" I asked, tugging her down and tucking her beneath my chin. "I thought you said you needed pointers?"

She ran her fingers over my chest before pushing up on her elbows to look at me. "Well, that's never happened before. The few times I did it, there was, er, no real *finale*."

I barked out a laugh. "That fucker didn't come, and he let you think it was because you weren't good at it?"

"Something like that. But you've always given me more credit than I deserve," she said, her voice just above a whisper.

"Or maybe you've just been with someone who didn't see

you the way he should." I wrapped my arm around her, and her cheek rested against my chest.

"This was a good first day for us, huh?" she asked with a chuckle, but her voice sounded sleepy.

"Damn straight. And now you're going to sleep like a champ until I wake you up for round two."

I pulled the covers over us and kissed the top of her head, closing my eyes and breathing her in.

It was the most content I'd ever felt in my life. And I was a pretty content dude, so that was saying a lot. I wrapped my arms around her tighter, wanting to keep her for as long as I could.

And sleep took us both.

The sun-filled room woke me from a sound sleep. I stretched my arms over my head and immediately missed the warmth of Reese beside me. I pushed to sit up, looking down beneath the thin sheet to see I was still fully naked. I blinked a few times before I realized my best friend was sitting on the edge of the bed, already dressed.

"Good morning. When did you get up?"

She turned around to look at me. "Hey. I've been up for an hour. I was just going to wake you up. We've got to get back home for Gracie's tea party."

She wasn't making eye contact with me, so I knew something was up. I ran my fingers over the scruff of my jaw as I waited for her gaze to meet mine.

"What's going on, Miney? You okay?"

"What? Yeah. Why wouldn't I be? Are you not okay? Are you freaking out?"

I chuckled. "Do I look like I'm freaking out?"

Her teeth sank into her bottom lip. "No. You look relaxed."

I leaned forward and grabbed her hand, tugging her over to me. "Tell me what's going through that over-worrying head of yours."

"I don't know. I don't want things to be weird. I figured you'd wake up with a lot of regret."

"Regret? I feel fucking fantastic. I can't wait to do it again."

Her head tipped back, and her face softened. "Yeah?"

"Hell, yeah. We can keep doing it until we break up, right?" I wanted her to feel in control of the situation.

She nodded slowly. "Yep. But I think we need some ground rules if we're going to keep this going and, you know, take the next step."

"Fuck like bunnies? Is that what you mean?"

"Have sex. Yes." She rolled her eyes. "We need rules, Chewy. Or this could get really messy."

"Are you worried I'm going to fall in love with you?" I teased before nipping at her bottom lip.

She put both hands on my chest and pushed up a little so she was looking down at me. "You aren't the one who confuses love and sex. That's me. So, we need to be smart. The last thing we need is me confusing what this is."

"And what is this, exactly?"

"This is two friends giving one another comfort before they go back to their regular lives." She shrugged. "You'll go back to filming and having sex with whoever the hell you want to, and Carl and I will most likely go back to planning a wedding again, and hopefully, our sex life will benefit from this break we've taken."

My hands fisted at the thought of that arrogant fucker getting the chance to touch her again.

Not happening.

"Fine. What are these rules?" I knew Reese well enough to know that she liked rules. Structure. She wanted to have a plan. There was no sense fighting it.

"We do whatever it is we want to do, but when we go to sleep, we go to our separate rooms."

"Why? We've slept together a million times."

"But we weren't having sex. Sleeping together will make it too intimate. We're already fake dating, and now we're throwing sex into the mix. We need to have some boundaries in place so it doesn't get… confusing."

It was already fucking confusing.

"I slept with you last night. You didn't seem to mind when you were grinding up against my cock at two o'clock in the morning, and we were making out like teenagers. And I'm fairly certain you weren't complaining when you were shaking and gasping for air after you came for the second time on my fingers."

"Oh my gosh." She jumped out of bed and stood there watching me with her arms crossed over her chest. "This is what I'm talking about. And we haven't even had sex yet."

"So, let me get this straight. If I bury my head between your thighs or we dry-hump until we both go over the fucking edge—we can sleep in the same bed? But the minute my dick enters you, there is no sleeping in the same bed? You do realize how insane this sounds, right?"

"We only slept in the same bed last night because there was only one bed. But now that we're trying the friends-with-benefits plan… that has to change. If we're intimate, we need to sleep in our own beds."

"I see." I pushed to sit up, my back against the headboard. I glanced down, unable to miss the tent beneath the sheets because the reminder of waking up to her rubbing all over me had me going hard all over again. "So, no sleeping together while we're having the benefits. Got it. Any other rules I need to be made aware of?" I didn't miss the way her eyes slowly perused my body, stopping at the sight of my dick, who was practically pointing her out and begging her for some attention.

"Well…" She shook her head, looking away from the elephant in the room… aka my raging boner. "We should keep this between us. If our family finds out that our fake dating situation has added in the, er, benefits, that will give everyone the wrong impression."

My tongue swiped out to wet my bottom lip, and her eyes zoned in on my mouth. "Got it. We can have some fun, but there's no sleeping in the same bed, and it all has to stay between us."

Well, I'd already broken that rule. But telling her that would mean telling her that I went to my brothers for advice on how to actually date her. And that would freak her the fuck out.

So, I'd keep that to myself.

Rule number two was already broken.

And I planned on breaking rule number one by the end of the week.

I'd never cared much for rules.

eighteen

. . .

Reese

WE'D MADE it back to town after we'd set some boundaries, and we were acting perfectly normal now, even if my body was still humming from the multiple orgasms I'd received the night before. Maybe this really could work. We'd hurried home and changed clothes, and the only thing that was different was that Finn insisted on sitting in the bathroom and talking to me while I got dressed.

Apparently, now that he'd seen my boobs, he couldn't get enough of them.

Go girls.

They'd never been all that noteworthy. They were small and perky, so I didn't mind them, but they'd never garnered much attention. Carl was a self-proclaimed *boob man*. It hadn't gone unnoticed by me that Christy Rae Lovell had a giant set of porn-worthy knockers. He'd always teased me that he'd get me a boob job as a wedding gift. I wasn't actually sure if he'd meant it as a joke or if he was hoping I'd bite at the offer. He'd always ended the conversation by saying that I was perfect just the way I was, so I certainly didn't feel pressure to do it. But I wasn't interested in changing them at this point in my life, though I'd never say never. Maybe someday I'd want some big ladies to show off—today just wasn't that day.

And my best friend was a super fan, so I'd enjoy this moment while it lasted.

Early November was one of my favorite times of the year. The town would soon be transitioning over to Christmas décor the day after Thanksgiving. But for now, fall was still surrounding us.

Finn and I parked a few blocks away and walked to the Tipsy Tea. I glanced in the windows of some of my favorite places. Once Upon a Time was my favorite bookstore, and the window display was always decorated for the season. There were hay bales with pumpkins and several fall-themed books set up there. We both chuckled when we passed Cottonwood Café because Mrs. Runither had hired Maggie to paint the front window, which currently read: *Fall into Cottonwood Café… We put the spice in pumpkin spice.*

"Never a dull moment with that woman," Finn said with a chuckle.

We walked past Garrity's, Finn's family's bar, and there was a bench out front with two scarecrows sitting on it. Pumpkins and corn stalks were gathered at the entrance. Cup of Cove had kept it simple, with a sign hanging out front that read: *Happy Fall, Y'all! All Pumpkins Welcome!*

I'd slipped into a floral maxi dress with my cowboy boots, and Finn was wearing jeans and a button-up. The man rarely wore anything other than a hoodie, a tee, or a flannel… but his weak spot had always been little Gracie.

And she'd asked us all to come to this tea party, so we were going to show up looking nice for her.

Finn held the door open for me as I stepped inside The Tipsy Tea. Loud chatter came from the back room, and we made our way back there.

Gracie came running toward us wearing what looked like some sort of wedding flower girl dress with a pair of pink cowboy boots. Gracie Reynolds was my spirit animal. Equal parts bougie princess and small-town cowgirl.

She lunged into her uncle's arms and kissed his cheek. "I'm happy you came to my tea party, Uncle Finny. Now let me hug Ree Ree."

He rumpled her curls and laughed before passing her over. She put a hand on each of my cheeks as she settled on my hello. "Thanks for coming. You look real pretty."

"And you look like a real live princess."

Her jaw fell open. "That's what my Bossman and Links said. They thinks I am a real live princess."

She wiggled out of my arms and clapped her hands together. "Everyone is here, Miss Matilda."

I made my way around the table, hugging every member of the Reynolds family and their significant others. Finn motioned for me to take the seat between him and Brinkley. Gracie sat at the head of the table between her grandma and grandpa, and I glanced around, taking them all in. The guys all looked way too big for their chairs, but there they were, showing up for this little girl.

Matilda and two teenage girls who worked for her came around to fill our teacups. Gracie stood up and patted her dress into place. "Bossman, thank you for giving my family this special party. All of my favorites are here. I thought you'd never come home, Ree Ree. I waited forever and a few days for you to come back."

I held up my teacup and smiled. "I wouldn't miss this for the world."

Gracie sat down, and everyone started talking all at once.

Maddox, whom Gracie called Bossman, stared at the platters of tiny sandwiches and picked up his teacup. "So, this is the big experience, huh? Little sandwiches and a few drops of liquid in our cups?"

"Yep. Every little girl in Cottonwood Cove wants to have a

tea party here," Georgia said, leaning against him. "You killed it, Bossman."

"Didn't Brinks sneak a frog into her tea party, and a few dishes got broken when he escaped, and all her friends freaked out?" Cage asked, raising a brow, while Gracie was talking a mile a minute to her grandparents.

"I wasn't really the tea party type. Mom insisted on me throwing my seventh birthday party here. I wanted to have a pirate party." She shrugged.

"Of course you did. That's why you're marrying Captain Jack Sparrow." Lincoln barked out a laugh.

Everyone chuckled, and Finn leaned over to fill me in that Captain Jack Sparrow was Lincoln's pseudonym when he travels and doesn't want to be recognized.

"So, I think you guys have a real shot at the Super Bowl this year." Maddox studied the tiny triangular sandwich, and his gaze narrowed like he'd never seen such an odd piece of food.

"Baby, it's cucumbers and cream cheese," Georgia whispered.

"Hmmm… do five-year-olds eat that?" He raised a brow.

"It's the experience," Hugh said, reaching for a triangle of his own and popping the whole thing into his mouth, and Lila laughed.

"It is all about the experience," she said.

"So, what's going on with the lovebirds?" Cage looked between me and Finn, and my cheeks burned.

"All is going well."

"Yeah? I heard Jessica made quite a scene last night," Brinkley said. "I'd like two minutes alone in a back alley with that girl."

My head fell back in laughter because she wasn't joking, which made it funnier.

"Miney handled her just fine. She didn't back down at all,

which probably bugged Jessica more than we can even imagine." Finn piled several sandwiches onto his plate.

His hand came around my shoulder, and he grazed his thumb along my collarbone. I didn't miss the way Cage watched the movement and then smirked when his gaze locked with mine.

He freaking knew something was up because the Reynolds brothers always knew what was going on with one another.

I looked up to see Alana smiling at Gracie, and I was grateful that at least she didn't know what was going on.

Siblings were one thing. Parents would be another. They would never understand what we were doing. Hell, I didn't understand it.

But I knew one thing—I couldn't wait to do it again.

"I'm not sure if Georgia let you all know, but she'd like to host Thanksgiving this year at their home," Alana said.

"Oh, man. She doesn't cook as good as you do," Cage groaned, shaking his head.

"Hey. I'm a great cook."

"Your specialty is gummy bears," Finn said over his laughter.

"I love Aunt Georgie's gummy bears. She gots all the colors at her house."

"Yeah, my dentist just said I have my first cavity, and I'm fairly certain it's from all the jars of candy you keep at the house," Hugh said.

"You do know that you don't have to eat handfuls every time you come over, right?" Maddox smirked.

"Mom is coming over to do most of the cooking. I just thought it would be fun to have a pickleball tournament."

"It's freaking Thanksgiving. Can we not turn it into a competition? I just want to eat good food and watch the game." This came from Cage again, and Brinkley balled up her napkin and tossed it at him.

"First Thanksgiving as a couple," Finn said, grazing his lips against my ear, and I sucked in a breath. "I know what you're going to be thankful for after tonight."

"Finn," I hissed over my laughter, looking up to meet his gaze. "You talk a big game."

"How about we get out of here soon?" He waggled his brows.

I nodded slowly before feeling eyes on me. I turned to see Hugh and Cage watching us with big, goofy grins on their faces as everyone else was involved in their own side conversations.

I raised a brow and looked between them. "You two are up to no good."

"I was going to say the same to you," Cage said.

"You do seem like you're in a hurry to get out of here." Hugh barked out a laugh.

"We're anxious to get home and take the horses for a ride," I said, reaching for my teacup and taking a sip.

"That's not the only thing you're going to ride," Finn said against my ear, and I spewed tea all over the table.

I coughed hard, and Finn rubbed my back as I reached for my napkin.

"Ree Ree, are you okay?"

"Yep. It just went down the wrong tube."

"Don't talk about boobs at the table. It turns me on," Finn whispered in my ear again, not a care in the world that I'd just embarrassed myself after the last thing he'd said.

"I said *tube*." I turned to face him and shook my head.

"Well, I guess you can't say words that rhyme with boob either."

"You're ridiculous. No more crazy talk until we leave here." I cleared my throat just as a loud ruckus had us all turning to see Mr. Larson walking into the back room, carrying what looked like a small version of a wedding cake.

It was three tiers with white icing and pink flowers

running around each layer of cake. There was a figurine on the top with brown curls, wearing a princess gown.

"Hey there, y'all. Miss Gracie, your uncle Finny sent over a special cake in honor of your tea party."

"You dicknut," Cage hissed under his breath. "You got a five-year-old a wedding cake. You know I don't like her to eat too much sugar because it always makes her cry after."

"She pointed it out to me a few weeks ago in the window at Larson's bakery."

"So, you just bought it for her?"

"Yes. Exactly. And so what if she cries a little after? You can get in touch with your feminine side, brother. Plus, everyone loves cake. So, let's cut the cake and get a move on." Finn stood and moved around the table to hug Gracie while everyone gaped at the sweet monstrosity. My chest squeezed as I watched him. He'd always been that guy. If we were with a group of friends in high school and someone said they were hungry, Finn would appear out of nowhere with a sandwich for them. He genuinely loved to do things for others, and it was one of my favorite traits about him.

But seeing him dote on little Gracie—well, that was hitting me with all the feels. Hell, my ovaries were getting in on the celebration. Finn would make a great dad if he had any desire to actually be in a real relationship. But he'd always said he was content being an uncle.

I couldn't imagine not being a mama, and I knew my biological clock was ticking. The fear in the back of my mind that the chemo may have hurt my chances and that I wouldn't ever get pregnant was there, but I always tried to push it away. My doctor said there was a very good chance I'd be fine. I was open to adopting, as well, if it wasn't in the cards for me.

It's funny, my being diagnosed with Non-Hodgkin's Lymphoma left me feeling an urgency about motherhood. But that was around the time that Finn started saying he'd never get married or have kids. Trauma does different things to different people, I guess. Carl had always said he wanted us to start a family as soon as we were married. We'd always been on the same page.

I shook myself from my thoughts when Finn handed me a piece of cake.

"Let's take some home so I can cover your tits with icing and take my time cleaning you up," he whispered close to my ear again.

Damn it. I was getting all sweaty and flustered.

He devoured his cake quickly and then stared at me as I scooped the icing onto my fork and popped it into my mouth.

"The sun is going to set soon. If you want to ride, we need to get going." He raised a brow.

Cage laughed so loudly that it startled everyone. "It's two o'clock in the afternoon. The sun's got a while, brother. But you two better run along before you lose daylight."

He oozed sarcasm, and everyone laughed, though they looked completely confused by the conversation.

I was scooping some more icing onto my fork when Finn jumped to his feet. "Love you all. We're out of here."

Finn rolled his eyes when I made my way around the table to hug everyone goodbye.

When did he get so impatient?

And why was I suddenly nervous?

We stepped out of The Tipsy Tea and headed to his truck. Once he got into the driver's seat and we were pulling away from the curb, I turned to face him.

"What was that about? Where's the fire?" I said over my laughter.

"The fire? It's in my fucking pants, Miney. I need to be inside you right now. I can't wait one more minute. And if you keep looking over at me with those gorgeous green eyes, I'll pull this truck over and fuck you right here in the cab. Give the whole town something to talk about."

My jaw dropped, my mouth hanging open as my heart raced so fast that I was certain he could hear it.

This was really happening.

I'd never had anyone want me the way Finn wanted me.

And I liked it.

A lot.

"Well, I suggest you get us home quickly, then. Show me what I've been missing."

"That's exactly what I plan to do."

He hit the gas, and I jolted forward a bit. "Buckle up, Miney. You're in for a good time."

My head fell back in laughter because I was already having a good time.

These last few weeks had been the best I'd had in a long time.

And I couldn't wait to see what would happen once we got home.

nineteen

. . .

Finn

WE WERE all over one another the minute we'd hurried into the house. I had her dress off of her and had dropped it somewhere on the floor leading to my bedroom. She shoved my shirt up and over my head, and I picked her up, her lean legs wrapping around my waist as I started running to the bedroom.

Laughter filled the air around us as her head fell back, and I continued to haul ass to get her to my room. I couldn't get there fast enough.

Had I ever wanted a woman more?

Never. Nothing close to this.

I tossed her onto the bed, her light brown hair falling all around her. She smiled up at me, her perfect tits covered in pink lace, matching the thong I was dying to peel off her.

"You really want me, don't you, Finn Reynolds?"

I kicked off my shoes and pushed my jeans down my legs, tugging my boxer briefs down along with them. I kicked my clothing out of the way and turned to face her. My dick had never been more eager, and it was about time she understood how badly I wanted her.

"What do you think?"

"Wow." Her tongue moved back and forth across her bottom lip, making me even harder. I wanted to taste her, have her lips around my cock again, but right now, I needed to be inside her.

To feel her tighten around me.

To hear her cry out my name when I took her over the edge.

"You sure you want this, Reese? This is your last chance to back out because once we start, I won't be able to hold back."

"I'm not backing out. You're going to show me what I've been missing and teach me some skills for my future husband." She waggled her brows.

What the fuck?

I didn't want to talk about Carl fucking Barley or the fact that if she went back to him, he was going to reap the benefits of what we'd experienced together.

I leaned down, hovering just inches from her mouth. "You've been making all the rules, but I have some of my own."

Her eyes widened, her chest rising and falling fast now. "Okay. Let's hear them."

"When we're in this bedroom together, or anywhere that our clothes are off, I don't want to hear a fucking word about your future husband. You won't talk about another man when I'm inside you, and you sure as shit won't be thinking about him."

She nodded slowly, looking stunned by my outburst. But a man had his limits. Yeah, I'd agreed to this fucked-up plan, but I was still shooting for a different outcome. So, hearing the mention of another dude did not sit well with me.

She looked puzzled, so I gave the briefest explanation without showing my cards. "When we aren't fucking, you can talk about your plan to win him back if that's what you want, and I'll do what you need me to do. But not when we're like this."

"That's fair. I'm sorry." Her words were labored and laced with desire.

"Don't apologize, Reese. Just don't let it happen again." There was no tease in my voice, and she pushed her hips up to press against my erection.

So fucking eager.

I leaned down and kissed her hard, my tongue sliding in and exploring her sweet mouth as I rocked myself against her. I wanted to take my time, but we were both so needy and ready. My hands tangled in her hair, tipping her head back and moving my lips down her slender neck. My fingers grazed over her lace-covered breasts and tweaked her nipples.

I covered her tit with my mouth and sucked right over the fabric. She groaned, her back arching nearly off the bed to get closer. I pulled back and looked at her. Her green gaze was so eager and trusting. Damn, I loved this girl in a way I couldn't wrap my head around.

More than a friend.

More than a lover.

Reese Murphy was… everything.

And she was going to be mine in every way.

My hand made its way around her back and I easily unsnapped her bra, tossing it to the floor. I traced my fingers along her tits—goddamn, I couldn't get enough. Her hard peaks responded immediately to my touch, and I took my time memorizing every inch. The swell beneath her perfect breasts and the pretty pink nipples were made for me. I circled her peaks with my tongue as she gasped and writhed beneath me. Hell, I'd barely touched her, and she was so ready.

And so the fuck was I.

My fingers trailed down her body, stopping at the bit of lace that stood between us. I slid the fabric to the side and hissed when I swiped along her slit and found her drenched.

"Fuck me," I groaned. I slipped my hand beneath the band of her panties and tugged them down her legs, kissing the trail from her thighs down to her ankles as I did so.

I moved to the nightstand, opened the drawer, and reached for a condom. I made my way back to where she lay on my bed, and she propped herself up on her elbows to watch me.

"I think it's too big."

"You can take it."

"You think so?" Her teeth sunk into her bottom lip.

"We'll take our time. I'm here for the long game, Reese," I said, but she didn't know the real meaning behind it. I was going to spend these next few weeks showing her just how good we could be together.

As more than friends.

I rolled the latex over my thick, throbbing length and climbed onto the bed, hovering above her.

"Okay," she whispered.

"We're going to start this way. Let you get adjusted to my size. And then you're going to be on top, so you can ride me like a prized fucking thoroughbred." I remembered her saying that she'd only ever had missionary-style sex. That was like only eating vanilla ice cream your entire life. I was about to change that.

My cock was like thirty-one flavors of orgasms.

"Is everything going to change between us after we cross this line?" she whispered.

That was the plan.

"Change isn't always bad. We're going to be just fine. But you're going to change the way you look at sex—that much I can promise you. And I can't wait to watch you fall apart with me inside you."

She tangled her hands in my hair. I moved between her thighs, my dick finding her entrance as if he belonged there. I kissed her for the longest time, our bodies rocking together, desperate for contact. I reached between us and teased her a bit before pulling back to look at her. She gave me the slightest nod, and I moved forward just a bit, and she sucked in a breath.

"You okay?"

"Yes. More please."

That was my girl.

I moved in slowly, inch by glorious inch, taking my time. Making sure she was okay. And with every movement, her tight pussy squeezed around me. Nothing had ever felt this good or this torturous in my life. My forehead pressed against hers as I fought the urge to push all the way in and bury myself deep inside her before we found our rhythm. Her hands came around and gripped my ass, urging me forward.

"Come on, Lover. Don't hold back on my account." Her voice was all raspy and filled with lust.

That was all I needed to hear. I propped myself up and drove the rest of the way into all that sweetness and warmth.

I stayed perfectly still, and it was both heaven and hell. She squeezed me like a goddamn vise, and I wanted to relish this moment. Yet staying still was painful. My desire to move was so strong that I fisted my hands in the sheets as I waited for her to adjust to my size. Her breaths were coming hard and fast, and I looked down, tracing my tongue across her bottom lip.

"You feel so fucking good."

She smiled, her eyes half-mast. "Now, show me how you work your magic."

I pulled back before sliding back in, slowly at first.

Over and over.

Faster.

Harder.

She met me thrust for thrust.

Her back arched, and I gripped both of her hips, setting

the pace. My lips sealed over her perfect nipple, taking turns between each breast.

A layer of sweat covered her sweet body, and I paused to push the hair away from her face. "You ready to ride me?"

"I was born to ride you, Cowboy," she purred, and I swear to fucking God, nothing had ever been sexier.

I rolled onto my back, and she settled above me. Her tan skin glistened in the sun that was shining through the blinds, and her long hair fell down her back.

She started to move, her eyes closed, her head tipped back, and she found her rhythm.

I couldn't stop staring at her in awe. Her tits bounced the slightest bit, her slender arms gripped the backs of my thighs, and little moans escaped those sweet lips.

My hand moved to her clit, knowing she was close.

I was moments from tumbling over the edge, and I sure as shit wasn't going to do that without her. She looked down at me, green eyes locked with mine, as I grabbed her hip with my free hand and bucked into her harder.

With a need I'd never experienced.

She fell forward, her mouth finding mine, and she kissed me hard as her entire body quaked and shook on top of me.

The walls of her pussy strangled my cock, and I thrust one last time before my vision blurred and a guttural sound escaped my lips.

And we both continued moving, riding out every last bit of pleasure.

Moans and groans and heavy breaths filled the space around us, and she collapsed, body completely limp against mine.

Reese Murphy had always owned my heart in a way I'd never realized.

And now she owned my body, too.

Because I would never get enough of this girl.

Maybe I'd avoided these feelings for years because I'd

thought she was happy with someone else. Maybe Reese had been the reason I'd never found anyone else. Because she'd been right in front of me the whole time.

She pushed up and looked down at me, a wide grin spreading across her face. "You lived up to the hype, Lover."

"I told you. There's lots more where that came from." I ran my fingers up and down the soft skin of her back.

"Good. Let's get dressed and take the horses for a ride." She climbed off of me quickly, startling me as she did so. I wondered if it had freaked her out that we'd crossed the line. But then she gathered her clothes and looked over her shoulder. "Bring a condom. I want to do that again on the beach right before sunset."

That was exactly what I wanted to hear.

The last two weeks had been the best I'd ever had. Reese and I had found a rhythm. She was working and had four clients now, which was keeping her busy. But not too busy for all the extracurricular activities we were having.

And by that, I mean mind-blowing, fabulous fucking sex.

I'd never had this much sex with the same person before, and I fucking loved it.

I knew every inch of her body. What made her shiver, what made her horny, what made her cry out my name.

I'd been reading the movie script that the producers had sent over along with the script for season two of *Big Sky Ranch,* and I was grateful that I didn't have any scenes with Jessica Carson. She'd done one final interview, but *The Hollywood Moment* had released the article with me and Reese, and no one had given Jessica's final Hail Mary the time of day. Charles and Sadie had informed me that they were trying to buy out her contract early. Otherwise, they would be writing her character off in a few months when her contract was up.

So, things were falling into place. People loved seeing me with a girlfriend, but that wasn't the reason that I was in this anymore.

Hell, I wouldn't have even agreed to any of this if it weren't for Reese. But now that I was here, I didn't want it to end. And with Thanksgiving tomorrow, my time was running out.

She was spending the day with that dick weasel, Carl, today, as all the furniture for his office had arrived. I'd been half tempted to drive over there and remind him that she was still with me. But my brothers had convinced me not to do it. Apparently, Reese needed to come to the conclusion herself.

We took the horses out every day after work now. We ate most meals together, and we fucked like bunnies at least twice a day. But at the end of the night, she would kiss me goodbye and go sleep in her room. And that bullshit rule was starting to piss me off. I wanted her in my bed all the time. I wasn't sleeping well lately because I'd wake up thinking about her.

"Hey," she called out as the door opened, and I closed my laptop and made my way to the front room.

"Hey, Miney." I scooped her up and spun her around, kissing her neck as she laughed. "How was Dr. Limpdick?"

She pinched my arm. "Not nice, Chewy. But I do have news."

I led her to the kitchen and poured us each a glass of wine while she moved to the fridge and started pulling out all the makings for a salad and got a pot of water boiling for some pasta.

As I said, we had a routine.

One I'd grown fond of.

I handed her the glass of Chardonnay, and she took a sip and watched me over the rim. "Carl broke up with Christy Rae Lovell."

A pang hit my chest as if someone had just stuck me with

something sharp. Thankfully, I was a damn good actor, and I made an effort to keep my face from reacting. "I see. What was the reason for their breakup?"

She set her wine glass on the counter and dropped the lettuce into a colander and started rinsing it. "He claims he misses me."

The fucking bastard. Of course, he does. What's not to miss?

I sipped my wine, moving to the stovetop to drop some penne into the boiling water. Was this it? Was she going to end things with me?

Now I was getting pissed. This fucker says he misses her, and she's going to bail on me?

"So, what does that mean? You're going back to him?" I shifted around, crossing one leg in front of the other as I leaned against the counter. I turned my baseball cap backward because I needed to do something to distract my hands from fisting.

"No, Chewy. We have a plan. I'm sticking to it. Unless you're looking for an early out from our arrangement?"

"Nope. I'm not bailing, Miney."

"Well, I told him that I'm happy with you," she said, before turning back to the sink. My shoulders relaxed for all of two minutes before she said her next statement. "I mean, we both know how this is going to end, so stop worrying. You'll leave after Christmas to go to Tokyo, and you'll go back to being single, just the way you like it. We'll end this fake relationship before you go, just like we planned."

"Yeah. That's the plan." I cleared my throat. Suddenly, I didn't like that plan anymore. It didn't give me much time to prove to her that she should be with me.

That she was my girl.

Always had been.

Always would be.

We continued cooking and ate dinner, but the conversation was over. I didn't like that there was an expiration date, nor did I appreciate that she kept bringing it up.

At the end of the day, how could she still want to go back to that asshole when we'd been so good together?

Now I was actually pissed off.

"You're awfully quiet," she said, standing and clearing our plates.

"Yeah. I'm a little tired. I think I'm going to call it a night."

We'd had sex every single night since the first time, so I knew she wouldn't like that I was bailing on her.

She studied me, a look of surprise crossing her features. She placed the back of her hand on my forehead and rolled her eyes. "No fever. You feel just fine."

I'd never been good at dealing with anger, so I'd walk away for now, and hopefully, by tomorrow, I'd be over it.

But she wasn't getting to spend one minute with my dick tonight.

I'd never been one to withhold sex, but I sure as shit wasn't gracing her with his presence tonight.

"Okay. Well, let me know if you need anything." Her green gaze searched mine.

"Nope. I think I just need some space tonight."

Yeah, that ought to get her thinking. I wasn't just some fake boyfriend she could use and then go back to Dr. Lame-Ass and use all her new mad sex skills on him. Hell, no.

None of it would work without me because we were just that good together.

Her gaze narrowed. "Some space? I see. Take all the space you need, Chewy."

And with that, she loaded the dishes into the dishwasher like they'd committed a crime against her. Handling the utensils aggressively as they banged around in the sink, slamming the door closed to the dishwasher with force, and then stomping through the room to get her coat.

"Where the fuck are you going?" I hissed.

She glanced over her shoulder. "I'm going out and getting *some space.*"

She was not going to pull the reverse pissed-off tantrum on me. I had two sisters. I knew this game better than anyone.

I was the one who was pissed.

She didn't get to be pissed.

"Don't let the door hit you in the ass," I growled as I stormed down the hallway to my bedroom.

I took a hot shower and came out to see if she was home, but the house was dark. I peeked in her room, and she wasn't in there.

The fuck?

I glanced out the window, and her car was still in the driveway.

Did she have that bastard come pick her up?

Was she going to cry on his shoulder about her fight with her fake boyfriend?

I was fuming as I sat up on the couch, waiting for her like some lovesick fucker.

That was exactly what I was now, wasn't it?

I was in love with my best friend.

My fake girlfriend.

Here she'd worried about her falling for me, and I'd been the one to fall.

I reached for the blanket my mom had brought over for me and Reese yesterday and shook it out to cover me while I sulked on the sofa. My mom had come over under the guise of bringing a present. I knew her well, and she'd come to see what was going on between us. She and Jenny were both suspicious. They'd been asking a lot of questions, and we'd denied all accusations that our fake relationship was anything more than that. We'd both acted offended that they'd think we'd do anything to risk our friendship.

They'd apologized, and we'd both felt pretty shitty for lying.

But now I was starting to wonder if I was the only one that thought this relationship wasn't fake anymore.

I scratched at my arms and looked down to see red spots covering my arms.

Motherfucker.

Could this night get any worse?

I texted my mom as I glanced at the clock and saw it was after ten o'clock at night, and I didn't want to call and risk waking her.

Hey. I have hives. I think it might be the new blanket. What do I do?

MOM

Oh, Finny. I'm so sorry. Check the tag. Is there wool in that blanket? I didn't think to check it.

I glanced down and found the tag, and sure enough, it was almost all wool.

Yep. It's wool. And now my hands are covered in spots.

I sent her a photo.

MOM

Take two Benadryl right now. I'm so sorry. I'm going to burn that blanket.

This is what happens when you buy a phony gift to come spy on your kid.

MOM

Very funny. Also true. I'm sorry. Do you have Benadryl?

Yeah. And that'll be good because it always knocks me out.

MOM

Warn Reese that you're taking it. It always makes your sleepwalking worse.

I wouldn't warn Reese because she was out partying with her ex. One day of Carl being single, and she couldn't get out of here quickly enough.

You got it. Love you.

MOM

Love you, honey.

I tossed the blanket in the laundry room and went to the bathroom to find the medication. I popped two pink pills in my mouth and fell face down on my bed.

I hoped that sleep would take me fast because I couldn't get my mind off where Reese was and what she was doing with him.

And I fucking hated that I cared so much.

twenty

. . .

Reese

I CAME BACK to the house close to midnight after sitting out in the stall with Millie for a few hours and reading on my Kindle. I was pissed at Finn, and I had no right to be angry. The way he shut down the minute I told him that Carl was single had pissed me off. I didn't say I was going back to him just yet, and he looked disappointed. Like he'd hoped the minute Carl ended things with his girlfriend, I'd just call off this sham of a relationship and crawl back to him.

How desperate would that be?

So, he'd gone completely quiet. Probably afraid to tell me that he wanted this to be done. Hell, he'd had more sex with me than he'd ever had with anyone, if what he'd told me was true. He was supposed to be the king of one-nighters until now. Maybe he was bored out of his mind and sick of spending his days with me. At least in a romantic way.

I knew this was going to be a huge mistake. We'd never fought much in the past, and if we had disagreements, we were able to come around fast. This was the reason I worried about breaking our pact.

Finn and I were different when it came to sex.

I mixed up the emotions between sex and love.

Finn just thought of sex as an act.

But I loved having sex with him. I was getting too attached. He was already my best friend, and now that we'd crossed this line, thoughts of having sex with Carl did not excite me.

The thought actually repulsed me, and that was a whole different situation I wasn't ready to deal with.

The man I'd thought I'd marry was finally single, and he wanted to get back together with me. He'd rubbed my arm today, and I'd cringed at his touch.

I didn't want Carl that way anymore.

Something had changed in me since I'd come home. Hell, maybe it all changed while I was away for a year, and I just hadn't realized it. I'd built Carl up in my head.

Or I'd just experienced something so much more powerful that now I didn't want anyone or anything else.

But Finn's reaction had stung. I think he thought I should have let him off the hook and been more excited about going back to Carl.

I tiptoed down the hallway and saw him lying in his bed. All of his clothes were still on, and he was sprawled face down on top of the bedding. I picked up the flannel throw blanket and placed it over him.

I made my way back to my room and changed into my pajamas before climbing into bed.

I was finally getting what I wanted, and now I didn't want it. What was wrong with me? Tears ran down my cheeks, and I pulled the comforter up around my neck and let myself cry. Because for the first time in my life, I didn't know what the future looked like, or what I even wanted it to look like.

I was exhausted, and my eyes grew heavy, so I let the darkness take me.

My dreams were not filled with thoughts of my ex-boyfriend, the handsome doctor I'd planned to spend my life with. Once again, they were flooded with thoughts of my sexy best friend. The way he touched me. The way he made me feel.

And I let myself drift away because it was the one place I felt completely at peace.

A creak on the floor woke me from a sound sleep, and the room was pitch dark, so I knew it was still the middle of the night. I lay perfectly still, and I felt someone approach my bed. I jerked up to see a dark figure standing there, and on instinct, I shot up and punched him in the throat, my foot coming out and kicking as hard as I could. He fell forward toward me with a gasp.

A blood-curdling scream left my throat as I dove out of bed and ran across the room.

"Finn!" I screamed as I hit the lights and turned around to see the man I'd just assaulted on the floor was my best friend, lying in a ball and groaning.

"Finn? Oh my God." I hurried over, and he was holding his throat and gasping for air.

I placed a hand on each side of his face, and he blinked up at me a few times.

"What the fuck, Miney? Did you just throat-punch me and kick me in the balls?" he yelled.

"I thought you were a stranger," I said, helping him slide over so his back could rest against the wall. He closed his eyes, and his free hand moved to his crotch.

Oh my God. I kicked him in the dick and punched him in the throat.

I was definitely the worst fake girlfriend of all time.

"Why would a stranger be in your room?" he said, his voice hoarse.

I'd probably damaged his vocal cords and his family jewels all within a matter of seconds.

Fight or flight was clearly a real thing.

"Why would you be standing over my bed in the dark? It freaked me out."

He groaned and shifted, pressing his back against the wall as he thought it over. "I don't know. I took two Benadryl earlier, so I must have been sleepwalking."

"I'm so sorry. What can I do? Do you want me to get you a glass of water?" I asked.

"No. Just sit here with me." He reached for my hand, placing his on top of mine as he set it back down on his crotch. "Maybe you can comfort the big guy. It's the least you can do after that vicious attack."

I chuckled, leaving my hand there because I'd hated that we'd fought earlier. It had been the first night we hadn't had sex since the day that we'd crossed the line. And I'd missed him, even though I'd just had dinner with him a few hours ago.

We'd definitely entered a gray area. At least I had.

"Why did you take Benadryl?"

"Because I was waiting up for you to get home from your date with Carl, and I used that fucked-up blanket my mom brought over yesterday. That fake gift from hell is actually wool, and you know I have sensitive skin."

I laughed so hard that a few tears escaped my eyes. "What are you talking about? First of all, I wasn't on a date with Carl. I was out in the barn with Millie and Han. But why would you care? You seemed thrilled that Carl was single again."

He looked over at me, his gaze softening now. "You were in the fucking barn the whole night? It's freezing outside."

"It's not cold in the barn, and I had a coat on. I didn't think you'd notice."

He looked away for a minute before his beautiful gray eyes found mine. "I noticed, Miney. And I wasn't thrilled that Carl was single again. I was worried that you were going to, uh, change the plan and bail on me."

I leaned my head against his chest and listened to the

sound of his heartbeat. "I would never bail on you, Chewy. Right now, this is the only place I want to be."

Had I said too much? Was it going to scare him off?

His arms came around me, and we sat there quietly. "Seeing as you just attacked me in the most violent way and all, I feel like I should be allowed to add a rule to our little arrangement."

"Anything," I whispered.

"I want you to sleep in my bed. I don't sleep well when you leave every night. Then tonight, when I was medicated, I wandered in here. Clearly, my subconscious was looking for you."

I sucked in a breath at his words.

Don't make more out of it than it is.

"I hated the way we left things earlier. And I'm sorry for throat-punching you and kicking you in the balls." My hand moved beneath his hoodie, desperate to feel the warmth of his skin. My fingertips traced along the lines of his chiseled abs. "So yes, I will sleep in your bed for as long as you want me to."

Forever, if you asked.

"Thank you. And now that Carl is single, we need to be clear on a few things."

"Okay," I said, tipping my head back to look at him.

"I won't share you, Miney. So, for as long as this fake relationship, or friends with benefits, or whatever the fuck you want to call what we have going on lasts, you can't be crossing any lines with Carl. That's a hard line for me."

"Are you being possessive of me, Finn Reynolds? You've never even been in a relationship, and now you're setting down a lot of rules on one that isn't even real," I asked with a chuckle as I pushed back to face him. "It might be harder than you expected for you to leave me when this all ends."

My voice was all tease, but I swear I was holding my breath and waiting for an answer.

A sign that maybe he was feeling confused, just like me.

Not just because he hated Carl and didn't want his pride to be hurt by me ending things earlier than planned.

His hand moved toward me as his thumb traced along my bottom lip. "All I want is for you to be happy."

What the hell did that mean?

Why did he have to be so cryptic?

I didn't know, and he looked exhausted.

"Okay, let's get you to bed. Can you get up?"

He reached for my hand, and we both pushed to stand. We walked out of the bedroom, his arm wrapped around my shoulder as we made our way to his bedroom.

Once we climbed beneath the sheets, we rolled on our sides to face one another. The room was completely dark, and Finn's hand found mine, our fingers intertwining.

"I'm glad you're here," he whispered, and I moved even closer.

Needing his warmth.

"Me, too."

And sleep took us both.

I woke up earlier than usual because my mind was still reeling from everything that had happened yesterday. About the fact that the man I had planned to marry had told me he missed me and wanted to get back together.

Yet, I'd hurried home to Finn because I'd missed him in the short time we'd been apart.

And then the way Finn had made it clear that he wouldn't share me with Carl, at least not during this time that we were pretending to be together.

But were we even pretending anymore? We spent every minute that we weren't working together. We were best friends. We had amazing sex. And now we'd agreed to sleep in the same bed.

What was fake about it?

But the thing I kept coming back to was that Finn and I wanted different things.

It could never really work.

So, I was just going to enjoy this moment while it lasted.

I studied his face. Long black lashes rested on his cheeks as his eyes were closed. His chiseled jaw was covered in day-old scruff. His red lips were plump and kissable. My hand moved beneath the blankets, stroking him over his joggers. He was already hard, per usual.

"Good morning." His voice was sleepy, his eyes still closed. "Are you wanting to apologize to my dick for the way that you treated him last night?"

I chuckled as my hand slipped inside his joggers, where there was nothing but his hard, thick erection.

"I definitely want to apologize," I said, my voice all breathy as desire stirred between my legs. "And I have a little surprise for you, as well."

"Tell me." His hand moved between my thighs, pushing my sleep shorts aside as he swiped his fingers across my heat.

"Remember when your giant condom tore after we'd had sex that first time on the beach and you were trying to get it off?" I chuckled. "I told you that I wanted to get on the pill just to be extra safe?"

"Yes. You mentioned that you'd started a few weeks ago."

"Yep. I've been taking it every day. And I wondered if you've ever been with a woman without a condom."

His eyes opened, meeting my gaze as if I'd just asked him the most serious question in the world. "I've never been with a woman without wearing a condom, because I haven't been in a committed relationship."

"Well, our relationship may be fake, but we're not with anyone else, so I guess that makes it committed. And we've still got another month together." I cleared my throat. Why was I so nervous? I wanted to feel Finn with nothing between us.

"You've been in one hell of a long relationship before this one. Did you and Dr. Prickdick always wear a condom?"

"Yeah. He has a thing about it. So, we never had sex without one."

"I'd be your first bare penis?" he teased, his finger slipping inside me as I continued running my hand up and down his length.

"And I'd be your first bare..." I sucked in a breath when his thumb moved over my clit and started circling it.

"Pussy, Miney. And it happens to be my favorite, so I can't think of a better deal for me. Are you sure about this?" he asked as he slowed down his rhythm to allow me to answer.

"I'm sure."

He stopped moving, and I did the same as we both pulled our hands away. He sat forward and tugged his hoodie over his head as I watched. He moved to his feet, dropping his joggers to the floor before turning toward me. I held my hands up in the air as he pulled my top over my head and then quickly found my bottoms and tugged them down my legs.

"I want you on top so you can feel everything," he said, moving to the bed to lie down and then grabbing my hips and helping me shift on top of him, one leg settling on each side of him. "You're so fucking beautiful."

Something had shifted between us. There was no humor this morning. We weren't rushing things, nor was he pulling out the dirty talk.

This felt... different.

I pushed up on my knees and wrapped my hand around his erection as my gaze locked with his. I slowly slid down, feeling every glorious inch of him. His lips parted, and he just watched me as I took him all the way in.

His hands moved to my waist as I started to ride him.

Slow and steady. His big hands splayed across my breasts and his thumbs teased my nipples. My hair fell down my back as we found our rhythm.

It wasn't desperate or frantic this time.

It was—perfect.

I'd never felt a connection to anyone the way I did to Finn. But in this moment, it was somehow stronger.

The kind of connection you would never get over.

The kind that brought you to your knees and made you weep if it was gone.

"Nothing has ever felt better," he hissed. "I love you so fucking much."

"I love you, too."

We'd said those words thousands of times. But this time, they felt like they had more meaning.

My body started to tingle, a euphoric feeling spreading through me. I moved faster, and his hips met me, thrust for thrust. My head fell back, eyes closed, just as his hand moved to my clit, knowing just what I needed.

He always had, hadn't he?

The most powerful force ripped through my entire body as I shook and quaked, going right over the edge and crying out his name.

Finn gripped my hips hard. Thrusting one more time.

And that was all it took.

He followed me into oblivion.

In this moment, I knew that I'd never feel anything like this with anyone else.

And I didn't know how to feel about that.

twenty-one

• • •

Finn

WE'D HEADED over to have Thanksgiving dinner at Georgia and Maddox's house, and we'd been late, so everyone gave us a hard time.

"Neither of you had to work today, so why are you late?" Cage eyed me suspiciously.

"Stop giving them a hard time. They're here, aren't they?" Georgia said as she hugged me and then moved to wrap her arms around Reese.

"We aren't that late," I said with annoyance because Reese couldn't seem to form a sentence without turning bright red, which made me the only one able to defend us.

"I mean, it's fine. But you are an hour late. We made it here from New York before you made it a few blocks from your house." Brinkley chuckled.

I was still making my way through the kitchen, hugging everyone, and Cage was not going to let it go.

"We do have a five-year-old to think of," my oldest brother grumped.

"I'm not hungry because Grammie gave me lots of snacks. But Daddy wants the turkey real bad." Gracie jumped into my arms, and I hugged her.

"You're fine, brother. The bird is still in the oven." Hugh pulled me in next.

Dylan walked toward me, her round belly leading the way. I'd been thrilled that my cousin and her husband were joining us this year. The rest of the Thomas family were all in Honey Mountain, but these two owned a hockey team, and they had a home game tomorrow, so they'd decided to stay in the city where they lived. Wolf didn't want her traveling that far for one day just to eat turkey, as apparently, getting around was getting tough on her, being so pregnant.

"If you'd been any later, I'd be holding baby Hugh in my hands." She laughed as she wrapped her arms around my neck, and her belly stood between us. She was naming her firstborn after my baby brother, Hugh, as they'd always been really close. We'd all been surprised when she'd gotten pregnant because Dylan and I had always been the two that said we'd be content just being great aunts and uncles. And now here she was, getting ready to be a mama. I knew she'd be amazing because she and Wolf loved each other fiercely.

"Sorry about that. We had an issue with the horses," I said, completely lying because everyone was watching me.

So, condom-free sex was my new favorite thing. I couldn't get enough of Reese or the feel of her without anything between us.

We had checked on the horses just before we were getting ready to leave, but when she'd bent over in the barn, wearing those tight jeans and her cowboy boots, I couldn't wait another second. I had to have her. So, we'd gone at it in an empty stall, which required another visit to the house, because we'd both had hay in areas where hay should never be.

"Oh, no, were the horses okay?" Georgia asked, because she completely believed my bullshit story.

Brinkley's eyes locked with mine, and she smirked. She was watching me like she'd just solved a murder mystery. I looked away quickly as I hugged Wolf, and my mother handed me a beer and winked.

"Hey, I need you for a minute." Brinkley glanced around to make sure no one was paying us any attention as she motioned for me to follow.

She stopped in front of the hall closet and opened the door and shoved me inside. Georgia and Maddox's house was custom-built, and of course, they had a window in their oversized hall closet with views of the ocean in the distance. It provided enough light to see one another, and I crossed my arms over my chest.

"What are we doing in here, Brinks?"

"What's going on, Finny?" She raised a brow, and I knew she was counting down in her head because she was not a patient woman. She'd give me a short time to answer before she started her torture tactics.

"I have no idea what you're talking about."

She reached up and pinched my upper arm so hard, I squealed. "Ouch. What the hell was that for?"

"Stop being a baby. And don't you dare offend me by lying. I wasn't born yesterday, you bastard."

I rubbed at my sore arm and gaped at her. "None of us were. That makes no sense."

"Cage and Hugh know what's going on, and you've left me and Georgie out. That's sexist. And rude. Have women not been through enough, for God's sake?"

I groaned. "This is not me being unfair to you for being a woman. You're acting insane. They don't know anything."

The door whipped open, and Hugh stepped inside. With both he and I in the closet and then you add in petite Brinkley, it was getting a little crowded. I stepped deeper into the abyss of all of Georgia's holiday boxes and luggage.

"Why are we in the closet?" he asked, before taking a long pull from his beer.

"I'm pissed that he told you guys what's going on but left

out me and Georgie. You know how I feel about picking sides between men and women."

"Ahhh... so you think he's a sexist pig for telling us that he has real feelings for Reese and not telling you? You aren't always the best secret keeper, Brinks."

"For fuck's sake. Apparently, neither are you. I told her you didn't know anything." I threw my hands in the air.

The door opened again, because heaven for-fucking-bid anyone in this family have a private conversation. Now it was Cage stepping inside, with Georgia right behind him, shoving themselves in and pulling the door closed.

"I figured it had to be something good, seeing as you're all packed into the closet." Cage pushed Hugh back a little so he could stand all the way up.

"Georgia, apparently, Finn doesn't feel that we should be in the know about his real feelings for Reese and that their relationship is not fake. Just as I suspected."

"Actually, I was the one who suspected it first," Cage hissed. "And don't be all righteous. He didn't want to tell you they were banging because you'd tell him that he had to confess his feelings to her first. And that would have run her off."

"Yes. The Reynolds men should always lead with the penis," Hugh said, crushing his beer can after taking the last sip.

"You're sleeping with her? Jesus, Finny. You should have established the relationship before you went there." Brinkley poked me hard in the chest. "This is why you come to us first and not these jackasses."

"Way to go, brother. Once again, we hadn't shared that. And I'd rather not be in the closet discussing this with you guys while Reese is out there." I ran a hand through my hair. "Her fucking parents are ten feet away. Can we not do this right now?"

"Well, you should have thought of that before you *did it.*

This is just like tip-of-the-penis-gate. You need to think before you act." Brinkley poked me in the chest again.

"All I do is fucking think about it, okay? This wasn't something I took lightly. I wouldn't have gone there with her if it wasn't—I don't know..." I hissed, trying to keep my voice low. "It's just more, okay?"

"Finny." Georgia wrapped her arms around me. "You love her, don't you?"

"I've always loved her, so I don't know how to tell what it means. But yeah, I've never felt this before."

"Do you see this as the long game?" Brinkley asked.

"Listen, she still has Carl in the picture. He's single again. She didn't want to end things with me early, so maybe that's a good sign. But at the same time, I'm fucking terrified. I don't know if I'm any good at this. What if I push for it and then I fuck it up?"

"Then we'll have to kill you," Brinkley said, her voice void of all humor before she barked out a laugh.

The door whipped open and in waddled a very pregnant Dylan. "Hey, what is the rule we have about family meetings?"

"Keep the talk short?" Cage asked, and she chuckled.

"If one goes, we all go. I'm offended that you've all disappeared and didn't invite me."

"Well, no one here was actually invited," I said. "They just keep coming in."

Dylan pressed about what was going on, and Georgia and Brinkley took turns bringing her up to speed, and I took Cage's beer from his hand and chugged it.

"We need to get back out there. Everyone is going to notice we're gone." I made an attempt at the door, and this time it was Dylan who pinched me.

"Don't you dare leave before I give you my two cents," she said.

"Aren't pregnant women supposed to be sweet?" Cage asked over his laughter.

"Yeah, you try having a giant human living inside you and then push him out of your penis and tell me if you'd be sweet." She raised a brow, and now the entire closet erupted in laughter.

"Okay, let's hear your two cents, Dilly," Hugh said as he winked at her.

"You're worrying about the wrong things. I get it. She knows what she wants—marriage, babies, all that stuff. And you've never thought about it because you've never been in love." She smiled and raised a brow. "I was very similar, Finny. My sisters all knew what they wanted. I'd never imagined my future that way. But here's the thing—you don't have to have it all figured out. Because when you really love someone, there's no running from it. Look at me. I've got a watermelon growing in my belly. Who'd have ever thought I'd be pregnant right now?"

"But this is Reese," Brinkley whispered. "She's family. You need to figure it out before you promise her the world, because if you hurt her, it's going to cause a shit storm in this family and in hers."

"And let's not forget Dr. Pricknuts. She had planned to marry the dude, and now he's single and wants her back. How do we know she isn't going to crush Finny's heart?" Cage said with a wicked grin on his face.

"Why the fuck are you smiling when discussing my heartache?"

"Just never thought I'd see the day that you'd be someone's little bitch." He barked out a laugh.

"Why does no one pinch him?" I grumped, just as a knock on the door had us all going silent.

Dylan pushed it open, and Wolf peeked his head in. "Dinner's ready, and everyone's looking for you."

"How'd you know where we were?" my cousin purred to her husband.

"I've always got my eyes on you, Minx."

"Good answer. Take some lessons, Finny," Dylan teased as we all piled out of the closet.

"Hey," Hugh said, just before I stepped out. We were the last two in there. "I doubted myself, too. But what I learned is, just because you've never done it before, doesn't mean you can't. It just means that you haven't met someone worth going out on a limb for. Maybe you've been single because you'd already met the one you were meant to be with. You just didn't know it. She'd been there the whole time."

I nodded. I'd thought that many times over the last few weeks. I clapped him on the shoulder, and we stepped out, hearing all the chatter coming from the dining room.

Reese was deep in conversation with Lila and Olivia, and my mom and Jenny Murphy were refilling wine glasses, while my father and Grant had just finished carving two turkeys and were setting the platters on each end of the table.

Everyone made their way to the dining room, and we found our seats. I was between Reese and Cage. We passed around the sides and filled our plates while we all chatted. Once we had piles of delicious food on our plates, my father raised his water glass, and we all did the same. Dylan had water, Gracie had chocolate milk, and the rest of us had wine or beer in our glasses.

"Another year to be thankful for good food, great friends, and my beautiful family. Thanks for hosting, Georgia and Maddox. Thank you to the Murphys for being here with us. Let's all take a minute to think about all the good in our lives," my father said, and Cage leaned close to my ear.

"I'm thankful that we finally get to eat some damn turkey."

I chuckled and elbowed him in the arm.

"I'm thankful for Grammie and Pops!" Gracie shouted. "And all my families and for Bob Picklepants."

I barked out a laugh because the fact that my oldest brother, with the heart of the Tin Man, had not only gotten his baby girl the cutest puppy, but he'd allowed her to name it that ridiculous name.

"Cheers to Bob Picklepants," Hugh said, holding his glass high.

"To Bob Picklepants!" everyone said together.

"Yeah, yeah, yeah. Let's eat." Cage rolled his eyes before cutting up the food on Gracie's plate beside him.

Reese piled mashed potatoes onto my plate, and I buttered a roll and set it on hers. I glanced up to see Brinkley smiling at me.

We spent the next thirty minutes going around the table saying what we were thankful for, and my mom couldn't stop talking about putting the tree up tomorrow and needing help with that.

Gracie was asking about pie, and we all laughed because we'd just consumed more food than anyone ever should in one sitting.

The doorbell rang, and Georgia left to go see who it was. We were still talking and laughing as we pushed to our feet to start clearing the plates.

"Umm, Reese. Carl is here to see you. He's in the front entryway."

What the fuck?

This guy had some nerve.

"How did he get through the gate?" Maddox hissed, arms crossed over his chest as he pulled out his phone to check the camera.

"I left the gate open while everyone was arriving." Georgia shrugged. "I must have forgotten to close it."

"I've got it. Thank you," Reese said as she glanced over at me.

"*We've* got it," I said, my voice firm. This guy thought he could crash Thanksgiving because he was now single?

Not a fucking chance.

"You don't have to do this," Reese whispered as she looked up at me. "I can ask him to leave."

"You shouldn't have to." I intertwined my fingers with hers, and we walked down the hallway toward the entrance.

Dr. Dipweasal stood in the foyer, holding a giant bouquet of flowers, looking unusually disheveled. His shirt was untucked, and his eyes were bloodshot. My family was in the bar business, so I could spot an intoxicated person a mile away.

"You've got to be fucking kidding me," I said, dropping Reese's hand as I moved in front of her. "You come to my sister's house with flowers for *my girlfriend* on Thanksgiving?"

Carl looked between Reese and me, and he cleared his throat. "Reese and I usually spend Thanksgiving together."

"Really? Were you with her last year when you cut her off for moving to London? And now you break up with your girlfriend less than twenty-four hours ago and you think you have a right to come here and disrupt our dinner?"

He glared at me, holding his chin high. "Reese, do you think you could step outside and speak to me for a minute?"

It was the moment of truth. Was she going to side with this guy like she always had? I crossed my arms over my chest and glared at him.

"Carl, you shouldn't have come here. Are you drunk?"

"I'm a mess. I'm lost without you. So yeah, I had dinner with my family, and I drank a lot. And here I am."

"You need to leave." She shook her head. "How did you get here?"

"I took an Uber, but he left. I was kind of hoping you'd give me a ride home."

That was it for me. He'd thought my girlfriend was going to leave with him?

"Who the fuck do you think you are?" I stormed toward him, pushing him up against the door.

"I can handle this!" Reese shouted, and I could hear the quake in her voice.

"Finn, he's drunk. Not a fair fight, brother," Hugh said, his voice coming from behind me.

"We'll give you a ride home," my father said, as he and Cage stepped up beside Hugh.

"Reese, can we talk first?"

"Are you fucking kidding me?" I hissed.

"For fuck's sake," Cage said. "Take the ride before you get a fist to the face. And after my brother strikes, there are a lot more of us standing behind him. Don't push your luck. You're lucky we're offering you a ride."

My father held up his keys and clapped me on the shoulder. "Go have some pie. We'll be back shortly."

Hugh, Cage, and my dad escorted Carl out of the house, and I turned to see Reese standing there with a tear running down her cheek.

As far as I was concerned, that would be the last tear she ever shed over that bastard.

twenty-two

. . .

Reese

IT HAD BEEN two weeks since the fiasco at Thanksgiving. I'd never seen Finn so angry. His mother had made a comment about what a great actor he was, making it clear that nobody there believed there wasn't more going on between us.

And they'd be right.

But I didn't know what exactly this was, and neither did he.

I'd been angry at Carl for coming there the way he had. It was disrespectful to Finn, and I'd told him as much when I'd finished the renovation of his office that following week.

Thankfully, there was no reason for me to be around him anymore, and I needed this time to figure out what I wanted.

Because at the end of the day, whether Finn wanted the same things I did didn't really matter. Because he'd shown me that there was a different kind of love than I'd realized.

I didn't know if he felt what I felt.

I didn't want to put that pressure on him.

He knew exactly who I was and what I wanted out of this life. That was the reason he'd always hated Carl. He knew that he didn't love me the way that I deserved to be loved. I couldn't see it then, but I saw it now.

But I also knew Finn. Knew that he wanted to travel the world and pursue his acting dreams. He'd never talked about wanting kids or wanting to settle down with one woman.

He'd always told me he'd be content being a fabulous uncle to my and his siblings' kids.

So, he'd need to decide if that had changed or not.

I wouldn't be settling for less than I deserved anymore, because being loved by Finn Reynolds had been life-changing for me.

Whether he wanted to stay with me forever would be his decision. I was going to enjoy every second of it while it lasted.

I'd been burning the candle at both ends lately, and I was feeling it. I'd taken on three more clients, and I'd had a few people hire me to decorate their homes for the holidays. That wasn't what I'd planned to offer, but right now, the more work I could take on, the better. I was growing this company, and I needed to push hard to get things going. I'd always been prone to getting run down, so I was doubling up on vitamins to keep my energy up and stay healthy. There was always this nagging fear that I'd relapse. That my world would come crashing down again. That my future wouldn't hold all the things that I hoped it would. So I was hyperaware of my body and how I was feeling at all times.

You go through several rounds of chemo, and it will teach you to look for red flags.

But tonight, I was surprising Finn. He'd been so supportive of my new business, fighting me when I'd insisted on paying rent to him and Maddox. Bringing me lunch at work all the time. Letting me live in his house while we pretended to be dating—when we were actually dating, we just weren't admitting it to one another.

I wanted to do something nice for him tonight. I'd made

him his favorite dinner, chicken marsala and mashed potatoes. I told him to go to the bedroom and wait for me after.

I'd snuck off to what used to be my bedroom to change into my outfit. The whole house was decorated for Christmas. Finn and I had spent the weekend after Thanksgiving shopping and decorating every inch of his home.

"Miney, are you coming?" he shouted from down the hallway.

"Hopefully soon. Be patient!" I yelled back, and he barked out a laugh.

I looked in the mirror and adjusted the two buns on top of my head before giving myself one more look-see. I couldn't believe I was doing this.

The gold bikini top left little to the imagination, barely covering the girls. And the bottoms had a gold strap that went around my hips, with white sheer fabric that formed a see-through skirt around the bikini bottoms. I'd turned myself into quite the sexy Princess Leia, and I couldn't wait to see the look on Finn's face.

"Are your eyes closed, Chewy?"

"Yes, ma'am." His voice was all tease. "You know I love surprises."

"Well, get ready, because this is going to be your favorite of all time, I think." I adjusted my straps as I stood outside his bedroom door.

"Better than when you dressed as Yoda in seventh grade when I begged you to be my sidekick?" he sang out.

"I think so."

"Better than when you covered yourself in one hundred purple balloons for the hundredth day of school, and I spent the entire day popping them every chance I got?"

"We'll see," I said as I walked into the room. There were a few candles lit on the dresser, and the light from the moon illuminated the space. "You can open your eyes now."

I leaned against the door frame, and he pushed up on his

elbows as his gaze raked me over from head to toe. "Are you fucking kidding me right now?"

"You like it?"

He was on his feet and charging toward me before I could react. He tossed me over his shoulder like I weighed nothing and then hurried to the bed. But when he dropped me down onto the mattress, he did it slowly, his gaze locked with mine. "You are already my every fantasy, Reese Murphy. But this… this is next level. Princess fucking Leia. Hell yes, I like it."

I bit down on my bottom lip because he wasn't looking at me like I was his sexual fantasy. He was looking at me like I was the only girl in the world. Maybe I was reading into it, wanting this to be more than it was.

"Good," I said, my voice just above a whisper as I tried to pull myself together.

"Get one thing straight before I worship every inch of your sweet body." He stroked the strand of hair that had broken free from one of the buns sitting on top of my head. "This is hot, no doubt about it. But seeing you when you come home from a hard day of work, doing what you love, building your business, all tired and exhausted… It's just as fucking sexy to me. Seeing you in your cowboy boots and a pair of worn denim after you take Millie for a long ride—so fucking sexy. There isn't a version of you that I don't want. I can't get enough of any one of them."

I sucked in a breath because he was saying all the right things. No man had ever made me feel so wanted. But I didn't know what it meant.

I knew that I didn't want to be with the man I'd been hell-bent on marrying.

I didn't want anyone other than Finn.

"I can't get enough of you either," I said. "So, we like having sex with each other. Although, I haven't had any competition because you've been sort of forced to be here with me."

I wasn't planning on having a serious conversation right now. My romantic relationship with Finn was kind of like this costume. It was fun and sexy, but it was temporary.

Thinking any differently about it would only hurt us both.

His brows cinched together as his gaze searched mine. "No one has forced me to do anything. I'm the one who forced you to put things on hold with Carl. No one is here against their will, Miney. At least I'm not."

Tell him that you don't want Carl anymore.

Just say the words.

"I-I—" I looked away. I couldn't handle the way those gray eyes were boring into me. Looking deep into my soul like they always did. But telling Finn the truth would make him feel obligated to me. I couldn't stand the idea of him feeling forced to be with me once this was all over. "I think we should just focus on tonight."

He nodded, looking like he was about to say something, but he stopped himself. "How about this… We don't add any pressure to this already-odd situation. We have a few more weeks together, and if at the end of that, you want to go back to your dickhead ex when I leave town for work and fall back into my old routine—well, then that's okay. But if we decide we aren't ready to call this off, that's okay, too. We're always going to be fine, Reese."

Was he trying to prepare me for the end?

I tugged his head down so his lips were hovering just above mine. "Too much talking. I don't want to talk anymore. I just want you to kiss me. Can you do that?"

"Hell, yes. It's my favorite thing to do these days."

And just like that, all my worries melted away as his lush lips crashed into mine.

It might not be forever, but right now, it was enough.

Finn and I had taken the horses out for a ride before I left for work, and he had his Zoom call with the director and producer of his upcoming movie. Finn's career had already skyrocketed, but now he was going to move from the small screen to the big screen.

That meant more travel, more opportunity, and more fans.

This moment in time that we were sharing was coming to an end, and we both knew it.

We raced back toward the barn, my hair whipping around me as my braid had come undone after we'd left the beach and hurried home. It was cold, as Christmas was just a few days away.

My time with Finn felt like a ticking time bomb getting ready to detonate and blow up my world.

One I'd grown so comfortable in.

Too comfortable.

We'd made a deal not to discuss the future until after the holidays.

My guess was that it would make it easier for him to call this done, right before he left for Tokyo. Why discuss that now? It would make things awkward.

We'd still be in one another's lives. We always would. He was my best friend.

But things would go back to how they used to be, and I couldn't stand the thought of him telling me about other women now.

How would I fake it and act like it didn't bother me?

We stopped in the barn and put Han Solo and Millie in their stalls as we made our way back outside.

"Not a bad way to start the day, huh?" he said, as his hand found mine, and we walked toward the house.

It was second nature for us to touch at all times now. But it had been even before all of this. It had always annoyed Carl that I'd had to make a conscious effort not to do it around him when we were all together, which wasn't often.

"Yeah. It's the best."

"You know, I'd love for you to stay here when I start shooting the movie in Tokyo. Millie likes it, and I think Han Solo would be lonely if she left. I'm going to see about another horse next week."

I nodded. I hadn't decided where I'd go, but I needed to figure out a plan. I couldn't stay here if we weren't together. Oh my God. The thought of Finn bringing a woman home and me just being the roommate… That would not work.

"Well, I'm not sure what I'll do. I've been looking at some options." That wasn't true. But I didn't want to look like I just expected him to let me stay here. Like I just expected this to all work out in my favor. "But I can still care for the horses no matter where I am. I'm definitely going to be in Cottonwood Cove, seeing as I have a business here now," I said as an awkward laugh escaped. I glanced up to see his jaw tense as he nodded.

"Silas is going to increase his hours. I wouldn't expect you to take Han Solo out every day once I'm gone. I know how busy work is, and I think you've been pushing too hard as it is."

Of course, he didn't need me. He had Silas all lined up to increase his hours. I was the only one who was hoping nothing would change.

"Well, that sounds like a good plan," I said as we stepped inside, and Finn put on a pot of coffee while I ran to the bathroom to fix my hair really quickly.

He was pouring it into a to-go cup for me because he knew I'd need it.

"Thank you," I said, as I leaned my backside against the kitchen counter. "I've got that meeting with Georgia and Maddox about doing the décor for the casita they're adding on to their place."

"You all right? You look a little pale." He studied me, his eyes filled with concern.

How did he always know when something was wrong? I was tired. I'd been working long hours and not sleeping nearly enough.

"I'm good. Between work and getting ready for the holidays, it's just been a lot."

He nodded before pulling back and grabbing a banana and a muffin and dropping them into a paper bag. "Take these and eat. I'll bring you lunch, okay?"

"I know you have a busy day. You don't need to bring me lunch."

"I'm never too busy for you, Miney."

"You're just hoping I'll let you have your way with me, aren't you?" I teased as he followed me out to my car. I looked up to see a few snowflakes starting to fall from the sky.

"I'm always hoping you'll let me have my way with you." He opened the car door, and I slipped inside. "Eat that breakfast, you got it?"

"Yes, sir. And are we still set to go Christmas shopping tonight?"

"Absolutely. And we can grab some dinner at Reynolds' afterward."

"Sounds like a plan."

He leaned over and kissed me hard. Like it was perfectly normal to kiss me goodbye. How would we just suddenly turn this off after this had turned into a full-blown relationship with my best friend?

He shut my door, and I drove the short distance to my office, parking in the back lot and walking around to the front door. Carl was leaning against the wall, holding a bag and a coffee cup from Cup of Cove.

"Hey, I was hoping to catch you real quick." He appeared nervous. We'd only spoken once since he'd made that appearance at Georgia and Maddox's house on Thanksgiving, and that was the day I'd finished the project at his house.

"Hi. Sure. I have a meeting in a little bit, but I have a few minutes." I opened the door and flipped on the lights, and he whistled as he looked around. I slipped my coat off and hung it on the hook beside the door.

"Wow. This looks great," he said. He'd never come by before, even though he'd continually said he was anxious to see the place. He'd never found the time, and I'd always met him at his house for our design meetings. Now that the job was done, there'd be no reason for him to come here anymore.

He handed me the bag and the coffee, and I motioned for him to take the seat on the other side of my desk. "Thank you for this."

"Listen, Reese. I've been really horrified by my behavior." He held his hands up to stop me from interrupting. "My behavior before that night, as well. I've been an asshole. You deserved better."

"Thank you for saying that. I think you and I just have this history, you know? Where we thought we would have a future together, but in reality, we wanted different things out of life. I think I convinced myself that if we both wanted marriage and kids, that was enough. But I realize now that I have dreams of my own, too. And I'm not upset with you anymore for dating Christy, because if you hadn't, we would have just fallen into that same routine as soon as I'd returned home. I'm happy with where things are going in my life now. And I want you to be happy, too."

He nodded. "I've been an idiot. I should have supported you when you left for London. I was being stubborn. Fuck, I messed up so many times."

"I think things worked out the way they were supposed to."

He studied me for a long moment. "Are you feeling all right? You look a little pale. You pushing too hard?"

That was the doctor in him. And with my history, it was

normal for everyone to worry. "I have been feeling really worn out. I didn't expect to have so many clients right away, but I'm loving it. And you know, I'm always afraid to even tell anyone that I'm exhausted because they will freak out and think it's the worst-case scenario. I thought of calling Dr. Roberts just to be safe, but you know he's good friends with my dad, so everyone will hear about it, and then all the drama will start."

He didn't hide the concern from his gaze. "Well, instead of saying anything or going to him, what if I run a full panel and just check your blood work and make sure there aren't any red flags? Maybe you've got mono or a virus. Let's rule out everything before we panic."

"Really? That would be amazing. And you could keep it between us. If anything comes up, then I'll go see Dr. Roberts. But I'm fairly certain it's just exhaustion. I have been going nonstop."

"It probably is. Stop by my office later today, and I'll have Janet draw your blood and get it over to the lab. With the holidays, it might take a bit longer, but we'll get all of it back shortly after Christmas. Then you can put your mind at ease."

"Thank you, Carl," I said. "And how about you? Are you doing okay?"

"I am. I think I'm going to take some time and just be alone for a while. You know if you change your mind, and you and Finn don't work out, I'll be here." He waggled his brows, his attempt to be funny.

I chuckled. The problem was, it didn't matter if Finn was committed to this or not in the long run. He'd shown me what I wanted out of a relationship and what it meant to truly be loved by a man.

And I knew that Carl and I did not have a future.

He pushed to his feet and clutched his chest. "I know that look very well. I get it. You've got it bad for the guy. I knew it the first time I saw you two together when you came home outside of Cottonwood Café."

"What do you mean?" I stood and followed him to the door.

"The way you looked at him after he'd kissed you." He shrugged. "You've never looked at me that way."

Finn and I hadn't even been a real thing back then.

"How did I look at him?" I chuckled as he pulled the door open.

"Like he was the center of your universe." He leaned over and hugged me goodbye. "He looked at you the same way. And you know what, Reese?"

"What?" I asked as he stepped outside.

"You deserve that. I know it. And I think you know it now, too." He held a hand up and walked toward the parking lot. "Don't forget to come by today. I want to run that blood work."

I waved. "I will. Thank you, Carl."

When I closed the door, I leaned against it and closed my eyes.

He was right. I did look at Finn that way.

Because Finn Reynolds was the center of my universe.

twenty-three

• • •

Finn

I'm going holiday shopping with Reese tonight. I got her that charm bracelet I told you about. You know, the one that supposedly says, "I want to date you for real."

HUGH

What was the gift that said, "I want to fake date you?"

CAGE

That's the gift of the penis, apparently.

You were the ones who told me that sex would make her want to date me, not fake date me, you dicksicles.

BRINKLEY

And this is why you don't go to a man for dating advice. Sex is never going to show a woman that you want to date her seriously.

GEORGIA

Hmmm… I'm not sure that's true. It made me want to date Bossman.

CAGE

I just sat down to have lunch, and now my fucking appetite is ruined. For fuck's sake, don't talk about your sex life on the group chat, Georgie.

BRINKLEY

This is the guy you went to for advice, Finny? He doesn't have a clue how to handle a woman.

CAGE

I'm on this thread, you know that, right?

BRINKLEY

I do. I just don't care.

HUGH

Maybe you should just tell her that you want to date her for real.

BRINKLEY

Really? You think? Duh. That's what I've been trying to say.

Because she's still not sure how she feels about Dr. Lamebrain, and I don't want to scare her off.

GEORGIA

I have to tell you something, but I don't want you to get upset.

Tell me.

GEORGIA

Maddox and I met Reese at the office this morning, and Carl was just leaving when we arrived. It may have been nothing, but I didn't know if you knew he was going to see her today.

CAGE

I thought she was done with his bullshit design project.

She is. I didn't know they were meeting today. This is what I'm talking about. We don't speak about him anymore, so I don't know where she stands with him or with me. Ever since we entered this gray area, she doesn't say much about him.

BRINKLEY

You're leaving to film a movie after the holidays. Don't you think you should be discussing this? You live together. You sleep together. You're best friends. I have news for you, Finny: You are dating her. You just aren't talking about it.

Yet she's still meeting with her asshole ex. Why? Because she is hell-bent on getting married. I don't fucking understand it.

GEORGIA

Well, she did talk to us today about renting the little house that Brinks and I have both lived in. She said she wants to find a place to rent after you leave. So at least she isn't moving in with Carl.

What? Why the fuck would she want to rent your home when she can stay in mine? And, of course, she isn't moving right in with him. She's been in my bed for weeks. But is that the plan? Once I'm gone, she takes a break and then goes back to him?

HUGH

You're jumping to conclusions. We don't know why he was there this morning.

It doesn't fucking matter. He's still in her life, waiting in the wings for the minute I'm gone. I brought her lunch, and she didn't mention seeing him.

BRINKLEY

I think the million-dollar question is, do you want the same things? She wants to settle down and start a family. Is that what you want, Finny?

I SCRUBBED a hand down my face. There was so much going on right now. For both of us. I was getting ready to leave the country for a month. Then I'd come back and start shooting season two of *Big Sky Ranch.* Was that even conducive to having a healthy relationship? Me being gone all the time?

This is new for me. But I know that I don't want anyone else.

CAGE

That's not very convincing.

That's why I need a really good gift.

GEORGIA

It's not about a gift, Finny. It's about putting yourself out there.

BRINKLEY

Yes. Pour your heart out. Put yourself out there. But I think you should get her some good gifts, too.

HUGH

You could fly her to Vegas and just marry her and be done with it.

CAGE

I hate Vegas. The last time I was there, I lost 800 bucks and my pants.

You were with me, and you didn't lose your pants. You willingly took them off and then jumped into the fountain like a moron while everyone cheered.

HUGH

Umm… I was also there, and you and I both followed him into the fountain without our pants.

BRINKLEY

Why does all the fun happen when Georgie and I aren't there?

CAGE

Because no one is scolding us and telling us what to do. #livingourbestlife

GEORGIA

It was Hugh's bachelor party. We were with Lila. Thankfully, no one got naked or arrested.

BRINKLEY

Anyway, you better make a move, Finny. Carl is going to swoop in the minute you leave. He already crashed Thanksgiving, and now he showed up at her office today. The writing is on the wall. Don't sit back and wait for it to happen.

She said she doesn't want to put any pressure on us and that we will talk about it before I leave. So, I'm trying to do what's best for her.

HUGH

That's a fair point.

GEORGIA

Trust your gut, Finny. You two are so good together. It won't matter that you're leaving for a while. You're meant to be together.

CAGE

I still think leading with the penis was a good plan.

HUGH

It always is, brother.

BRINKLEY

Not my go-to, but whatever. Maybe you can write her a letter to have after you leave, too.

GEORGIA

Swoon. I agree. You can have the talk and then leave her with the letter to read whenever she's missing you. I love that idea. And a cashmere sweater is always a win.

CAGE

Does she want a puppy? One of Mr. Wigglestein's many bitches will be delivering soon.

BRINKLEY

Do not get her a puppy right before you leave town. She'll hate you. You already got her the jewelry. That's going to be a winner. Women love thoughtful gifts.

HUGH

I got Lila new running shoes and leggings. Now I'm feeling like an asshole.

GEORGIA

She will love it, Hughey. But maybe get something pretty, too.

BRINKLEY

She liked my gold hoop earrings. I'll send you the link. But I think she'd like you to put a baby in her, if I'm being honest. It's all she talks about lately.

HUGH

Trust me… I'm trying. Can't wait to knock up my girl.

GEORGIA

That's romantic. Sort of. Maybe the wording is a little off.

CAGE

This is where I tap out. You've lost me, and I've got an office full of needy animals. They take priority.

Thanks for the pep talk. Love you, guys.

GEORGIA

You've got this, Finny.

BRINKLEY

Put yourself out there before she leaves. Don't wimp out.

HUGH

If you want to grab a beer later, come by Reynolds'.

I met with Silas to talk about some added responsibilities he'd be taking on once I left and also discussed the idea of bringing someone on to work for him if needed, as well.

I was still pissed that Reese had arranged for another place to live. Even if she didn't want to keep things going with me, we were still best friends. So why the fuck would she want to move out?

Unless she was planning to get back together with Carl after I left.

I stewed on it as I sat at my desk and looked over the itinerary for my trip to Tokyo, where I'd be filming through January and into part of February. I'd be gone a little over a month.

"I'm home, Chewy," Reese called out, and I heard the door close. I felt this sense of relief when she got home each day, which was not even logical to me. I'd always loved her. She'd been my best friend for as long as I could remember.

But this was different.

It was hard to breathe when she wasn't in the room.

I didn't know how I was going to be away from her for weeks, maybe months, when it was all said and done. And what if she did go back to Carl, and she married the dude like she'd always planned?

How would I even survive if I had to see them together?

I wasn't going to ask her about him stopping by today, because there'd be no reason for her not to tell me if there was nothing going on.

So, I'd give her the opportunity to tell me.

I came out of the office, and she rushed toward me, dropping her purse on the floor. My arms came around her as her body crashed into mine.

"Hey, are you okay?" I pulled back, finding her chin and tipping her head back so I could look at her. "What's wrong?"

"I just missed you." She smiled, and my shoulders relaxed.

"Yeah? Missed you, too. Busy day?"

"Yes. I had a few meetings, and I have two new clients." She pushed up on her tiptoes and kissed my cheek. "Come on. I'll tell you all about it on the way. Let's get our shopping done so we can have dinner and relax."

I grabbed my coat by the door and pulled it on before reaching for my keys and stepping outside. The snow was falling, and the driveway had a layer of white powder covering it. I loved this time of year.

I pulled the passenger door open, and she climbed in. I leaned down and kissed her hard as I reached for the seat belt and pulled it across her body. I studied her face, noticing she looked a little pale, and considering how cold it was, her face should be flush.

"You still look a little pale. Are you okay?" There was always that sinking feeling in my stomach when I worried about Reese. The worst time of my life was the day that I found out she was sick. The fear of losing her—it had scared me shitless.

"I'm just a little tired, Chewy. I've been working a lot. I feel fine. I promise."

"Should you see Dr. Roberts? Just to be safe?"

"Finn. Stop. I would go if I were worried about it. Being tired does not mean that I have cancer." Her gaze hardened like I'd just completely offended her. "Now, get in the truck so we can go buy lots of presents and go to Reynolds' for some good food."

I nodded slowly before closing the door and hurrying around to start the truck and crank up the heat.

"So, tell me about your day," I said, keeping my tone light as I waited for her to tell me about Carl.

"Well, your sister and Maddox came by early this morning, and we went over some design ideas for the casita."

And you asked if you could rent their home.

"Yes. What else did you talk about?" Reese and I had never had secrets. But now that we were sleeping together, she was suddenly tight-lipped with me? That didn't sit fucking well with me.

"I drew up some sketches, and they loved them. We looked at some different finishes, and—"

"Oh, for fuck's sake. You asked to rent their house. Why are you leaving that out?" I said, not hiding my irritation as I found a parking spot on Cottonwood Cove Drive downtown.

She chuckled. "Ah, I figured Georgie might mention it. I

was going to tell you. I just thought I'd wait until we have our little talk."

"The day before I leave? Isn't that what you requested? We wait until the last fucking minute to talk about it? But meanwhile, you go and rent another home? What's your deal, Miney?"

Her jaw fell open as she searched my gaze. She unbuckled her seat belt and slid across the seat before climbing onto my lap. She placed a mitten-covered hand on each of my cheeks.

"I need to have a plan, Chewy. You're leaving, and once you finish shooting the movie, you'll be shooting *Big Sky Ranch*. You're going to be gone for a few months, so I can't just be living in your house."

"Why the fuck not?" I asked.

"For a lot of reasons."

"Name one."

"We don't know what this is, what's happening between us. I'm an adult, and I need to have a home of my own. I can't be sitting around, waiting to see what happens. I'm not going to do that to you, Finn. You're my best friend. My favorite person. I love you so much, and I don't want you worrying about me. If you—" She looked away, glancing out the window as a tear ran down her cheek.

"If I, what?"

"You're leaving, Chewy. You're going to have women chasing after you. You're a freaking movie star now. You did me a favor. But we both know this isn't going to last forever. This isn't what you want." Now the tears were streaming down her cheeks.

I guess we were doing this now.

I used my thumbs to clear away the liquid. "How do you know what I want?"

"Because I know you better than anyone. And I don't think we want the same things." Her voice broke, and I swear a piece of my heart cracked at the pain that I heard. "I want you to want the same things I want. God, I want that so bad. But I won't ever ask you to be someone you're not. And I can't stand the thought of you not being happy. Or you being far away and feeling guilty because you want someone else, and you don't know how to tell me. We can't let that happen to us."

I wrapped my arms around her and pulled her close, stunned by how much she'd been holding in. Hell, I had been holding back, too.

"Miney," I whispered before she pulled back to look at me.

"I'm sorry. I'm just tired and emotional."

"Stop. I'm unsure where we stand, too. I don't know where you are with Carl. I mean, I'm not the one who has someone waiting for this to fail so they can swoop in."

Her pretty green eyes searched mine like she was stunned by my words. "You've got lots of people waiting to swoop in, Chewy. The whole world wants a piece of you. Your life is just getting started. And mine… mine is here."

"Mine has always revolved around you. I just didn't know what it meant back then. And now I know this for certain," I said, as my thumb stroked her bottom lip. "I don't want anyone else. When I'm away from you, I miss you like crazy."

"I don't think that's enough." She shrugged. "It'll fade."

"This isn't a fucking fling. I've loved you my entire life, Reese Murphy. That will never fade."

She pushed forward again, hugging me tight. "Let's just enjoy this time together, okay? And then we'll see what happens. You don't need to make me any promises. But just know that I'm going to be fine. I'm going to move into my own place when you leave. And we'll just take things one day at a time."

She'd already given up on me.

But what she didn't know was… I'd never give up on her.

Or on us.

twenty-four

. . .

Reese

DOWNTOWN WAS LIT with white twinkle lights that crossed back and forth over the street. The light posts were covered in garland, and red and white poinsettias hung from above. Holiday music was piped through the speakers, and everyone was out shopping tonight. The snow had lightened up, and Finn and I had already found a few gifts for our siblings. We'd stopped in The Tipsy Tea and bought a few things for Gracie. As we strode down the street toward Reynolds', Finn stopped in front of Cove Jewelry.

"Come on. Let's go in and look," he said.

"What? Why?"

"I want to look in here together. Humor me."

I stepped inside when he held the door open for me. "Hey, Mr. Clark."

"Well, if it isn't my two favorite troublemakers." The older man came around the corner and hugged each of us. He had to be in his early eighties now, and I swear the man used to be taller, but his smile was as big as ever.

"Who are you calling troublemakers?" I teased.

"Oh, I don't know. The girl who mailed water balloons when she was eight years old. And the boy who ran naked through downtown in high school." He laughed so hard that a few tears ran down his kind face.

"It was one water balloon. Finny here bet me that I wouldn't do it. I waited until after Mr. Milford had picked up the mail that day. I don't know why Alicia Rogers felt the need to turn me in." I couldn't hide the smile on my face, even if I'd been completely beside myself back then, convinced I'd have a police record and never go to college. Damn, we'd had so much fun growing up in this town.

"Well, Alicia Rogers's favorite hobby is judging others." Mr. Clark barked out a laugh.

"She'd been so proud, thinking I didn't know the mail had already been taken out of the box. But when Alicia called the police… Holy shit balls." Finn was laughing so hard, a wide grin spread across his face. "You made me promise to visit you every day in the slammer."

"Well, I had a wild imagination back then. Luckily, they just made me pick up trash at the park for the next few weekends. It was a fair trade. And then this one…" I flicked my thumb at the charming bastard beside me. "He gets nothing but a slap on the hand for running naked through downtown."

"I wore body paint, and I had a sling over my—*johnson*." He smirked.

"I always knew you two would end up together," Mr. Clark said.

"Yeah? How'd you know?" Finn asked as he walked around, looking at the jewelry in the glass cases.

"It was the way you looked at one another, even way back in the day. Like, as long as you were together, nothing else really mattered. Never saw you look at Dr. Barley that way, Reese."

Awkward.

But also very true.

It had taken me a while to realize I was hopelessly in love

with my best friend. I think I'd settled on a future with Carl because it seemed… easy.

Possible, even.

I loved him in the way I thought mattered.

And I'd thought my world was ending after he started dating someone else, and I was coming home with no plan.

But in the end, it had never been Carl.

After being home, I realized that I didn't miss him.

I missed the idea of him.

I didn't like being single. I wanted a partner. A best friend. A lover. Someone to raise a family with and laugh and grow old with.

And now that Finn had shown me how good sex could be, the connection that I felt to him—I knew what I had with Carl didn't compare in any way. I wasn't myself with him. With Finn, I could just be me. I could ask for what I wanted and not feel ashamed to have dreams of my own.

But now I had a whole new set of problems because Finn was leaving soon. The man was going to have temptation every which way he looked. I believed him when he said he loved me. I'd never felt more loved by anyone in my life than by Finn Reynolds.

But he'd tire of the distance. He would be traveling the world for his career. He'd go back to being with different women and remembering how exciting it all was.

And I couldn't ask him to give me something that wouldn't make him happy.

I loved him enough to let him go figure it out.

If he came back to me, I'd be here waiting.

Because now that I'd had him, no one else would compare.

But I wasn't going to say any of that to him. I'd move into my own place and focus on work and being okay with being alone.

"I agree with you," I said, and his head snapped up to look at me. "I never looked at Carl the way I look at Finn."

His gray eyes locked with mine, and his lips turned up in the corners. "It's because you already knew you belonged to me."

"Maybe," I said, feeling this pull toward him that was impossible to avoid lately.

"Do you have that gift wrapped for me, Mr. Clark?"

"I sure do, Finny boy. Let me go grab it from the back for you."

"What did you get?" I asked as he stepped closer and wrapped one arm around my lower back, tugging me against him.

"It's a surprise."

"For me?"

"Yep. And you don't get it until Christmas morning." He nipped at my bottom lip, and I tugged his head down to kiss me.

We used to do this just to put on a show for people when we first came up with the idea to fake date. But now, I wanted to kiss this boy everywhere I went.

"Well, somebody needs to call the fire department if you two keep going like that."

We pulled back and laughed, and Finn reached for the small box wrapped in black paper with a white satin bow on it. He dropped it into the large shopping bag from The Tipsy Tea.

We said our goodbyes, and he wrapped an arm around my shoulder as we walked toward Reynolds'.

"Is that where Carl got your engagement ring?" Finn asked.

"Yeah. He bought it from Mr. Clark."

"Man, I hated that ring," he said as we waved at a few locals passing by.

I laughed. "You really didn't care for it. I remember you making that very clear from the minute I got it."

"It wasn't your style at all. It was plain."

"Some call that classic," I teased. But the ring had been very much Carl's style. A perfect princess-cut diamond solitaire on a platinum band. It was beautiful. But Finn was right: It wasn't really me at all.

"Classic, my ass. You're too good for something that basic." He tugged the door open, and country music seeped outside. Finn leaned down close to my ear. "You deserve a ring that shows how much the man you're marrying loves you. How well he knows you. A ring that when you slide it onto your finger, you know it's forever."

I sucked in a breath. My legs were frozen in place. "And what kind of ring is that, Chewy?"

"I think you'll know it when you see it." His lips grazed my ear. "I guess some things you're going to have to see to believe, Reese Murphy. But I've never been afraid of a challenge."

He was saying all the right things.

And damn, did I want to believe him.

"Merry Christmas, beautiful," his deep voice whispered from between my legs. The room was still dark, but there was some light coming from the bathroom, so Finn must have gotten up. I blinked a few times, and a loud laugh escaped my lips.

My legs were bent, and he was propped up to look at me, wearing a Santa hat on his head. "Ho ho ho. Don't say no."

"Oh my gosh. Chewy! Why are you wearing a Santa hat?"

He pushed up on his knees. The man was stark naked, wearing nothing but a red hat with white fur circling the edge with a matching white ball hanging off the tip. My gaze moved down to see his erection, ready as always.

I couldn't get enough of this man.

What was going to happen next week? I'd just go back to my sexless life?

"It's Christmas. I couldn't wait to give you your gift, but then I saw you there, sleeping like a fucking angel, and I wanted to give myself a gift." He leaned down and kissed me.

"A gift for you, huh?"

"Damn straight. Waking you up with you coming apart on my lips. There is no better gift you could give me."

We'd had sex last night, and I'd fallen asleep naked in his arms, barely able to keep my eyes open. I couldn't remember a time that I'd been this tired.

Yet I was ravenous for him.

Maybe that was why I was worn out. Maybe my blood work would just show that I'd had way too many orgasms over the last few weeks.

Exhaustion by orgasm. I was here for it.

"I'm going to miss you, Chewy." I couldn't stop myself from saying it. We'd been confessing all the things lately, and I knew that goodbye was coming soon.

"It's not goodbye, baby. It's just, *I'll see you in a few weeks*. I promise you, I'm not going anywhere."

I nodded, fighting back the lump in my throat. Why was I such a weepy mess lately?

"As much as I love the idea of your face between my legs… I need to feel *you* right now."

"Oh, yeah? How about I take you out by the tree, then? We can turn on the fireplace, and I'll let you feel every inch of me. And then we'll open presents."

He never could wait. Not when he was a kid, and not any time since.

"I like the sound of that." I yawned, and he scooped me up, wrapping the blanket around me as he strode naked through the house, carrying me like some sort of present. He set me on the couch and walked over to the fireplace and turned it on, all while giving me a wonderful view of his toned ass. It was impossible not to laugh when he turned around, wearing that ridiculous hat and looking like a Greek god with his tan, glistening, chiseled body.

He dropped down to sit, pulled the hat off his head, and unwrapped me from the blanket before settling me on his lap.

"Merry Christmas, Miney," he said as I shifted so that I was straddling him.

"It certainly is." I waggled my brows before lifting up and positioning myself just above him.

He groaned as I slid down slowly, my gaze locked with his. Pops of citrine danced in his gray eyes in the firelight flickering from behind me.

I took my time at first, sliding up and then coming back down at the same speed. And then his hands found my hips, and his lips found my hard peak, and my body surrendered.

He took control, guiding me up and down his shaft as he set the pace. Our breaths filled the air around us. My head fell back as my entire body started to tremble.

"Finn," I cried out.

He thrust into me a few more times as I exploded around him. A feral noise escaped his lips as he followed me right over the edge. We rode out every last bit of pleasure. My head fell against his chest as we both panted, waiting for our breaths to slow.

"I fucking love you, Reese Murphy," he said as his arms came around me, holding me against him.

Our hearts were both racing.

Bodies covered in a layer of sweat.

The light from the fire danced on the walls around us.

I closed my eyes and wondered what it would feel like if Finn would be mine forever.

twenty-five

• • •

Finn

I CARRIED Reese to the bathroom, with her legs wrapped around my waist as she chuckled. I set her feet down on the floor, and I cleaned myself up before grabbing a washcloth and turning on the hot water. I dropped to my knees and gently pushed her legs apart, taking my time to clean her up.

"Can I ask you something?" she said.

"Of course. We've never had secrets." It was meant to remind her because she still hadn't told me about that fuck-face coming by her office.

"Are you this way with everyone?" She shook her head when I looked up and waved her hands around. "I just mean, if you met a woman and had sex with her, do you carry her around and then clean her up? It feels so intimate to me."

Did she not get that everything about this was different?

I pushed to my feet, my hand landing on the side of her neck. "No. I've never done this with anyone. I've never woken someone up with my head between their legs or waited anxiously for them to come home. I've never had sex this many times with one person, nor have I craved it the way I do with you. Everything about this—about you—is different. Why is it so hard for you to believe that?"

"I do believe it. I just know that things are about to change. And I don't want to put expectations on anything where feelings get hurt," she said, looking away from me.

She was convinced that I would hurt her.

I understood it. My track record sucked.

"Listen, I know you have your doubts. But I've never lied to you, Miney. I wouldn't be saying these things if I didn't mean them. But I don't know that you can say the same."

Her gaze snapped in my direction. "What do you mean?"

"I mean that I don't know how you feel about Carl. About me. Not really. I know that he is still in the background, waiting for me to leave."

"I'm trying really hard, Finn, not to make you feel obligated to me." She let out a long breath. "Here's what I can tell you without any hesitation… I've never felt like this. I've never been so happy. So comfortable in my own skin, as well as with another person. I love you in a way that I never thought I could love someone. But, and it's a big but…" She paused, motioning for me to go ahead with my joke because she knew me better than anyone.

"You know I like big butts," I teased because I couldn't help myself.

"I set you up for that."

"Tell me what the big but is, Miney."

"This movie deal. Your show taking off. Distance. Travel. Temptation. Change. That's all waiting for us. And I don't want anything to ever come between our friendship, so I think we need to let things play out. See how we feel when we aren't together."

"Always so fucking practical," I said. "I'm not worried about it. You'll see. I'll prove it to you if that's what you need."

"I'm not worried about me, Finn." Her gaze was so empathetic it made my chest squeeze. Of course, she wasn't worried about herself. She was loyal as hell; we both knew it.

"I want you to be happy, and I don't ever want to hold you back in any way. I was in a relationship where I was the one who was held back. I won't be that person, not when I love everything about you just the way you are. So, let's just take this one day at a time."

"All right. I can do that." I kissed the tip of her nose. "But I want to remind you of something."

"Okay, let me hear it."

"You aren't the only one that went without sex for almost a year. Do you not find it strange that I had such a hard time when you moved to London? Your boyfriend met someone new. But your best friend"—I pointed to myself—"was lost without you, Miney. So, the distance doesn't scare me. I've already proven that when I'm not with you, I'm not looking for anyone else. I'm waiting for you. And that was before I fake dated you and got to have all the sex with my girl," I said, keeping my tone light.

Her eyes blinked several times, and she smiled. "That's impressive. I'm not going to lie."

"Just giving you something to think about." I nipped at her bottom lip and kissed her hard before pulling away. "Can I give you your presents now?"

"Yep. But can I at least put on one of your T-shirts so I'm not unwrapping gifts naked?" She chuckled.

"I can live with that. And then I'll unwrap you when we're done."

"You're insatiable." She led me out of the bathroom and down the hall, where she slipped into one of my oversized tees, and I pulled on a pair of joggers.

The sun was just coming up as we settled in front of the tree. She handed me a package, and I reached for one I'd gotten for her.

"You open first, Chewy," she said, rubbing her hands together after she handed me the package. I tore the paper off and pulled out a large scrapbook. I opened the front cover to see a photo of me in my first school play.

"It all started with *Peter Pan,*" she said, leaning her head against my shoulder as I flipped the pages. She had newspaper clippings and photographs of every single role I'd ever played. Big and small. Magazine articles that had been cut out over the years about some of the small roles I'd taken. Interviews and quotes and reviews from different sites. It was all pasted in here with photos of me scattered around. Several pictures of my family and Reese attending different events for me.

The last few pages were dedicated to *Big Sky Ranch,* with all the articles and interviews and clippings she'd pulled for the show and for me. Several photos of me on set, along with photos of the cast. The final page was the article of Reese and me, with a photo of us. The title of the article read: *Hollywood's 'IT' Boy and his Small-Town Girl.*

I looked up at her, unable to find the words at first.

I shook my head. "This is unbelievable. It must have taken so long to put this together."

"I worked on it while I was living in London last year, but I'd been collecting everything for years to make you one big scrapbook."

"I love it. Thank you. This means the world to me." There was a lump in my throat, and I shook my head. I'd become a sappy bastard with this girl.

"Well, you mean the world to me, Finn Reynolds." Her voice was all tease, but her eyes told a different story.

Reese and I were the real deal. Whether she believed it or not, I didn't know. But I knew it. She feared it. Which I understood because loving someone like this opened you up to a lot of hurt. I remember feeling that fear deep in my soul when she'd gotten sick. So I couldn't blame her for being fearful.

She'd had her share of heartache.

It was my job to show her that we were different.

"All right. Your turn."

She pushed up on her knees to face me. She closed her eyes and opened her hands. She'd always loved surprises. I placed the large white box with the black satin bow tied around it in her hands. Her eyes sprung open, and she set it on the rug in front of us and untied it. Inside, she pulled out the white cowboy hat I'd seen her looking at a few times at Buttons & Boots downtown. It was suede and the same color as her cowboy boots.

"Oh my gosh, you got me the hat! I love it. Do you know that I've been looking at this for two years before I even left for London?"

My eyes widened. "No. If I'd known that, I would have gotten it for you two years ago."

She placed it on her head and smiled at me. "I love it. Thank you so much."

"Well, if you're out there riding Millie every day, you need a good hat, right?"

"Right. I'm never taking it off."

"Good. I plan on fucking you in this hat in about thirty minutes."

She chuckled, her cheeks flushed pink. She loved when I talked to her that way. She leaned forward and grabbed another package and handed it to me.

I unwrapped the red paper covered in tiny snowmen. When I pulled the lid off the box, there were a pair of brown chaps inside, with darker brown stitching down the sides. I raised a brow as I pulled them out.

"I guess you'll be wearing these in thirty minutes, as well," she said over her laughter. "Although, I sort of imagined us riding down to the beach just before sunset, and you wearing nothing but these chaps. You know, it'll give me really easy access."

Now it was my turn to bark out a laugh. "I'll tell you what, Miney. I'll wear these chaps and nothing else, and you wear that long floral skirt you love and your cowboy hat and nothing else, and we'll ride as fast as we can down to the beach."

"Oh, yeah. Well, thanks for giving me a skirt in this fantasy."

"I don't want you getting that sweet pussy all irritated by riding bare. But I'll have that skirt up and over your head the minute I lift you off that horse and you mount this one." I waggled my brows.

"God, you have a filthy mouth, Chewy."

"You love it, don't you?" I tugged her close. "Knowing all the things that I want to do to you."

"I don't mind it." Her teeth sank into her bottom lip as a wide grin spread across her face. I kissed her hard before pulling away. We spent the next ten minutes giving one another a few more presents. She'd gotten me a nice black sweater along with a pair of jeans and a baseball cap. She also got me socks that had her face all over them and my favorite candy. I gave her the cream cashmere sweater my sisters had recommended and a few design books that I'd seen her looking at.

"All right. Last one." I reached for the small package in front of the tree, the one we'd gotten from Mr. Clark's store.

"I've been dying to know what's in here." She smiled as she studied the box.

"Open it."

She pulled the bow off and lifted the lid of the box. It was a gold charm bracelet that I'd been working on with Mr. Clark for a while now. Since she'd come back to Cottonwood Cove, actually.

She studied each of the charms. One was a heart that said Chewy on it, there was a *Harry Potter* book charm, a circular charm covered in citrine stones with the word *Miney* engraved inside. There was a gold horse charm and one of the sun, and it was engraved with the words, *Before the sunset,* as that had always been our favorite time together.

"Chewy," she whispered as she studied each charm, taking her time with them. "Before the sunset. This is my favorite."

I laughed as she continued gasping over each one. "Ahhh… it's perfect. You really are the most thoughtful guy I've ever known. And I like that nobody knows it but me."

"That's because I'm not very thoughtful to anyone else but you and my mama, of course."

"You always were a mama's boy, weren't you?" She held the bracelet against her wrist for me to clasp as she continued studying it.

"Yeah? And what am I now?"

"Well, you're a Christmas miracle, Finn Reynolds. And, at least for today, you're all mine."

I pushed to my feet and scooped her up, running down the hall with her and dropping her onto the bed.

"We've got to be at your parents' house soon, right? Gracie gets up early."

Her tongue swiped along her bottom lip, and I nearly came undone at the sight of her. "Yeah, but we've got a little time. Merry Christmas, Miney. Thanks for making this the best one yet."

She smiled, her eyes watering with emotion, as my mouth crashed into hers.

Because Reese Murphy was the best Christmas gift I'd ever received.

Christmas morning at my parents' house was pure chaos, and I wouldn't change a thing. We were heading to Reese's parents' house for presents and an early dinner later today, but we'd all always been here to watch Gracie open her gifts in the morning. She and Cage always spent Christmas Eve night at my parents' house because my mom had a lot of traditions that she liked to do with her granddaughter that Cage would never be able to pull off.

"Yeah. Mom actually sprinkles reindeer shit out in the snow," Cage said as he glanced over to see his daughter in the kitchen, helping our mom put the muffins into a basket.

"It's not reindeer shit, you dick banana. It's reindeer food," Hugh said, over his laughter.

"So reindeer eat glitter?" Maddox asked.

"They definitely don't eat glitter. They're animals, not paper cutouts," Lincoln said, shaking his head with a goofy smile on his face.

"It's just something fun for kids. She did it for all of you, and she's doing it for our granddaughter." Dad walked in on the conversation, carrying a large platter of waffles and pancakes.

"Well, if we're supposed to think they eat glitter, then one would imagine that they shit glitter, right? That's how the body works. If you eat it, you'll shit it out." Cage pressed his tongue against his cheek as if he'd just told us something that we didn't know.

"Really, genius?" I said as I shook my head. "I had no idea that's how it worked. You must be a doctor."

"My daddy is a doctor," Gracie said as she came around the corner and held her arms out for me to scoop her up. "That's why we're getting to babysit Maxine. Because she has 'ziety, right, Daddy?"

We all turned to gape at Cage.

Brinkley sauntered over, moving next to Lincoln with a wicked smile on her face. "I heard. Your daddy is now offering babysitting services to local pigs with anxiety. Who knew you were such a tender-hearted guy?"

He huffed and crossed his arms over his chest before glancing at his daughter. "Martha Langley asked me to watch

Maxine while I was standing at Cottonwood Café with Gracie. She knew I'd have to say yes. And now she's claiming that the pig can't be with anyone aside from her, Joe, or me. So now, every time they travel, I have to house this beast."

The room erupted in laughter as we all took our seats.

"I think it's nice that you're helping them out. They're a nice couple, and they love Maxine, so you're giving them peace of mind when they travel," our mother said as she winked at Gracie.

"That thing has mounted my leg twice. It's not normal. I think it's fixated on me." He scooped some fruit onto Gracie's plate and then his own.

"I'm definitely coming over to visit when she's at your house. I think it's sweet of you to watch her," Georgia said.

The rest of the conversation was about Lincoln and the fact that everyone but me would be traveling to the Super Bowl to see him play, because I'd be gone to Tokyo by then. They were the underdogs for this game, but I'd learned a long time ago to never underestimate Lincoln Hendrix.

Everyone was talking at the same time about everything under the sun, and then Brinkley turned to me and asked the million-dollar question, which made everyone stop talking and turn their attention to us.

"So, what happens when you leave, Finny? Have you two figured that out yet?"

"Well, are you finally admitting that this isn't a fake relationship?" My mother raised a brow, and my father barked out a laugh.

"It's not fake," I said with a shrug. "I don't think it ever was."

Reese's eyes doubled in size, and a slow smile spread across her face. "It never did feel fake, did it?"

"I don't think you could have given me a better Christmas gift than that," my mother said as she beamed at us.

"So, what happens next?" Cage asked. The douchedick was putting us on the spot.

Reese waved her hands around, acting like this was no big deal, but I knew she was nervous about it. "We're just taking it one day at a time. Finn's whole life is about to take off. He's leaving for Tokyo to film a major motion picture. And I'll be here, building my business."

Everyone was quiet again, and I cleared my throat. "None of that makes a difference. You'll see."

My mom's gaze locked with mine, and she tilted her head to the side.

"I don't know, Reese. I'm putting my money on Finn. That right there is a man determined." Mom pointed her fork at me and smiled before popping a piece of French toast into her mouth.

And like the saying goes… Mama knows best.

twenty-six

. . .

Reese

NEW YEAR'S Eve would go down as the most romantic night of my entire life. Finn and I bundled up and took the horses for a ride. He'd claimed he wanted to just go down to the beach before sunset like we always did, but when we'd gotten down there, he'd had a fire going with a teepee and food and hot chocolate and champagne.

I'd had to work downtown, as I'd been hired to decorate for the Cottonwood Cove New Year's Eve party. Finn and I were planning to go there later, but clearly, he had other plans that I hadn't known about.

We climbed off the horses, and I took it all in. The roaring fire crackled a few feet from us, and we tied the horses to a tree behind the teepee.

"When did you do all this?" I asked, shaking my head with surprise.

"While you were working. The guys all came down and helped me. Hugh and Lila ran by and started the fire right before we got here."

"Well, aren't you just full of surprises?" He'd always been a spontaneous, fun guy, but he was also thoughtful and romantic, and I'd loved every minute of it. But I was also a realist. Things were going to change drastically for us. We'd been playing house these last few months, and I knew we were happy in our bubble.

But our bubble was not going to be contained any longer. I needed to be prepared for whatever happened. Protect our friendship and my heart at all costs.

Finn was a dreamer. He wanted to believe nothing would change, and as much as I wanted that to be true, I knew better.

"Come on." He guided me toward the blankets in front of the fire, which sat on top of a tarp to keep dry, and the food was laid out on two platters. "Let's eat."

"Did you make charcuterie boards?" I couldn't hide the humor in my voice. These were far too fancy to be made by a man.

"Lila had them put together at the restaurant." He held up the champagne and the sparkling water, and I pointed to the water. I'd been feeling more tired than ever, and trying not to let anyone know how I was feeling was exhausting. Carl had texted me on my way home tonight that he wanted to meet me tomorrow morning to go over the results. I had a pit in my stomach because the fact that he didn't just say everything was fine meant that it wasn't.

But I wasn't about to ruin one of my last nights with Finn. He was flying out to Tokyo the day after tomorrow. I'd just have to make up an excuse to sneak away tomorrow to find out what was going on.

We clinked our glasses together. "Happy New Year, Miney."

"Happy New Year. I don't think we've ever spent a New Year's apart, now that I think of it," I said, thinking back on all the ways we'd brought in the new year.

"Yeah, last year was pretty epic being in London."

"It was. And we had a few wild ones in college," I said, and we both looked away at the same time as the memory of the year I'd been diagnosed with cancer was a memory I didn't like to think of often. Finn had given up his New Year's to sit with me during chemo treatments that year. Carl had been away at school, and Finn had always been there.

"Yep. I can't imagine ringing in the new year without you."

"Thanks for spending one of those at an oncology center with apple juice and my mom, dad, and Olivia pacing around and crying. That couldn't have been much fun for you."

"Are you kidding? My parents ended up coming and smuggling champagne in for your parents, and Liv was on the phone the entire time with that guy who desperately wanted to date her."

My head fell back in laughter as I piled some salami and cheese on a cracker and handed it to him. "Um, the fact that she sits on a call for hours telling someone that she doesn't want to date them is madness."

"That's when you decided to cut back on your classes and pursue acting, huh?" I asked, because I'd always known that as much as that time in my life changed me in many ways, it had also changed Finn.

"Yeah." He looked up, his eyes locking with mine. "I think the thought of losing you had me going out of my mind. I guess that's when I decided that life was short, and I needed to make every day count."

I nodded. "I get that. I felt the same way. Like I had this second chance, you know?"

"It's interesting, right? How people's perspectives change when things like that happen. When you're faced with the really hard stuff—the way you choose to process it." He cleared his throat, gazing off at the water.

"What do you mean?"

"Well, your first thought when you were diagnosed was the concern about how it would affect you having children. I mean, you'd mentioned that you wanted to be a mama one day over the years, but it hardly came up much before that time. Once you got sick, it moved to the forefront of your mind. But for me, I'd never thought about it much until then. But seeing you sick… Knowing that the outcome might not be what we wanted… It did something to me, Miney. I decided that moving forward, I'd make a conscious effort to never let myself love anyone the way that I loved you in that moment. Obviously, I love my family, and I can't take away the people that I already loved. But the thought of kids or loving even more people—I didn't want to ever feel that way again. And then a few years later, my dad got sick. Fuck. It's much easier to keep things casual, you know?"

"Loving people always comes with risk, Chewy." I swiped at the tear rolling down my cheek. "That shouldn't stop you from living. From loving."

"Yeah. Well, I think some loves are impossible to run from." He winked.

"Thanks for being there with me every step of the way." I tried hard to swallow the enormous lump in my throat.

"Always. And we made the best out of a tough situation, didn't we?"

"We sure did. We were playing that Hollywood game where we picked names out of a cup and had to describe them to one another. Even though I swear you let me win because you missed too many easy ones."

"Please. Do I strike you as a guy who would give a win away?"

Not to anyone else, but to me, yes.

"I think you would always give me the win." I reached for his hand and squeezed it.

This mix of fear and hope weighed heavy on my heart.

And it wasn't fear of all the things that I should be nervous about at the moment. That my test results could possibly mean the cancer was back.

That I would need to do rounds of chemo again.

Another year of pure hell.

No. My fear was that I couldn't have this fairy tale that we were currently living. That it wouldn't last.

That he'd leave, and we'd go back to just being friends again.

That nothing else would ever measure up to this.

To us.

"Well, since we're talking about things, there is another theory that has dawned on me over these last few months—hell, maybe over the last year since you've been gone."

"What's that?" I asked as I pulled off my hat because the heat from the fire was warming me up. Or maybe it was the heat from this man.

"Maybe the real reason that I've never had a serious relationship is because the only girl I'd ever wanted was always taken. We'd friend-zoned one another, and I never found anyone that compared to you. But these last few months, Miney, they've changed me."

My bottom lip quivered. "Finn, you can't say things like that to me."

He tugged me closer. "It's the truth."

"Please don't make promises that you might not be able to keep," I said as a tear ran down my face. "I don't want to hope for something that could change the minute you're gone. I couldn't take it, okay?"

"What are you so afraid of?" he asked, his voice harder now than I'd ever heard it.

"I thought my heart had broken when Carl and I ended, but I was wrong. It was beating just fine after everything went down. But this, you and me…" I motioned my hand between us. "This would break me."

I shook my head and used the back of my hand to swipe at my tears.

"You've got to trust me, Reese. I'd never hurt you."

"I know that. That's part of what scares me. You'd suffer

because you were afraid to hurt me. That's why I just want you to go and see how you feel. We've been in this bubble together for the last few months, but that's not realistic. You need to be out there, doing your thing, Finn. I'll be here. I'm not going anywhere."

The thought of ever being an obligation to this man would be the worst thing that could ever happen to me.

But the thought of being the one he wanted, the way that I wanted him, would be the best thing that could ever happen to me.

And I was afraid to hope for that because I'd seen the other side when things don't work out. When you're twenty years old and sitting at an oncology center on New Year's Eve, getting a chemo treatment.

Life wasn't always fair. So, the best you could do was prepare yourself for what might be coming.

"Why is it so hard to believe that you're it for me?" He ran the pad of his calloused thumb over my bottom lip.

"I don't know. Maybe things feel too good right now. Maybe being ridiculously happy terrifies me." I sniffed.

"You'll see." He smiled that charming grin that stole the air from my lungs. "But I still think you should stay at my house when I leave. I like the idea of you being there."

"I'll tell you what," I said before taking a long pull of my bubbly water. "If you come back from Tokyo and you still feel like this after that time apart, I'll move back in."

"Deal. Don't unpack."

"So cocky," I said as he handed me another cracker with jam and cheese on this one, and I took a bite and groaned. "This is so good."

"You can't talk about my cock and then groan and say that the cracker is good." His tongue swiped back and forth along his bottom lip.

"I said you were *cocky*." I chuckled.

"I heard you. I'll show you cocky later when I put those

chaps on for you and let you ride me in nothing but your cowboy hat and boots."

"Don't threaten me with a good time," I teased.

"I never would." He popped a raspberry into his mouth. "So, tell me about the business. It's growing quicker than you expected. Do you think you should bring on some help?"

I thought it over. "Yeah, at some point. But the beginning is all about grinding, right? I'm starting a business. I need to put everything I make back into it for right now."

"Miney. Why is taking help so hard for you? Let me invest in your business. Let me help you get things going."

"You already did. You bought a building, Finn. I think you've gone above and beyond."

"Yet you keep trying to pay rent when we already had a deal to wait a year."

"That's sort of a normal business expense." I laughed. "I've got this. I promise."

"I don't like seeing you work so hard. You're running yourself into the ground."

"I'm young. You work long hours when you're on set."

He nodded. But I saw the look in his eyes. He was worried I'd get sick again. There was always that nagging worry in the back of everyone's minds, mine included.

"I'm fine. I promise. And I love you for caring so much."

"Well, I love you, and that's why I care so much."

"You always have to one-up me with the fancy words, don't you?"

"Whatever it takes to impress my girl," he said, and butterflies fluttered in my belly.

"You've already impressed me. How are you feeling about this movie? About being gone?"

"I feel okay about it. I wish you could come with me, but I know you've got your own dreams to chase here, and I wouldn't ask you to give that up. So, I'll put my head down and go work hard for a few weeks, and then come home and show you what you've been missing."

"I will miss you, Chewy. I used to feel so guilty when I was in London because you were the person I missed the most."

"Yeah? That year was an eye-opener for me, too. It's the longest we'd ever been apart. And I, uh…" He paused and looked over at the fire, and I waited. My heart raced a little, wondering what he was going to say. "I didn't do so well, Miney. I didn't sleep well on the days that we didn't speak."

"I felt the same. Like I'd lost a limb."

I pulled off my coat because I was either burning up from this fire or from the man beside me. His coat had been off for a while because Finn was never cold. He loved the colder temperatures and the snow and the mountains. I slid over toward him, and he pulled me onto his lap.

"Well, we can't have that, can we? I think we have something pretty special." He kissed my cheek.

"What we have is nothing I've ever experienced with anyone else."

"Good. I want to keep it that way." His fingers were in my hair, and he tipped my head back and kissed me. I melded against his body as his tongue found mine. And I wished I could freeze time and stay right here forever.

Finn had left to go see his brothers, and I'd texted Carl and told him I'd meet him at Cup of Cove for a quick coffee. I didn't mention the blood work to Finn because he'd just worry that I was sick. He was leaving in the morning, and that was the last thing he should be thinking about.

I made my way to the table near the entrance when I saw Carl waving at me. It was weird that just a few months ago, I thought this man was the love of my life, and now I just felt —nothing.

Sure, we had a history, and I loved him in a friendship sort of way. Maybe that was the way I had always loved him, but I just didn't know any different before now.

"Hey," he said, and the look on his face had my stomach dropping. What could he have found out? The blood work was just to rule out anything else, right? Or was there something there that made it obvious something was wrong? "I got you a hot chocolate."

I sat in the chair across from him. "Thank you. You don't look so well. Did the blood work show something?"

My heart was racing as he studied me.

"I don't know, Reese. I guess it depends if you wanted to get pregnant."

Pregnant?

Pregnant.

I couldn't speak.

Couldn't think.

I was prepared for him to say that I had mono.

Strep throat.

An immune disorder.

Or some sort of infection.

A baby?

A beautiful baby.

Joy coursed through my veins just before this unsettling feeling spread through my body.

If I was afraid of making Finn feel trapped before, I'd just forced him into a corner in the worst way. Now he'd feel obligated to me.

My bottom lip quivered first before I let the tears fall.

This was what I'd always wanted.

But Finn had this exciting career starting, and I was freaking pregnant?

He'd never had a serious relationship, and now he was

tied to one that hadn't even started out as real for the rest of his life.

He'd never forgive me.

It was too soon.

Carl grabbed my hands. "Is this not good news?"

Why did he sound so pleased?

Had the sound of his voice always irritated me?

"It's not that. Of course, it's not that. I'm thrilled. A part of me wondered if I'd ever be able to get pregnant. It's just, Finn and I are so new to dating, and I don't know if he's ready for all of this. He's leaving for Tokyo tomorrow. I-I just don't know what he'll think."

"I'm here for you, Reese. I'd raise this baby with you if you asked me to."

What?

That made me cry harder.

This was not how I ever imagined finding out I was pregnant would be. My ex-boyfriend delivering the news and then offering to raise the baby with me because I wasn't certain that the man I loved would be ready for all of this.

"I'm in love with him, Carl." I whimpered, and he held my hands from across the table, and I saw the tears streaming down his face.

My God, I'd made a mess of everything.

"Why are you crying?" I asked as I tried to pull myself together.

"Because I just realized right now that I've lost you forever."

I pulled my hands away to swipe at my face, and I shook my head. "I'm sorry. I'm sorry that you had to come here and tell me this. I'm sorry that I'm falling apart in front of you. This is just all wrong for so many reasons."

"Don't be silly. I would do anything for you." He held his hands up and sniffed. "In a friendship type of way. I get it. Your heart belongs to him now. Hell, it probably always did. I just forced the situation by ending things with you. I guess it gave you the time to actually explore those feelings."

"I guess so." I nodded, reaching for the napkin and dabbing at my eyes.

"Well, I mean, at least we know you're not sick. You just have a baby in your belly, which is why you're so tired. You've always wanted to be a mom. And it sounds like you want to be with Finn, so maybe this isn't so bad."

"It's not that it's bad, Carl. Of course, I want to be a mom, and the idea of having a baby with Finn is amazing—" I looked away because this wasn't fair to be talking about this with my ex-boyfriend, who was suddenly willing to raise another man's baby with me after rejecting me for taking the job of my dreams. "It makes me happy to think about, but the timing is tough because we're still figuring things out, you know?"

"Well, if it helps, I told you that I see the way he looks at you. Hell, I've always seen it. I was trying everything I could not to see it, long before you two got together. He's in love with you, Reesey. I think he always has been."

I nodded. "I know that he loves me. I don't doubt that."

"Then what is it? Just tell him."

"I don't want him to be with me for the wrong reasons, Carl. So, I'm asking you as a favor, as a man that I consider my friend after all the years we've been together. Please don't tell anyone. I want Finn to know first, but I'm not ready to tell him. He needs to go on this trip with a clear mind. And we'll see how he feels once we've spent some time apart."

"Of course. I won't say a word. And I'm here if you need me."

"Thank you so much," I said as I pushed to my feet and swiped at my face one last time.

He stood and hugged me. "You're going to be just fine."

"I will be. Thank you so much for everything. I'll see you soon."

I had to pull myself together before I went home.

I wasn't ready to tell Finn what was going on.

Because I knew Finn. He'd cancel the trip. He'd worry about me being alone.

I needed to give him this time to make sure that he came back to me because he missed me, not because we were having a child together.

We were having this baby, but I needed to know that he loved me either way.

The way I wanted to be loved.

The way I needed to be loved.

twenty-seven

. . .

Finn

I WAS FUCKING FUMING. I'd left Cage's house after saying goodbye to everyone, and I drove through downtown and saw Reese's car parked outside of Cup of Cove. I was going to surprise her and stop in, but the fucking joke was on me.

I'd parked my car and didn't even make it across the street because there she was, right in front of the window, holding hands and crying with Carl fucking Barley. After everything we'd talked about, this was where she went on my last day home?

I got in my truck and told Siri to call Cage. I could have called Hugh, but I didn't want someone talking sense into me. I wanted someone that would be pissed off right along with me.

"Miss me already?" he said over Bluetooth.

"Far from it. I saw Reese's car parked at Cup of Cove and was going to go grab a coffee and surprise her, but she was sitting at a table with Dr. fucking Douche and crying. I can't fucking believe this, man."

He was quiet for a moment, which was very out of character.

"Maybe it was closure?"

"They've had closure. She's been with me for months. I don't know what the fuck to think. I'm leaving. She's worried about me not being able to handle the distance, and she's holding hands and crying with that dicksack while I'm still here? What's she going to do when I'm gone?"

"Okay, first off, you don't know what it was about."

"Does it fucking matter?" My voice boomed through the cab of my truck. "She didn't tell me she was going. She's not being honest, so something must be going on."

"You know, you could just ask her before you get all worked up. This is fucking Reese, brother. She's your best friend, and you're both clearly in love with one other. She wouldn't be doing anything behind your back."

"Yeah? Well, why didn't she tell me about him coming by her office the other day? Why didn't she tell me that she was meeting him today?"

"Ummm… maybe because you'd react like a fucking lunatic. You clearly hate the guy, and she has a history with him. Listen, I've done this shit before where I let my pride get in the way." He cleared his throat. "Don't do that. Just fucking talk to her."

"Fuck, dude. I didn't call you to be the voice of reason. I called you because you're the cynical, irrational, bitter sibling."

"Sorry to disappoint. It's Reese. I think she deserves a chance to tell you what's going on."

I nodded, even though he couldn't see me. "Fine. I'll give her a chance to tell me where she was before I lose my shit."

"That's not exactly what I was saying you should do."

"It's the most I can do right now. I'm pissed. She's never lied to me. I've poured my fucking heart out to her these last few days, man. And she's doubting me? I'm not the one sneaking around with my ex."

"You don't have an ex."

"Fuck you," I growled.

He laughed. "All right, take it down a notch. This is not you. You don't get all worked up and out of control. You're Finn fucking Reynolds. Come on, brother. Get it together."

I pulled into my driveway and stared out at the barn, white flakes falling from the sky. I was leaving tomorrow for Tokyo. This role was the biggest thing to ever happen to me in my career after the success of *Big Sky Ranch*. Things were taking off for me, and I should be fucking happy. But my stomach was twisted up over all of this.

I felt like a lovesick puppy.

This was bullshit.

"Got it. I'll be fine. I'm going to go check on the horses, and I'll call you when I get to Tokyo."

"You call me before if you need me, okay?"

"Don't get sappy. It doesn't suit you."

He barked out a laugh. "Good. Fuck off. Call me when you call me. Maybe I'll answer. Better?"

"Much. I'll talk to you later."

I climbed out of the truck and made my way into the barn. Silas was there, and he'd just finished raking the stalls.

"Hey, you're off tomorrow, right?" he asked.

"Yep. You've got my number. Text me if you have any issues. But you've got Cage's number if there is any sort of medical emergency and Hugh's number for anything else."

"I do. And Miss Reese told me she'll be taking them for a run daily just like she always does. But I'll run them, as well, if needed."

I nodded. Reese would be up here every day, but she wouldn't stay at the house. Why the fuck not? My mind was racing with thoughts I didn't want to even consider. Was she going back to him? Did she just not want to tell me?

"Sounds good. Thanks for taking care of everything."

"Always. Have a safe trip. I'm going to head home." He clapped me on the shoulder before walking out. I heard tires roll up on the gravel driveway, and I turned to see Reese getting out of her car and greeting Silas with a hug.

She waved at me, but I shoved my hands into my pockets as she walked toward me.

Light brown hair bouncing around her shoulders, dark jeans and cowboy boots, and her black down winter coat zipped all the way up. Her lips were turned up in the corners until she got closer and took me in. Her face straightened as she studied me.

"Hey. What's wrong?"

"Nothing. Where were you?"

"Where was I?"

"Did I stutter? Where the fuck were you?" So maybe I wasn't keeping calm the way I'd planned, but this was the best I could do.

Her eyes widened. "What's with the attitude, Chewy?"

"Why are you avoiding the motherfucking question? Where. The fuck. Were. You?"

The hurt on her face was impossible to miss. My gaze locked with her pretty green eyes, and I didn't miss the bit of puffiness beneath them. But I already knew she'd been crying, didn't I?

Because she'd been cozied up to her ex-boyfriend, crying in a coffee shop twenty minutes ago.

"I don't know what's going on with you, but I'm not going to be spoken to like that." She turned on her heels and stormed in the opposite direction.

"Yeah, you don't like answering questions that don't suit you, do you?" I shouted at her.

She whipped around. "I don't like answering questions when someone is demanding I tell them where I was. You're not my boss, Finn. I don't work for you."

"I'm more than aware I'm not your boss. I'm just your best friend, right? And your fuckboy? But nothing more."

Her shoulders sagged, and a tear streaked down her

cheek. "You're much more than that, and you know it."

I stepped toward her, softening my tone. "Tell me where you were."

"You're making this a bigger deal than it is." She used the back of her hand to swipe at the falling tears. "I met Carl at Cup of Cove. We just had some last-minute work things to talk about. For his office design."

She couldn't look at me, so I knew she was lying.

"So why keep that a secret? Why keep the fact that he stopped by the other day a secret? Since when do you lie to me, Reese?"

Her mouth fell open, and she shook her head. "It's not what you think, Finn. You've got to trust me."

"Like you trust me? Hell, you don't believe that I'm all in. That I can be faithful to you. You won't even discuss the idea of it until I come back. Yet, you want me to trust you?"

"It's not that I don't trust you." She moved toward me, reaching for my hand and pressing my palm to her cheek. "I don't want to make you promise something that you can't deliver. I want you to be happy because I love you."

"I don't know about that, Miney. I think you're the one who isn't sure about this. You've got someone lined up, waiting for me to leave town, don't you? You're already packed and ready to go. You've got one foot out the door, and I haven't even left town. I'm guessing you can't wait for me to leave so you can jump back into the sack with that piece of shit."

She dropped my hand and stepped back, tears streaming down her face. "If you think that, then you don't know me at all."

"Maybe I don't."

"Wow. Maybe this is just your way of getting out of this before you leave, huh? You can head to Tokyo guilt-free and fuck whoever you want."

"Sure. It's what you thought I'd do anyway, right? Just

living up to your expectations."

She placed her hand on her heart, and a sob escaped her lips. I wanted to rush her and wrap my arms around her, but I didn't. I couldn't. She didn't want me, and that hurt like hell.

"I'm going to head to the rental house early. I think we could both use some space right now."

"You sure you aren't going to Carl's? You may as well just tell me now. It's a small town, remember? Word travels. I'll hear about it."

She let out a long breath. "Have a safe trip, Chewy. Whether you believe it or not, I love you."

She turned around and made her way into the house. I walked out to the truck and climbed back in. I threw it in reverse and sped down the driveway. I needed to get out of here.

Couldn't believe this shit was happening.

This was fucking Reese.

I knew her better than I knew myself.

And she'd fucking ripped my heart from my chest.

I made my way to Reynolds', and Lila told me Hugh was down in his office.

"Hey," I said, closing the door before dropping into the chair across from his desk.

"What happened? You look like shit."

I spent the next thirty minutes filling him in on all of it. Reese being with Carl. Her not wanting to tell me what was going on. The horrible things I'd said to her. And the things she'd said back.

He sat back in his chair, not saying a word. He just listened.

"You want my opinion, or do you want me to just take your side?" he finally said, intertwining his fingers as he leaned forward on his desk.

"Both."

"Well, I'll always have your back, you know that. But this

is not some woman that you don't know, brother. This is Reese. You've been best friends since fucking birth. She wouldn't lie to you if she were sleeping with Carl. It's not who she is. You know that. I don't believe there's anything going on there, and I think you overreacted."

"So why not tell me that she met with him? Why lie about it?"

He blew out a breath and shrugged. "She didn't lie. She just didn't offer it up. There could be a lot of reasons why, but none of those are because she's playing you. That girl is madly in love with you. If she wanted to get back together with Carl, she'd never have crossed the line with you. I don't think she knew it at the time, but I'm guessing something inside her knew it. Just like something inside you knew it was right."

"Yet she doesn't think I'm capable of having a relationship with her. She insists that I'll go away, and she won't even stay at the house because she has so little faith in me."

"Is that really what you think, Finny?"

I scrubbed a hand down my face. "I don't know what I fucking think. I'm going out of my mind over this girl. I can't think straight."

He chuckled this annoying, cocky sound, and I wanted to dive over the desk and tackle him. He saw the look on my face and held up a hand. "There you go again, overreacting. I'm not laughing at you. I'm laughing because you've got it bad. I know it. You know it. But she doesn't know it yet, brother. And it's fair of her to be cautious."

"What? I thought you were on my side."

"I am. Always. But, Finn, come on, man. You've never had a relationship that lasted longer than a few drinks and a fun weekend. She's scared to death. You're a fucking movie star. You've always had women chasing after you. She lives here. She wants the fairy tale, brother. The picket fence and the kids and the whole nine yards. Of course, she's fucking nervous. I can't really blame her. She isn't saying that she's going to date anyone or run back to her ex. What did she actually say? Be honest. What did she ask you to do?"

I leaned back in my chair and thought it over. "She didn't want us to make any decisions before I left about—us. She told me to go to Tokyo and have the time of my life, and if I missed her the way she would miss me, she'd move back into the house when I got home next month. She said she didn't want me to go there feeling pressure with her living at my house, and that if I came back and didn't feel the same way, we'd go back to being best friends, or some shit like that."

"You dumb fucker." He threw his hands in the air. "She's worried about you. She doesn't want you to feel trapped. But that sure as shit doesn't mean she doesn't want you to come back and want the same things she wants. That's why she said she'd move back in with you if you still felt the same."

"Of course, I'll feel the same. She's driving me fucking crazy. She's all I think about."

"She doesn't want to hear it, Finn. She wants you to show her. Go to Tokyo. Find a way to show her that you miss her every fucking day. Show her, for fuck's sake. It's not a lot to ask. She's giving you a pass to figure it out. She already knows what she wants. She wants to make sure that you want the same fucking thing. Because she loves you enough to let you go if you don't."

"Goddamn it. Should I go to the rental house and bring her home with me? Try to talk to her?"

He laughed so loud that it bellowed around the small office. "I think you've gone caveman one too many times already. Demanding her to come home with you right now will not go over well."

"How do you know?"

"Because I'm married to a woman, and we have two sisters, and I've always been more in tune with this stuff." He winked with that cocky grin on his face.

"Please. You fucked up plenty of times with Lila." I crossed my arms over my chest.

"I did. And I finally listened to what she needed from me. Stop talking. Stop demanding. She told you what she wanted. Just trust her and give it to her."

"Ugh," I groaned, running my hands through my hair. "I'm not good at this shit, am I?"

"No. But you've got the right girl. She'll wait for you. Send her a text now and tell her you're sorry. That you overreacted. That you're going to respect her space and miss her every day you're gone. That you'll be back, and you can't wait to move her back in. Can you do that?"

"I can do that. Do you think it's too late? Did I fuck everything up?"

I pulled out my phone and typed out the text in my own words.

"If it were anyone else, I'd be worried. But this is Reese, and I know how much she loves you. She's as loyal as they come, brother. Just do what she asked you to do and stop having a temper tantrum."

"So where is the part where you're actually on my side?"

He pushed to his feet. "This is me being on your side. I'm helping you fix things with the girl you love. Now, let's go grab some beers and take them to your place, and I'll help you pack up."

"You're just afraid I'll pull some more caveman shit and go over to that house and throw her over my shoulder and bring her home."

"Maybe, but you're smarter than that. You know what you need to do. Now you just need to do it."

I nodded and followed him up the stairs and through the restaurant.

He was right.

I was going to do whatever it took to show her I was all in.

And that was going to start today.

twenty-eight

. . .

Reese

I'D SPENT the night at my parents' house instead of going to the rental house. I'd cried hard to my sister, thankful she was home from her interview in the city.

I'd filled her in on our fight, and she'd grilled me about why I hadn't told him I was meeting with Carl. I couldn't tell her the reason either. Because Finn deserved to be told the news that I was pregnant first, whether we were together or not.

But not yet.

I wanted him to go have this experience and work on this movie without worrying about me. Which I knew he would do the minute he found out I was pregnant.

But the things he'd said to me had been so hurtful. Liv had insisted that he was just lashing out because he thought I didn't want him anymore.

How could he think that?

She'd even come back in when she'd heard my muffled cries through the walls, and she'd climbed into bed with me.

His text made me feel a little better, but I hated the way things ended. He'd apologized, insisting he would be back and that he wanted me and only me, and I was going to hold on to that.

Maybe right now, space was what we both needed.

I had a lot on my mind. I was going to be a mama.

It was something I'd always wanted, but this wasn't how I saw it happening. I had a new business that required a lot of time and energy, and I was moving some of my things into Georgia and Maddox's rental house today. My parents were offended that I wasn't staying with them, but Liv had quickly jumped on board and said she'd be over there often, too, and that it was important for adults to have their own place.

I made my way into the kitchen and poured myself a cup of water when I was dying for coffee. But now that I knew that I was pregnant, I needed to find out what things I could and couldn't have. I had a little human growing inside me to care for now.

A lump formed in my throat because I was overcome with how happy I was carrying a baby. A baby that was part me and part Chewy.

In my wildest dreams, I'd never allowed myself to even think about that as a possibility up until a few weeks ago. But even then, I was afraid to think about it. To hope for it.

"No coffee?" my mom asked as she walked in with a stack of clean dish towels from the laundry room.

"Nope. I'm trying to cut out the caffeine because I've just been drinking it too often."

She raised a brow. "I thought you said you can't function without a cup first thing in the morning?"

"Yeah, well, that was before I started this health kick."

"Did someone say health kick? Mom says I need to eat healthier," my father said as he walked in and made his way over to the coffeepot.

I envied him. But until I did my research, I'd abstain.

"I said that you can't be eating all that candy every night." My mom chuckled and swatted him with a towel.

They were so cute. Ridiculously in love. They couldn't stand to be away from one another for long, and I'd always admired their relationship.

The family they'd created together.

"You're right." My father wrapped his arms around her from behind. "I've got all the sweetness I need right here."

Swoon.

"Oh, man." Liv made a gagging, vomiting sound and shook her head as she walked through the kitchen. "It's too early for all that. Plus, as your offspring, we don't want to see that. It's too much. Get into a fight or something. Eat some pistachios, Dad. The way you chew them always annoys Mom."

I fell forward with a laugh and shook my head. "Leave them alone. They're sweet together."

"If a man told me I was all the sweetness he needed, I would junk-punch him. I don't need to be anyone's sweetness. Sweeten your own life, dude. Not you, Dad, but if another man said it to me, I'd be disgusted."

My dad rolled his eyes. "I wouldn't worry about anyone saying that to you."

My mom and I both chuckled, and Liv rolled her eyes.

I glanced down at my phone to see a text.

CHEWY

I'm heading to Tokyo. Was scrolling through my phone and found this photo of the first time we flew on a plane together. Remember the summer our families went to Maui? I miss you already, Miney.

A picture of me and Finn on an airplane, when we were ten years old, came through. He was wearing a Hawaiian shirt with a baseball cap and a big grin. I had on a white summer dress, two braids in my hair, and I was rocking quite the gap between my front teeth.

"What are you looking at?" My dad took the seat beside me and glanced down at the phone.

I handed it over, and my mom and sister both took turns looking.

"That was such a fun trip. Didn't Cage get stung by a jellyfish?" my father asked.

"Oh, yes, he did. And he did not take it well. He had an epic meltdown," Olivia said over her laughter.

"Yes. Finn was chasing him around, telling him he needed to pee on his foot," my mother said with a big smile on her face. "So, he's off to Tokyo. What happens after that with you two?"

"Inquiring minds want to know," my sister said, waggling her brows.

"We're taking it one day at a time. I'm going to move my clothes over to the rental house today and get settled. Georgie said it's fully equipped. They just use it now for family and friends that are visiting, but they agreed to let me rent it for as long as I need it."

"It's silly to pay for a place when you can live here for free." Dad sipped his coffee.

I wasn't going to go down this road again.

"I love you guys, but I'm twenty-nine years old, and I need my own place. Plus, they gave me the same deal they gave Brinkley, which is a dollar a month, and I pay the utilities." I shook my head and laughed.

There wasn't much else to say.

I'm also having a baby that'll be here in less than nine months.

I had no idea how far along I was, so I definitely needed to go see someone and start planning for the future.

"Well, I'll grab my truck and help you move your things over," my father said as he pushed to stand and leaned over to kiss my cheek.

"Moving is so not my thing." Olivia shivered dramatically. "I've got to prep for an interview, anyway."

"I hardly have that much to move over. I didn't bring a ton to Finn's house."

My chest squeezed at the mention of his name. It was the first day in a while that I didn't wake up to his handsome face. To his smile. To taking a ride down to the water right after we got up and moving.

"You're leaving Millie over there?" my mom asked. She'd been unusually quiet since I'd come home last night, which meant she was stewing, trying not to fire off rapid questions and have me shut her down. Or maybe Alana had told her Finn and I were taking a break. I wasn't offering anything up because I wasn't totally sure what would happen over the next few weeks.

"Yep. I'll go ride her every day before work. I'm going to head over there now and take her out. I'll meet you there in an hour?" I asked my father.

"I'll be there, sweetheart."

I grabbed my keys and my coat and made my way out to my car. I drove around the corner and pulled over, letting the tears fall again.

I cried for all that was unknown about my future.

I cried because I missed Finn.

I cried because I'd made a real mess of everything.

I cried because it crushed me that he thought I'd go back to Carl.

I cried because I was having a baby with the man I loved, and I didn't know how to tell him.

And then I reached into my purse and pulled out some tissue and cleaned myself up.

You've got this.

One week had passed, and it felt like an eternity. But every single day, I received a text message the minute I opened my eyes, and they continued to come in throughout the day.

Every single day, there was a photo of me and Finn at different stages of our lives.

Together.

Always together.

I hearted each of the texts as they came in, but I hadn't responded. I wanted to give him his time to figure out what he wanted. I wasn't going to tell him how much I missed him right now. How I cried myself to sleep every night. How my body ached for him. How I missed his touch. His laugh. His smile. Hell, I missed the way he smelled.

How twisted was that?

I sat at my desk and scrolled through all the photos and the texts that had come through this week.

Monday

CHEWY

I miss your face.

CHEWY

I dreamed about you last night. About your body and the little sounds you make when you're pressed against me, sleeping.

A photo came through of us on the first day of kindergarten. We were holding hands, and my head was tipped back in laughter, and he was just smiling at me. It was one of my favorite pictures of us. I printed it on my little phone printer and set it on my nightstand with the photo that he'd sent of us on the airplane.

CHEWY

The food is good here, but it's a little spicy. I miss taking the horses out with you. I think of you every night before the sun sets. It's our time. Always has been, always will be.

CHEWY

It doesn't matter where I am. I think of you nonstop.

CHEWY

I got hit on tonight, and I let her know I was practically married. Because, in a sense, I am. You have my heart, and you always will.

He sent a selfie of him holding up his phone with the vibrant city behind him and his handsome face smiling at me. I printed it and slept with it clutched to my chest.

Desperate times call for desperate measures.

Monday evening, there'd been a knock on my door and an enormous vase filled with yellow daffodils and yellow roses was handed to me.

The card read:

There are no citrine flowers, so this is the best I can do. There are 29 daffodils and 29 roses (pending Janine at Cottonwood Blooms counted correctly). One of each flower for every year that I've been lucky enough to call you my best friend. You are that and so much more. I will love you forever, Miney.

Xo, Chewy

Tuesday

CHEWY

I ate some sort of porridge this morning and got a bad case of the shits on set. Not a good look. I was running to the shitter between scenes. <poop emoji> <head exploding emoji> <fire emoji>

CHEWY

It's beautiful here. I wish you were with me. There is no one that I want by my side other than you. I ache for you, Miney.

CHEWY

I'm glad that you keep hearting these texts, so I'll keep them coming. But I wouldn't mind hearing from you either. A sign of life. Can you throw me a bone?

I'd laughed at that. And of course, I responded.

I'm giving you time to figure things out. But I miss you so much, Chewy. I'm here, and I'll continue to be here. Always.

CHEWY

That's all I needed to hear. I'll keep blowing up your phone because you're all I think about.

CHEWY

Well, I think about your <cat emoji> often, too. About your perfect tits and your gorgeous legs and the way I wish they were wrapped around me.

Only Finn could be comfortable sexting me from Tokyo in a one-sided conversation.

CHEWY

Just answer me with one word. Do you think about me and touch yourself?

Yes. No more questions. Keep the texts coming and go be a movie star.

CHEWY

That's easy. I'm lying in bed right now, and I'm thinking about you. Thinking about the sound of your laugh. Do you know it's my favorite sound in the world?

My chest squeezed at his words. He'd sent a few more photos on Tuesday. One of us on Halloween with me dressed as Hermione and Finn dressed as Chewbacca. We were sitting at his parents' kitchen table with all our candy between us. I smiled at the memory. He'd always take all the Snickers, and I'd go for the jelly beans. I printed that one, along with the other one he'd sent of us in high school, going to homecoming our junior year. We'd gone to every school dance together up until our senior year, when I started dating Carl, and Finn got to bless a few of the girls in our class that had been dying to go with him to a dance. My pile of pictures was growing, and I'd stopped at the craft store after work on Tuesday to get a new scrapbook to keep them all in.

I'd arrived home to find a package on my doorstep. When I'd opened it up, there was a box inside called *the pleasure pleaser*, and I'd opened it up to find a hot pink vibrator. I'd laughed so hard, and when I'd pulled out the card inside, it read:

This will hold you over until I get home. Twenty-eight more days, Miney. I hope you still want to move back in with me, even though I was a stubborn ass. I will love you for the rest of my life, just like I always have.

Wednesday

CHEWY

Damn. I'm not sleeping well without you. It's not the kind of lonely where I want to find someone else to keep me company because it's the kind of lonely where I crave only one person. Only you can make me whole. I don't want anyone but you.

That had caused me to crack. I'd sat at my desk and sobbed when I'd read it. I couldn't not respond.

I feel that same kind of lonely. I only want you. Twenty-seven days, Chewy. I'll see you soon. I love you.

CHEWY

Work is hard. The hours are long, but the director is great. My costar, Melanie Starwood, has three kids. They are all on set. Her husband is here, too. They're really great. This can be a family business, Miney. People make it work. I've never craved Hollywood. I craved the creativity of acting. I miss our life in Cottonwood Cove, but I thrive on set. No reason we can't have both. Together. I want that. We can hire someone to help you at work so you can travel with me when you want to, and when I'm not filming, we'll be home. I see it, Reese. I see it all with you.

He sent me a photo of him with Melanie's three kids. Two boys and a little girl. They were all laughing in the photo and looking at Finn like he was their favorite person. I knew that look well because he was my favorite person. I rubbed my belly and squeezed my eyes shut. I already loved this little baby so much, and I knew that Finn would, too.

I see it, too. Go make some magic, Finn Reynolds.

THURSDAY
CHEWY

I brought that shirt of mine that you liked to wear around the house. It smells like you. Violet and amber. I sleep with it on my pillow every night. That's not creepy, is it?

Not creepy at all. I sleep in your favorite flannel every night. I stole it the night I left. I pretend that you're with me when I fall asleep.

At lunchtime, Mrs. Runither had walked in carrying a bag of food. She'd told me that Finn had called from Tokyo and said he knew I was working too much and that it was cold outside, and I needed mac and cheese and some cornbread. I'd fought back tears because I'd been exhausted and hungry but hadn't stopped to go grab lunch. I swear that man knew me better than I knew myself.

CHEWY

> Today, I had to shoot a solo shower scene. Nothing quite like being practically nude (while covering my dick with some sort of sling, XL of course, <winky face emoji>) and letting them film my ass in front of the entire camera crew. I asked Melanie's husband, Tony, to snap a photo on his phone of my ass so I could send it to you. He said to tell you, "It's a fine ass, and you should know that this ass only belongs to you."

He sent said photo of his chiseled ass, along with a selfie of him and Tony giving me a thumbs-up. I'd printed it up and taped it right into the scrapbook.

Today was Friday, and he'd sent a photo of him and me at the London Bridge when he'd come to visit. He said it was his favorite because the time we'd spent apart that year had been the most difficult in his life, and seeing me again had been the happiest. I had a lump in my throat as I'd read his words. Being away from Finn had been horrible for me, too. I'd missed him more than anyone. The only time I'd had a breakdown about Carl was when I'd learned he was dating someone else. But I'd come to realize that it had never been about missing him. It had been more about feeling rejected.

But I'd always missed Finn when we weren't together. It was a deep longing. An ache that could only be filled with him.

I pushed to stand because today I had my first appointment with Dr. Judy Green. She'd been my gynecologist since I'd been in my early twenties, and I'd last seen her when I'd asked to go on the pill. Today's meeting would be very different. I locked up the office and drove the short distance over to see her.

I spent the next hour peeing in a cup, getting weighed and measured, and she even used a sonogram to show me the baby's heartbeat. My guess was that I'd gotten pregnant the night Finn's condom broke, as I was about two months along. She told me everything looked great, and I was healthy, and the baby was healthy, as well.

I asked for a copy of the ultrasound so I could share it with Finn when he got home. It felt strange keeping such a big secret to myself right now. But I knew if I told him what was going on, he'd be on the next plane home. It was who he was.

Why had I doubted that?

Doubted that he really loved me the way that I loved him.

I'd been unfair to him. Judging him for never having a relationship and questioning if he was capable. I'd had a relationship with one man for most of my adult life, even agreeing to marry him—only now realizing I was never happy with him.

I hadn't known what love was.

Who was I to judge?

So, at the end of the day, it just comes down to love and finding the person that fits. The person that knows you and loves you exactly for who you are. There wasn't one thing I would change about Finn Reynolds—aside from willing him to be here right now.

But all good things were worth the wait.

Finn had proven that he was definitely worth the wait.

twenty-nine

• • •

Finn

I'D BEEN on set for hours, as our schedule was brutal. I had ten more days until I was home. Until I could finally kiss my girl and tell her I was all in. I'd kept up with texting her all day, every day. Sending photos of us together over the years that were saved on my phone.

Years of memories.

Years of loving this girl.

I'd just made it back to the hotel, and I opened my phone to see that she'd responded to my last text and photo, which was pretty hilarious, if I do say so myself.

> This photo makes me laugh every time. Senior year, prom. You went with

> Dr. Pretentious, and I took Lucy Baker. But I did all I could to photobomb every picture you two posed for.

The photo I'd sent was Carl looking like an uptight asshole, Reese laughing because she knew I was behind them, and me making a face and crossing my eyes in the background.

I'd texted her several other texts throughout the day, and I was thrilled to see that she'd responded to this last one.

MINEY

Can I FaceTime you?

I wasn't even going to respond. I was dying to see her face. This was the first time she'd asked to speak on the phone, and FaceTime would make it even better. I dialed the phone and dropped down onto the bed, leaning my back against the headboard. It was almost one o'clock in the morning here, which meant it was almost nine in the morning there. The phone connected, and I waited for her face to come into view, and there she was. The prettiest girl I'd ever laid eyes on.

My heart raced at the sight of her, and for whatever reason, I found it difficult to speak at first.

She was sitting in a stall out in the barn, hay beneath her fine ass and a braid hanging over one shoulder.

She didn't speak either.

She just smiled, and then the tears started falling down her gorgeous face, and she just waved.

I pushed away the lump in my throat. "Hey, Miney."

She nodded and swiped at her cheeks and then started laughing. "I don't know why I'm crying. I'm just really happy to see you."

"Yeah? I'm glad I'm not the only one who's been tortured by this crazy plan of yours."

She smiled and tucked a loose strand of hair behind her ear. "You're not the only one."

"Did you just go for a ride?" I asked, feeling an unexplainable peace come over me now that I was looking at her.

"Not yet. I was waiting to see if you called first."

"You call, I come, right? Works the same way with the phone. You ask, I'll call. Every fucking time. I'll always show up, Reese."

"I know you will. I was wrong to worry that you didn't know what you wanted. I'm far from a relationship expert. I just had all these fears that you would feel obligated to me because this all started off not being real. So, I worried that once you left, you'd realize this wasn't for you." Pops of gold and honey danced in her green eyes as the sun shone in through the barn doors.

"I think it was always real for me, if I'm being honest. From that first time I kissed you, something shifted in me."

"What shifted?" She smiled.

"I actually think that you insisting we take this time to figure things out was not the worst idea. It gave me a lot of time to think. And I realized that I've never enjoyed being with any woman the way I enjoy being with you. I'm pretty sure that the reason I never dated anyone seriously is because my heart already belonged to you. I just didn't know it at the time. So, you dated Carl for years, and I did what I did during that time. But from the minute my lips crashed into yours, I knew I was done for, Miney. You own me. I don't want anyone else. I don't think about anyone else. And it doesn't matter if I'm thousands of miles away or in bed beside you. You are all that I want."

She nodded as the tears fell, running down her cheeks.

"You are all that I want, too."

"Are you sure about that? Do you want to tell me why you didn't mention that you were meeting with Carl? Is there something going on there that I should know about?"

She shook her head. "There is nothing going on there. I wouldn't lie to you, Chewy, you know that. I'm sorry I didn't tell you, and I promise to tell you why I met him when I see you. Can you trust me on that?"

"Of course, I can. If you tell me there's nothing to worry about there, then that's all I need to hear. But that goes both ways. I'm telling you that you have nothing to worry about, so you need to trust that."

"I'm not a Hollywood movie star," she said, and her voice was all tease.

"You're everything, Miney."

Her eyes widened, and she tilted her head to the side. "So are you, Finn Reynolds."

"Well, it looks like we're finally on the same page. And now we've got to wait ten more days until I get to see you."

"Ten days. We've got this. You probably need to get some sleep. You must be exhausted."

"How about you do me a favor?" I asked, my voice heavy in desperate need of sleep, yet I wasn't ready to hang up with her.

"Anything."

"Take me on a ride down to the water."

She chuckled and pushed to her feet. "That's easy enough. I've missed our rides."

"I've missed them, too."

"Take me to the last place I was buried inside you, and you rode me with that white cowboy hat on your head and nothing else. Tits bouncing, lips parted," I said, and she gasped before holding her finger to her lips. "Good morning, Silas. I'm just chatting with Finn in Tokyo."

"I can see that," the man said as he barked out a laugh. "Your girl is three shades of red, Reynolds."

"Didn't know we had an audience," I said as I waggled my brows at Reese through the phone.

"Okay, give me a minute to get saddled up," she said, and I was fairly certain she tucked the phone into her cleavage, and I groaned. The phone moved, and she faced it out as she started trotting through the grassy field toward the pines and the water.

"Sorry about that," I said over my laughter when she turned the phone to face her.

"That's okay, you big perv. We're alone now. Tell me all the things you miss."

And that was exactly what I did.

We laughed, and we talked, and she sat on the beach with me until my eyes grew heavy, then we said our goodbyes.

And I fell asleep dreaming of home.

Dreaming of Reese.

One month away had felt like an eternity. But I'd continued sending texts all day long, finding photos that I knew she would love and sending her gifts that would make her smile at least once a day.

But we'd spent the last ten days FaceTiming when I'd get off work. It had helped to see her beautiful face those last days we'd been apart, but nothing would compare to holding her in my arms.

Hell, I hadn't had sex in a month, and I was horny as all get-out, but I didn't even care about that at the moment. I just wanted her with me. Near me.

My world had been off-kilter these last few weeks, and Reese had a way of making everything better. I landed in San Francisco, and my brother-in-law, Maddox, had a helicopter waiting for me to fly me home so I could get there quicker. When I landed on the rooftop of Lancaster Press, I pushed the door open to see Reese running toward me.

Arms pumping, hair flying in the wind as she crashed into me on a whoosh, and I wrapped my arms around her. We just stood there, with the wind whipping around us, the pilot strolling past us with a chuckle as he moved toward the door to the building—and I just held my girl.

She pulled back and looked up at me. "I'm so happy you're home."

"Me, too," I said, leaning down and kissing her hard. "Let's get out of here."

With my hand on the small of her back and my huge

duffle slung over my shoulder, I guided her toward the door. We went down the back stairs and out to her car. She tossed me her keys because she knew I always preferred to drive.

All the way home, she asked endless questions about Tokyo and the cast that I'd been working with. I asked about the new client she'd taken on yesterday.

"They are such a cute family. It's a second home for them, so they are pretty much giving me creative freedom." She leaned her cheek against the seat and smiled at me. "I'm super excited that I get to do their kids' rooms. Their son, Stephen, wants a superhero bedroom, and their daughter, Alicia, wants a rainbow room."

"Man, I would have loved to have you decorate my bedroom as a kid."

"Your mom is so talented. You guys all had the cutest bedrooms growing up. She's the reason I wanted to be a designer. Remember how I'd go hang out with her when she was redoing rooms or decorating for the holidays?"

"Oh. I thought you were there for me?"

Her smile lit up her entire face, and she nodded. "I was always there for you."

I pulled down the long driveway and parked in front of the barn before stepping out of the car and coming around to open her door. It wasn't snowing any longer, and we probably had a few hours of sunlight left before it tucked behind the clouds.

"What do you want to do first?" she asked, tipping her head back as my arms came around her.

"I want to do *you* first. And then I want to take the horses down to the beach and sit with you before the sun sets."

"I can work with that," she said, and I grabbed her behind the knees and flipped her over my shoulder. I jogged toward the house as her laughter filled the air around us.

It was my favorite sound.

And she was my favorite girl.

My only girl.

Always had been. Even before I knew it myself.

I didn't stop until we were in the bedroom, and I dropped her down onto the bed, her hair spilling all around her. Her green eyes blazed as I unzipped her coat, and she lifted enough for me to pull it off. Next, I bent down and pulled off her cowboy boots before removing every last stitch of clothing from her gorgeous body.

"Get naked," she said, her voice husky as the corners of her lips turned up.

"Yes, ma'am." I was stripped down in no time, and I pushed her back on the bed before hovering above her. "How do you want me first?"

"Any way I can have you."

"Yeah? Well, I want you in every way there is. But right now, I just need to be inside you. I need it like I need my next breath."

"Me, too," she whispered, raising her hips and teasing me.

That was all I needed to hear. My mouth crashed into hers, and my cock throbbed at her entrance. My heart was beating so fast, I was certain it would rip from my body.

This need.

This urgency.

I'd never felt it before, and I fucking loved it.

I pushed forward, and her head fell back, and my lips sealed over her nipple.

Fuck me. I'd memorized every inch of these tits, fantasizing about them every single day since I'd been gone. They were a little fuller than I'd remembered, and I couldn't get enough. I licked and sucked, groaning when she bucked against me, urging me to push all the way in.

I just wanted to savor every fucking second as she clenched around me.

I was buried inside her, and I didn't move. I pulled back to look at her, pushing her silky hair away from her face. Her cheeks were flushed, her lips parted, and her eyes filled with need.

"I love you. I mean it, Reese. I fucking love you." My breaths labored as I fought the urge to fuck her senseless and make sure she knew just how much she meant to me.

"I know you do. I see it. I feel it. And I love you just as fiercely." She gasped when I shifted the slightest bit. "Now, stop talking and have your way with me, Cowboy."

"Music to my fucking ears."

I pulled out and drove back into her, over and over. She met me thrust for thrust as we found our rhythm. She tugged my head down so my mouth was sealed over hers. And nothing had ever felt better.

This overwhelming feeling moved through my body, coursing through my veins.

She groaned into my mouth, and I pulled away to look at her. Her back arched off the bed, and I gripped her hips as we moved faster.

Our breaths were the only audible sounds flooding the room.

My hand moved between us, knowing exactly what she needed.

Where she needed me.

My thumb found her clit and applied the slightest bit of pressure, making little circles and watching as her eyes fell closed.

She bucked up against me with a need that I understood, because I felt it deep in my soul.

"Finn," she cried out as she shattered around me. Just seeing her body shake and tremble had me driving into her one more time before I exploded and followed her right over the edge.

Just like I always would.

thirty

. . .

Reese

WE'D COME DOWN from our high before looking out the window and realizing we needed to get moving if we wanted to see the sun go down.

We'd bundled up, and I'd tucked my scrapbook that I'd been working on these last few weeks into a backpack and asked him to carry it for me.

I'd assumed he'd noticed my breasts were fuller because he couldn't stop touching them. The rest of me didn't look any different yet, and I checked every day to see if my belly was showing at all. There was the slightest bump that no one else would probably notice, but I was looking for it.

And as we saddled up and started riding toward the water, I couldn't wait to tell Finn the news. I wasn't afraid anymore. There were no doubts or insecurities between us now.

That time apart had taught me a lot.

Time.

Distance.

Space.

All the obstacles life might throw at us.

None of it mattered because what we had was unbreakable.

Finn Reynolds was a part of me. He was probably the part of me that told me to leave for London. To change course and make a change.

He was slightly ahead of me, and he looked over his shoulder and winked, and my stomach fluttered as my head fell back in laughter when I chased after him.

We tied the horses to the tree, and Finn pulled the blanket that he'd brought for us out of the saddle bag and set the backpack down.

"We're just in time." He offered me a hand, and I slid down Millie's side until my boots hit the ground.

He gathered a few branches and piled them on our makeshift bonfire and tossed a lit match into the mix, and the flames grew as we settled together on the blanket, looking out over the water. Amber and citrine and gold were layered in front of us like a watercolor painting. I leaned my head against his shoulder and breathed in the crisp air mixed with his minty, manly, sexy-as-hell scent.

"That right there," I said, pointing at the colors in the sky. "The color in the middle is citrine at its finest. Only second to the perfection that is the ring around your steely, pewter eyes."

"Fine. I believe you. Citrine is a real color."

I chuckled and sat up. "I want to show you something I've been working on since you've been gone."

"Show me." He turned his baseball cap around, and the move was so sexy I had to squeeze my thighs together to stop the ache that was building there.

Pregnancy hormones were clearly a real thing. We'd just had sex, and here I was, fantasizing about him again.

I unzipped the backpack and pulled out the black leather book with a silver engraved plate on the front.

"Chewy and Miney. The story of us," he said as his fingers traced over the words.

He flipped to the first page and barked out a laugh at the photos of him and me as newborns and the chat bubbles that I'd filled in for each of us.

Mine read: *Hottie alert. Look at the thighs on that dude.*

His read: *She may look like a fragile bird, but someday, that girl will kick my ass on a horse.*

We huddled together as he turned every page, and we literally watched as we grew up right before our eyes. There were birthday parties, Halloweens, Disney trips, the first day of school pics, and dances. Pictures from college and Finn's acting gigs and my time in London. The photos he'd been sending me every single day over the last thirty days were all included in the book.

"This is fucking amazing." He studied every single photo and read all the notes that I'd written around them.

"Yeah?" I pushed up on my knees and placed my hand on the page he was currently looking at so he wouldn't turn it too quickly. "So, this last one is something that I wanted to show you in person."

"Is it a nude?" He waggled his brows.

"Better than a nude."

"I don't know, Miney. You naked is impossible to beat."

"Turn the page and see for yourself."

My heart raced, and I let out a long breath that I hadn't even realized I'd been holding as I pulled my hand away. He reached for the corner, turning it slowly and then staring down at the page in front of him.

A photo of our son or daughter was on that page with a note that read: *This is our future. Our baby. A perfect mix of you and me.*

"Reese," he whispered, and I heard the break in his voice. I startled when I saw the tears streaming down his cheeks. Finn had only cried twice in all the years that I'd known him.

He'd cried when I'd been diagnosed with cancer and when his father had been diagnosed years later.

But I was fairly certain these were happy tears.

"This is what I was meeting with Carl about. I was feeling really tired before you left, so he'd offered to run my blood work so I wouldn't have to go to Dr. Roberts and get everyone all worked up. I found out I was pregnant the night before you left."

He looked up at me, his gray eyes darker than I'd ever seen them. The fire light lit up the space around us, allowing me to see all the emotion there.

"I was horrible to you that night."

"I should have told you the truth, but I was scared you wouldn't have left for Tokyo. That you would have stayed with me out of obligation."

"You could never be an obligation to me. That's like saying that breathing is an obligation. And we're having a baby," he said as he shook his head and swiped at his face. "I'm so fucking happy."

"You are?" I said, and now I was crying, too. I'd held it all in for so long and it felt so good to get it all out. To share this with him.

"There is nothing better in the world than what's happening here between us. And now we get to bring this little human into the world and raise him or her together. Damn. You found the only thing that would be better than your naked body." He barked out a laugh.

"Did you just compare my naked body to our baby?"

"My two favorite things in the world," he said, staring down at the book. "Man, we're going to make some beautiful babies together, Miney. It just feels right, doesn't it? Like it all makes sense?"

"It does. You sure you're ready for all this?"

"Not one doubt in my mind." He kissed me hard. "Damn. We have a lot to do. I want to get our baby their own horse so we can all ride down here together."

"Chewy, our baby is the size of a passion fruit. They won't be riding a horse for a long while."

"Well, we can't get our kid a horse that we don't know when they're finally ready to ride. Hell no. I'm not trusting some wild beast with our child. We need to get it now and make sure it's trained."

"That's the priority, huh? Not the fact that I live in a rental house up the street at the moment?" I shook my head and laughed.

He lunged forward, laying me back on the blanket. "You won't spend one more night in that goddamn rental house. I shouldn't have allowed it that night. I should have apologized and demanded you come home."

"That's a total caveman apology," I said, running my fingers over his scruff.

"Marry me, Miney. Right now. Let's call Father Davis and get married right here."

My bottom lip quivered because there was nothing more that I wanted than to marry Finn and raise a family and grow old together.

"Our mothers would never forgive us."

"Do you want a big wedding?"

"No. I just want you."

"Well, then, we invite the family, and we get married right here in a couple of days. I already got you the ring."

"You did?"

"Yep. I'd met with Mr. Clark the day before I left. I wanted you to know how serious I was about… us. But then we had that fight, and I figured it would be an inappropriate time to propose, considering you packed a bag and left."

I shook my head. "I'm sorry, Chewy."

"That was on me. But this time, it's just right, you know? Who knows you're pregnant?"

"Nobody. I mean, no one aside from Carl." I winced. "I wanted to tell you first, so I haven't told a soul."

"That had to be a tough secret to keep these last few weeks."

"Yeah, but my boyfriend was sending me all these texts and flowers and vibrators. He can be very distracting."

"Sounds like my kind of guy."

"He's definitely my kind of guy."

"How about we don't tell anyone why they're coming over? We order food from Reynolds' and just invite the family to a Sunday dinner here. And we have Father Davis waiting for us down here by the water. We can tell them we're getting married and having a baby all at the same time."

"That's quite the Sunday dinner." I waggled my brows.

"Wouldn't have it any other way."

"Me either."

"Reese Reynolds has a nice ring to it." He nipped at my bottom lip.

"It does. Forever has a nice ring, too."

"You were always my forever. It just took us a little bit to figure it out." He kissed me before pulling back. "I love you, Reese."

"I love you more."

And I tugged his lips back down to mine.

Because once you realized that you'd found your forever, you wanted to start living it right now.

And that was exactly what I planned to do.

epilogue

• • •

Finn

REESE and I had never done anything by the book. We'd been the best of friends long before we were ever lovers. We didn't become lovers until we were fake dating. She moved out of my house after she found out she was pregnant. And we were having a wedding that everyone thought was a Sunday dinner. Oh, yeah, and we were also going to announce that we were having a baby, too.

Being conventional was boring.

I was a big believer in trusting your gut. If it feels right. If it feels good.

Do it.

Hugh and Lila had brought in boxes of food, and we were setting it up on the kitchen island. My parents were asking me a slew of questions about when I was leaving next week to start shooting *Big Sky Ranch,* but I wasn't ready to answer all their questions just yet. I had bigger things on my mind.

Much better things.

The fact that I was going to marry the only girl, the only woman I'd ever loved. And this wasn't a casual kind of love. This was an *I'll burn down the world for you* kind of love. The kind that you know is forever.

Georgia and Maddox were talking to Reese's parents.

Brinkley and Lincoln were home for a couple of weeks as he'd wrapped up his season. They'd made it to the Super Bowl, and though they didn't walk away with the win, it was still an amazing year for the Thunderbirds.

My brother-in-law was one hell of a player.

Cage was currently trying to explain to me why he brought a fucking pig to my house for Sunday dinner.

"Dude, I can't make this shit up. Maxine is fixated on me now. If I don't bring her with me, she goes batshit crazy. Martha and Joe better get home soon because I'm done with piggy daycare."

"Ridiculous. I think you like it. She's the only woman you seem to want to spend time with." I smirked because guess what? I didn't fucking care that he brought a pig to my house, which technically meant that he'd brought a pig to my wedding.

He just didn't know it yet.

"I'm done with women for a while."

"Yeah? Does that have anything to do with the story that just broke on the internet?"

"I have no idea what you're referring to." He smirked. He knew. He'd texted me about it an hour ago.

"Well, I just saw it. Do you think it's true?" Brinkley asked, looking around like what we were talking about was a top-secret mission for the FBI.

"It's public record. And where there's smoke, there's usually fire," I said.

"Are we talking about Presley Duncan?" Hugh asked as he walked into the huddle.

"I believe that's Presley Wellington. And no, we aren't talking about it." Cage cleared his throat.

"Right. Because it's no big deal that the love of your life's world has just imploded. Why would we talk about that?" Brinkley raised a brow.

"Oh, I heard." Georgia shoved her head into our little circle and whispered, "What a douche potato. How do you cheat on Presley Duncan? She's the whole package. Smart, beautiful, and she was the only person who could ever put Cage in his place."

"For the last time, her name is Presley Wellington. Let's not refer to her as the love of my life because that makes it sound like my life is over. I've got Gracie and Maxine. I'm doing just fine."

"Ah, a five-year-old and a pig," I teased. "And I don't know that she'll be going by that last name with the scandal around her husband. I'm guessing she'll be taking her maiden name back and leaving that—what did you call him, Georgie?"

"A douche potato."

"Don't ruin the potato by putting a douche in front of it. This conversation is over." My older brother hissed just as Lila walked over.

"Are we talking about Presley Duncan?"

We all started laughing because Cage threw his hands in the air and groaned.

"Yes, baby," Hugh said as he stroked the hair away from her face.

"Well, Mrs. Runither came into the restaurant right when I was leaving, and Hugh was loading the car with all the food. She told me Presley's dad is in the hospital. He had a stroke. When it rains, it sure does pour, huh? I feel terrible for her. We'll drop some food off for the family tomorrow."

I glanced at Cage and noticed the way his jaw clenched. The way his shoulders stiffened. He could deny that he cared all he wanted, but we all knew that he still did. Even if they'd had a horrible breakup and completely cut one another out of their lives.

I knew my brother.

He was worried about her.

"Keep me posted on Frank, please." Cage cleared his throat.

Reese came in, carrying Gracie in her arms. She was wearing a white dress covered in little flowers that ran down to the floor with her boots beneath it. She had her cowboy hat on her head, and her gaze locked with mine.

"You ready to do this, Chewy?"

"I love when you call Uncle Finny Chewy." Gracie's head fell back in laughter as she jumped down to her feet.

"All right, we have a little surprise for everyone before we eat. Come on outside. It won't take too long. Bring your jackets if you're cold." I sent a quick text to Father Davis, who was waiting for us down by the water, before sending a text to my cousin Everly, because I had a few surprises for everyone today.

With Reese's hand in mine, we led our families down through the field and into the pines. The timing, well, it was perfect.

Just the way we wanted it.

The sun was getting ready to go to sleep, and we were going to say our vows right before it did.

Under the last bit of citrine-colored sunshine.

"Look how gorgeous that sunset is," Georgia said as she and Maddox walked beside us.

"It's something." Maddox glanced over at me like he was trying to figure out what I was up to.

My parents and Reese's parents were talking a mile a minute and never questioned why we were all going for a walk.

Brinkley, on the other hand… She never missed a beat.

"What's going on, Finny?"

"You know what, Brinks? You're going to have to wait to find out."

"That is never okay with me," she huffed, and Lincoln

wrapped his arms around her from behind and chuckled as we made our way through the pines.

It was quiet, which surprised me, considering there was a small group waiting for us just a few feet away.

When we came through the other end of the tree line, there stood all my cousins and their husbands and their kids. Reese's cousins were there, as well, but considering they were a small group of four, the Thomas family was large. I didn't know how they'd kept all the kids so quiet, but they had. Dylan was there, holding baby Hugh, with Wolf standing beside her.

"Oh my word. What are you all doing here?" my mother gasped, and everyone started hugging one another.

"We have no idea. Finny said we needed to be here, and we came." Dylan shrugged. "Although, we didn't know we wouldn't be allowed in the house and that we'd be hidden out in the trees like criminals."

Wolf barked out a laugh. "We're on a beach, baby. We're hardly being hidden like criminals."

"I peed in the trees already. It feels a bit scandalous when you're wearing a dress and carrying a newborn." She raised a brow.

"Don't act like it's your first time peeing in public," Everly said over her laughter as she hugged me. "Happy to be here for whatever this is, Finny."

"We're so happy you included us." Ashlan kissed my cheek.

"Fine. We're happy to be here," Dylan said as she kissed my cheek, and Reese gushed over the baby.

"Listen, if it's important to you, it's important to us," Vivi said, giving me a hug while holding her little girl in her arms. She was adorable and looked just like her mama.

Uncle Jack made his rounds, shaking everyone's hands, and Cage gave up and tied Maxine to the tree before crossing his arms over his chest. "Can you tell us why we're all down here now, please?"

Reese looked at me, and I reached for her hands, moving to stand in front of the group. I called out to Father Davis, and he came walking out from the other side of the pine trees, and everyone's eyes widened when they saw him.

"We wanted you all to be here today because we're getting married." I put my hands up before anyone could say anything. "We wanted to do it last week, but it was important for us to have you here."

"This is exactly what we want for our special day. Surrounded by the people we love, in our favorite place, at our favorite time of day," Reese said, smiling up at me.

"Before sunset," I said, winking at her. "So, thanks for being here. Let's do this."

There were some whistles, and everyone clapped their hands and watched as we stood in front of Father Davis.

He did a short intro and said that we would each be reading our vows to one another. He motioned for Reese to go first.

"Finnegan Charles 'Chewy' Reynolds, you were my fairy tale before I even knew it. You have been my best friend and my ride or die for my entire life. You were there when I was delivered the worst news of my life and learned I had cancer." Her voice shook, and a tear streamed down her cheek. A lump formed in my throat, but I squeezed her hands and nodded. Because together, we could and would get through anything. "And somehow, you made that awful day my most memorable New Year's Eve. You have celebrated my wins and picked me up during my losses. You have cheered me on through every up and down in my life. You have shown me what real love is and that I should chase every dream that I have. But I've come to learn that the only thing I really want to chase is the cute boy in the baseball cap who rides horses like he was born to and then goes off and becomes a big movie star. You are my dream come true, Finn Reynolds. I have loved you since my earliest memory, and I will love you for as long as I'm on this earth."

There were sniffs and gasps, and Reese didn't even try to stop the tears from falling.

"Damn, girl, you're a hard act to follow," I said as the group erupted in laughter.

"Go ahead, Finn," Father Davis said.

"Well, we've done just about everything backward, and I've got to say, backward is the new forward." I chuckled. "I cannot recall a single day in my life that you weren't in my thoughts. Not a single day where I didn't love you fiercely. We started this relationship by lying to everyone and pretending that we were a couple when we weren't. But you see"—I glanced out at our families with a big smirk on my face—"that was mistake number one. Try fake dating someone you're already in love with. That poor bastard, Carl, didn't stand a chance." I winced and made an apologetic face at Father Davis.

"Continue," he said, over more laughter.

"You see, Reese and I loved one another before we even knew what it meant. My dad has always told the story about the first time that he saw Mama and all the hair on his arms stood on end, and he just knew she was the woman for him."

"Damn straight!" my father shouted over more chuckles.

"Well, we've given him a hard time over the years, as we've all made fun of how hard and fast he fell. But it hit me when I was in Tokyo that I think I fell for Reese Murphy before I knew what it meant to fall. When we were meeting out in that treehouse before the sun went down every single day. Desperate to spend just a few more minutes with my favorite girl." I leaned down and rested my forehead against hers. "I'd already given you my heart, so I spent many years being single because my soulmate and I needed time to figure out what this was between us. But the minute the opportunity came—fake dating didn't make much sense, did it, Miney?"

She shook her head, and her bottom lip wobbled. "Nope."

"Because my heart has always been yours. You are my best friend, my confidant, and the love of my life."

She sniffed as tears streamed down her face. "You're the love of my life."

"Can I tell them the good news?" I whispered, and everyone laughed again because apparently, I was a loud whisperer.

She nodded and smiled. "Please do."

I pulled back to look at everyone, with Reese's hand intertwined with mine.

"We wanted to bring you all here to be part of our special day, which we didn't want to wait to make official because, to us, we've already waited way too many years being apart. So, we're not spending one more day not letting everyone know that we're madly in love. That we found our forever, and we wanted to start living it right now."

"Cheers to that! It's about time," my mom and Jenny said at the same time as tears streamed down their faces.

"Yep. We'll be cheering real soon, I promise." I looked down at Reese and winked. "But we also wanted you to know that we're having a baby. And let's just hope he or she is going to have their mama's pretty looks and big brain."

Reese's head fell back in laughter. "And their daddy's swagger and charm."

"Wow. Go big or go home," Cage said, his eyes wide. "But I'd like to point out that I did predict this would all happen, and I believe several of you owe me some money."

"Ahhh… announcing the pregnancy during the ceremony is new for me." Father Davis leaned close to my ear, and I barked out a laugh along with everyone around us. "But congratulations. I'm happy for you both."

"Thank you. It's the happiest day of our lives, and there's just too much to celebrate."

"Well, without further ado, do you have the rings?"

I glanced over at my niece. "There is only one person that we trusted with those rings, and I believe Auntie Ree Ree asked you to keep a secret, and it looks like you did."

Gracie came walking over, wearing her pink cowboy boots and pink cowboy hat. "I've got the rings, Uncle Finny. And I didn't even tell Daddy the secret."

"I'm wounded." Cage clutched his heart.

"Well, she's only known the secret for about fifteen minutes. Don't be too hurt. But good job, Gracie girl."

Father Davis said a few more words, and I slipped the citrine yellow stone set into a solid gold band with amber color stones surrounding it. Reese stared down at her hand and smiled up at me.

"It's a sunset that I can have with me at all times." Her voice shook. "There is no one who knows me the way that you do, Finn Reynolds."

"I plan on keeping it that way." I offered her my hand, and she held up the buttery gold band for me to see before she slipped it onto my finger.

I studied it and then realized it was engraved on the inside.

To a lifetime of sunsets with you.

I don't remember the rest of the stuff that Father Davis said because I was too busy staring at my girl.

Everyone we loved was here, but all that really mattered was that Reese and I were here.

That we'd found our way to one another.

"I now pronounce you husband and wife," Father Davis said, and everyone howled and cheered.

It was exactly what we'd wanted today to be.

I kissed my bride and dipped her down low.

And when I pulled her back up, we turned to look at the sky as the sun was just setting behind the clouds.

"You ready for forever?" she whispered.

"Absolutely, I am. Happy wedding day, Mrs. Reynolds."

She smiled, her eyes wet with emotion, and I dipped her back and kissed her again.

Just before the sunset.

THE END

Do you want to see Reese give Finn a SWOONY surprise… Click here for an exclusive BONUS SCENE!

Read Reese's Swoony Surprise for Finn

Are you ready for the final book in the Cottonwood Cove Series? Presley Duncan might be the only woman who can bring Cage Reynolds to his knees. After the Storm is a Second Chance, Single Dad Romance, available now for Pre-Order!

Pre-Order After the Storm

acknowledgments

Greg, thankful to call you mine. I'm forever grateful to be on this journey with you. Love you SO MUCH! Thank you for supporting me and encouraging me to chase my dreams.

Chase & Hannah… My greatest gift is being your mom. You are the reason that I work hard, and the reason that I chase my dreams, because you both inspire me more than you know! I love you to the moon and back!

Willow, Thank you for always making me laugh, and for listening and encouraging me every step of the way. And of course, thank you for being the friend who is willing to read all three books of a certain series for me, and then fill me in in real time, so I can mentally prepare. Who could ask for more? I love you so much and am so grateful to have you in my life!

Catherine, thank you for your friendship and all of your support! Cheers to making many more memories together for years to come. Thankful to be on this journey with you. Love chain forever! Love you!

Kandi, I truly love being on this journey with you! Thank you for pushing me, inspiring me to work through the tough days and for cheering me on every step of the way. I am forever grateful for you! Love you my sweet friend!

Pathi, I can't put into words how thankful I am for YOU! Thank you for being such an amazing friend!! Thank you for believing in me and encouraging me to chase my dreams!! I love and appreciate you more than I can say!! Love you FOREVER!

Nat, I could not be happier to be on this journey with you!

I am so excited for all the memories we will get to share and I feel so lucky to be working together again! Thank you for supporting me and most importantly, thank you for your friendship! So grateful for you! Love you!

Nina, I don't know how I ever made a decision without you. Thank you for always being there for me. From the little things to the big things. Thank you for encouraging me in every way! I am forever grateful for your friendship and to be on this journey with you! Cheers to many more years together! Love you!!

Valentine Grinstead, I absolutely adore you! You are such a bright light and I am so thankful for YOU! And I will forever love our date night in Paris!! Love you!

Kim Cermak, You complete me. LOL! I'd truly be lost without you! Thank you for all that you do for me every single day!! I absolutely adore you!!

Christine Miller, I am so grateful for you! Thank you for making my life so much easier and for all that you do for me!! I am SO THANKFUL for you!

Sarah Norris, thank you for the gorgeous graphics, for all of your support and for always being willing to help! I am incredibly grateful for YOU!

Meagan, Oh how I adore you! Thank you for being an amazing beta reader and an amazing friend! Your support means the world to me!! Thank you so much!!

Kelley Beckham, thank you for setting up all the "lives" with people who have now become forever friends! Thank you so much for all that you do to help me get my books out there! I am truly so grateful!

Amy Dindia, You are the absolute sweetest and I'm so thankful for you. Thank you for creating absolutely perfect reels and TikToks for me. I am endlessly grateful for you!

Logan Chisolm, I absolutely adore you and am so grateful for your support and encouragement for this book! Your graphics are gorgeous and I just absolutely love working with you! Xo

Doo, Abi, Meagan, Annette, Jennifer, Pathi, Natalie, Caroline and Diana, thank you for being the BEST beta readers EVER! Your feedback means the world to me. I am so thankful for you!!

Hang, Thank you for bringing Reese and Finn to life in the swooniest way! I love these covers and I love working with you!!

Sue Grimshaw (Edits by Sue), I would be completely lost without you and I am so grateful to be on this journey with you. Thank you for being the voice that I rely on so much! Thank you for moving things around and doing what ever is needed to make the timeline work. I am FOREVER grateful for YOU!

Ellie (My Brothers Editor), So thankful for your friendship! I am so grateful for our chats and for all the laughs! Thank you for always making time for me no matter how challenging the timeline is! Love you forever!

Julie Deaton, thank you for helping me to put the best books out there possible. I am so grateful for you!

Jamie Ryter, I am so thankful for your feedback! Your comments are endlessly entertaining and they give me life when I need it most!! BEST COMMENTS EVER!! I am so thankful for you!!

Christine Estevez, thank you for your eagle eyes and being the last set of eyes on my book! I am so thankful for you! Your friendship truly means the world to me! Love you!

Crystal Eacker, I am so thankful for you! Thank you for doing whatever is needed! For making forms, beta audio reading, taking photos and making graphics!! You are such an amazing support and I'm forever grateful!

Jennifer, thank you for being an endless support system. For running the Facebook group, posting, reviewing and doing whatever is needed for each release. Your friendship means the world to me! Love you!

Paige, I am so thankful that the book world brought us together! I love our chats about decorating, renovating, books, kids, life, and everything in between! Most of all, I am thankful for your friendship! Love you!

Rachel Parker, I am endlessly grateful for your friendship! I love our chats. I love our LIVES! I love my Charlotte updates! And… I love you!

Sarah Sentz, thank you for always being so supportive and for making time to chat with me on every release! Thank you for helping spread the word about my books. I am forever grateful for you!!

Ashley Anastasio, I am forever grateful for your support and friendship! I appreciate all the love for my books!! It truly means the world to me!! So thankful for you!!

Kayla Compton, I am so grateful for your endless support! I love that you and I share a love for our favorite lake!! Thank you for spreading the word about my books and all that you do to support me!

Mom, thank you for loving Finn & Reese and for cheering me on every step of the way! I am so thankful that we share this love of books with one another! Ride or die!! Love you!

Dad, you really are the reason that I keep chasing my dreams!! Thank you for teaching me to never give up. Love you!

Sandy, thank you for reading and supporting me throughout this journey! Love you!

Sammi, I am so thankful for your support and your friendship!! Love you!

Marni, I love you forever and I am endlessly thankful for your friendship!! Xo

To the JKL WILLOWS… I am forever grateful to you for your support and encouragement, my sweet friends!! Love you!

To all the bloggers, bookstagrammers and ARC readers who have posted, shared, and supported me—I can't begin to tell you how much it means to me. I love seeing the graphics that you make and the gorgeous posts that you share. I am forever grateful for your support!

To all the readers who take the time to pick up my books and take a chance on my words…THANK YOU for helping to make my dreams come true!!

keep up on new releases

Linktree Laurapavlovauthor
Newsletter laurapavlov.com

other books by laura pavlov

Magnolia Falls Series

Loving Romeo

Wild River

Forbidden King

Beating Heart

Finding Hayes

Cottonwood Cove Series

Into the Tide

Under the Stars

On the Shore

Before the Sunset

After the Storm

Honey Mountain Series

Always Mine

Ever Mine

Make You Mine

Simply Mine

Only Mine

The Willow Springs Series

Frayed

Tangled

Charmed

Sealed

Claimed

Montgomery Brothers Series

Legacy

Peacekeeper

Rebel

A Love You More Rock Star Romance

More Jade

More of You

More of Us

The Shine Design Series

Beautifully Damaged

Beautifully Flawed

The G.D. Taylors Series with Willow Aster

Wanted Wed or Alive

The Bold and the Bullheaded

Another Motherfaker

Don't Cry Spilled MILF

Friends with Benefactors

follow me

Website laurapavlov.com
Goodreads @laurapavlov
Instagram @laurapavlovauthor
Facebook @laurapavlovauthor
Pav-Love's Readers @pav-love's readers
Amazon @laurapavlov
BookBub @laurapavlov
TikTok @laurapavlovauthor

Printed in the USA
CPSIA information can be obtained
at www.ICGtesting.com
LVHW071934260923
759342LV00003B/392